THOSE WE DO NOT SEE

ANGIE GALLION

Those We Do Not See
Red Adept Publishing, LLC
104 Bugenfield Court
Garner, NC 27529
https://RedAdeptPublishing.com/
Copyright © 2024 by Angie Gallion. All rights reserved.
Cover Art by Streetlight Graphics[1]

This is a work of fiction. Names, characters, places, and incidents either are the product of the author's imagination or are used fictitiously, and any resemblance to locales, events, business establishments, or actual persons—living or dead—is entirely coincidental.

---

1. http://StreetlightGraphics.com

For my parents. You are missed.

July 8

Chapter 1

Brit Addams glances toward the passenger seat. Jason's fingertip traces the seam on her jeans, moving up her thigh toward a promise. She shivers, and the car rolls forward onto Highway 54. The world stops turning, two hours before a July noon. His finger, light and enticing, is full of heat as the car inches forward, rolling through the stop sign.

An impact. The terrible screeching of metal, the shock of the airbags as they deploy followed by the stopped-time silence when her mouth and nose fill with powder. She can taste it and feels its grittiness on her tongue.

The airbag hits the side of her face. She was looking at him. He was staring straight ahead, as if he were not driving her to distraction with his touch, so the passenger airbag hits him in the face. When the powder clears, blood smears on his airbag as it deflates in the same moment his hands rise to cup his busted nose.

Brit didn't see the other car coming.

She looked. She knows she did. Confident that the path was clear, she rolled through the stop sign. The flesh of her thigh still tingles beneath her hand, the memory of a touch.

Brit presses her hand hard against her thigh, trying to stop feeling his touch, that caress that set her skin on fire the second before the other car hit them. *Me,* she reminds herself. She has to remember to say she was alone, or Zack will know.

It happened so fast. She looked.

Her mind rolls, spinning, as she tries to remember, tries to understand the seconds that led to the collision.

"Go," she says, nearly pushing Jason out of the car. "You can't be here."

Jason climbs out the passenger side and leaves a smear of blood on the door handle. It was supposed to be over, and if Zack catches them together again, a broken nose will be the least of their problems. He steps onto the shoulder and walks away, head down and blood dripping through his fingers.

Reaching for the handle to wipe away Jason's blood, Brit watches his silhouette grow smaller. *Go faster.*

Deep in the recesses of her mind, she is aware of the flashing lights coming to rest and blocking the road while her hand wipes at the drying blood, spreading it into the fibers of her jeans.

She needs to exhale. Finally, her held breath escapes her lips. The next incoming breath stings her nostrils, and she gags on the powder clogging her airway.

Far down the road, a figure continues to move away, jogging and still holding his head down.

Go faster.

Brit pulls her phone from her pocket and pushes the button that dials her boyfriend.

"Zack?" she whimpers into the phone.

"What's wrong? What's happened?"

"I've had an accident," she says in a ragged breath.

"Where are you?"

"Fischer Road at 54." She closes her eyes and tries to get her heart to stop racing.

"What were you doing over there?"

Chapter 2

Officer Cliff Rathborn reads the scene like the schematic for an electrical system, understanding the meaning of the skid marks. The red Honda Fit faces west but sits in the eastbound lane of Highway 54. The driver applied the brakes with force. The rubber is straight and flat, then the marks make an abrupt shift north and skitter and jump across the roadway until the place where the car came to rest.

The white SUV, a Nissan Rogue, was making a right-hand turn from Fischer Road onto 54. The collision forced the white car off the road and onto the shoulder. It plowed into the stop sign and bent it to a forty-five-degree angle, as if the driver applied the gas at the point of impact. That would make sense, based on the angle of the sign.

Cliff hates this intersection. The curve right before Fischer Road makes it a treacherous stretch. People drive too fast, and it's hard to gauge distance and speed going through it. Many times, a driver has asked, "Where the hell did that come from?" in the aftermath of a collision at this junction.

His car is parked, with the lights looping to warn oncoming drivers. He moves to check the occupants, mentally filling in the 523 accident report—cataloging the locations of the vehicles, noting the weather, and observing the skid marks from where the red car tried to avoid the collision. He glances up to confirm the sky is clear as he reaches the red Honda. Conditions are dry. Sniffing the air for the odor of fuel, he scans the roadway for signs of a breached gas tank. There is fuel in the air but expired as exhaust, not as the sharp tang of fresh gasoline.

The woman is covered with blood, and one eye is swollen closed with a shard of black plastic extending out. Similar shards stick out from her T-shirt. Cliff assesses her as he opens the door, counting the pieces of shrapnel in the blink of an eye. The woman stirs. Cliff's stomach rolls. Her one working eye flutters, opens, and finds him.

"Hey, Cliff."

His heart hammers at her knowing his name. She smiles, a blood-smeared caricature. In the shape of that smile, he recognizes her. The young woman works at Chick-fil-A, one of two who staffed the drive-thru when he came by.

"Hey, Dee. You're gonna be okay." His voice is thick and slow, like molasses in winter.

She tilts her head, as if to say, "Don't lie," or maybe just to see him better. The movement exposes a gaping wound in her neck that makes Cliff understand the cause of the bloodless cast to her lips and the pale sheen of her skin.

"Did you have breakfast today?" she asks, and her eyebrows draw together in pain or confusion.

"Yeah. I missed you." His voice doesn't break or waver.

Cliff had missed her. He had missed that smile. Three or four times a week, when his patrol took him through the Thomas Crossroads area around breakfast time, he pulled into the Chick-fil-A, where he could get his chicken grilled and without a bun. He always ordered the same thing, and Dee or the other kid who worked the outside line at the drive-thru always knew what he wanted before he even reached them.

"Wish you hadn't taken the day off," he says, trying for calm when his mind is still cataloguing all those pieces of shrapnel, counting the lacerations.

Dee smiles and nods. She coughs, choking, unable to catch a breath. Cliff places a hand on her face, and she settles, her muscles relaxing at his touch.

"Paramedics are coming, Dee. Just hold on."

Chapter 3

Brit closes her eyes and lowers the phone from her face, as if she doesn't hear the question. *What was I doing over here?* They were just driving, looking for a country road that they could turn down and park. She stares down the road, where she can no longer see Jason moving away.

When the heat inside the car becomes overwhelming, she pulls the handle to open her door and pushes. It won't budge. Fear grips her. She is trapped. Her eyes scan the car and come to rest on the smeared blood on the handle of the passenger-side door.

"Go!" she told him, and he went—through the passenger-side door.

Brit climbs over the console and swipes at the blood on the deflated airbag. She stumbles into the blazing sun, which is burning down like an oven set to broil.

The phone vibrates in her hand. Zack's face, smiling and rakish, lights the screen. *Shit.* She pushes the button to decline the call and drops the phone into the grass. Then she walks into the street, trying to make sense of what has happened. *I could just leave. We could run away and start over somewhere else.*

Ten feet away, across the highway, a red Honda sits, crumpled and facing west in the eastbound lane. Brit stares for several moments before knowledge seeps through the narrow corridors of her mind. That's the car that hit her. None of it makes sense. If it was going west, they would have been in different lanes altogether. She didn't cross into the westbound lane. The car hit her on the driver's side, not the passenger side. That was why her door wouldn't open. She would have seen the car if it had been coming from the west because she was looking at Jason. Brit didn't look the other way because he was touching her thigh, and she just wanted to get to the road where they could park, hidden by the trees.

She drops her head and pushes her hands through her hair. Everything will be different now. Somebody may be badly hurt in the other car. They probably are, or they would have come out of their car and yelled at her for being an idiot, the way Zack will when he comes and sees what she did. Zack will know about her and Jason. He'll kick her out at best and kill her at worst. He's not going to tolerate any of this.

Beneath her feet, the stark black skid marks stretch out. None of the details make sense. She looked. Nobody was coming. The skid marks are for a car that was going the other way. Her mind silences and shuts down.

Chapter 4

Cliff rips his eyes from Dee's face and scans the vehicle, taking in all the shards scattered through the cab. The shrapnel came from the driver's shredded airbag. He stands, holding pressure on the wound on her neck, and carries on a one-sided conversation.

"I was sad they got rid of that peach milkshake, Dee. You know how I love that."

Through the windshield, he watches as the woman from the other vehicle climbs out of the passenger side. She stands unmoving for several moments. Dee's warm chin relaxes on his wrist. The other woman studies her car, its placement on the embankment, and the stop sign tilted at a forty-five-degree angle, before raising her face to look across the street toward the red car. Her head tilts, as if she is trying to make sense of the situation, and she walks around the front of her car to the driver's side, where she stops, standing in the middle of the westbound lane, and stares dumbly down the road. He cannot see her face.

She's like a stone statue. Cliff needs to get her out of the road and to a safe location to be assessed, but his mind is reeling from the slow and erratic rhythm in Dee's neck and the desire to remove the shrapnel from her eye. He hesitates.

"They should just keep it all year, don't you think? We're in Georgia, after all."

Dee doesn't answer. There is so much damn shrapnel.

He calls out, "Hey, get off the road!" careful not to lose his connection with Dee as he strains to look over the roof line. The woman in the street does not move. She doesn't seem to hear him.

When the first ambulance arrives, Cliff motions them toward the red Honda.

"Her name is Dee." He isn't sure why he said that. They don't need to know her name to treat her. Dee's in critical condition, and he wants every available effort focused on her.

They reach Cliff, and he gently removes his hand from Dee's neck, exposing the wound. Her head lolls. Cliff steps aside, allowing EMT Tommy McSwain to take his place. He hovers, invested in the outcome.

"I got no rhythm," Tommy calls.

Cliff raises his eyes and steps back, out of the way of the paramedics.

A car honks and blows past the woman in the road. She jerks and shambles toward the shoulder, staring, but remains on the asphalt.

"I'll be right back, Dee. You just hold on, okay?" He doesn't think she can hear him, but he says it anyway, completing their one-sided conversation.

He imagines that she nods, although he's no longer able to see into the car. Tommy and Kennedy are working together to stabilize her.

Cliff walks toward the other woman as he scans down the road for oncoming traffic. She's walking in an unsteady line as if trying to leave the scene. *Is she drunk or just wobbly from the shock of the accident?*

Chapter 5

Flashing lights draw Brit's eyes to a police car, and she stares, marveling that it's there. She isn't sure when it arrived. For several minutes, she sat there, unbreathing, before she stepped onto the asphalt. That cop is coming toward her. His lips are moving, but she can't make out anything he's saying. Blood roars in her ears.

A car honks and swerves past her, and its wind lifts her hair. *Move.* It takes a few seconds for the message to reach her feet, but finally, she shambles toward the shoulder. She turns to follow Jason. If she can catch up to him, they can make a plan.

"Miss, I need you to stop."

The voice has authority, and Brit cowers to a halt. She knows the sound of authority and braces herself for impact. But it's not Zack, and for a moment, she's confused.

"Miss, I'm here to help. Paramedics are here. Are you injured?"

Words. Just words that don't make sense. She turns from him and looks down the road. The bobbing body moving away is visible again now that she's no longer sitting. Her feet itch to run, to catch up to him, to run away.

"I need you to stop walking, miss."

She stops and sways, her mind spinning.

"Why don't you sit down?" the officer asks.

Her knees buckle, and she drops hard onto the grassy shoulder, and her gorge rises. She fights it down.

"Can you tell me your name?" He kneels in front of her.

Brit wants to scream. She wants to scream and never stop. He leans toward her, moving inches from her eyes, and she's unable to look away.

"What is your name?" His words are slow, the way Zack asked, "What is his name?" before he punched her in the stomach and told her she was a whore.

"Britany Addams," she says and closes her eyes.

"Do you have a driver's license, Britany?"

"It's in the car, in my purse."

"I'm going to grab your purse for you, okay?"

She nods, even though she doesn't think he's asking permission.

The sun roasts her skin. Sweat beads in her hair and rolls down her back. The heat dries her eyes until they itch to close, but she sits, unblinking, staring at the place where Jason is putting distance between them.

"Miss Addams, I have your purse."

Brit reaches up to take it from his bloodstained hand and lowers her head to look inside. She pulls out her wallet, but her fingers begin to shake, and the tremble moves up her arm. When she can't get the license to come free, she shouts. The policeman takes her wallet and plucks the license easily from its slot and hands the wallet back to her.

"Here you go, Ms. Addams."

The trembling subsides as she focuses on the horizon far down the road.

"Have you been drinking today, Ms. Addams?"

She shakes her head.

"Was there somebody else in the car with you today?"

Brit blinks. She can no longer see the figure of the man walking away. He has been eaten by the shimmering waves of heat rising from the ground.

She shakes her head.

"Any drugs, Miss Addams? Do a little toking before heading out?"

She shakes her head and is grateful when he leaves. Seconds pass. Minutes roll forward.

Traffic begins to move past the two damaged vehicles, and Brit sits straight and tall, refusing to bow under the scrutiny, refusing to look at the woman lying beside the red Honda. Exhaust fumes overpower the smell of metal and airbag powder.

She had looked.

But she isn't certain. She had been looking at Jason, and he just got out of the car and left.

"You told him to go." The words slip past her teeth before her lips can clamp down, and she bites hard to keep them trapped.

The heat of the sun burns her skin. Every exposed cell feels torn. The dry grass beneath her ankles is brittle and broken. The lights flash from blue to red and back again. The scent of the asphalt, overlaid with the acrid odor of fuel and torn metal, stings her nostrils. Her stomach roils, churning with guilt and anxiety. Her unblinking eyes ache in the brilliant light.

Brit's hands are on her thighs, stretching flat against the spread of blood on her jeans. She breathes only because her heart continues beating.

Chapter 6

Cliff places cones to stop traffic before sliding into his cruiser to search the database with the woman's driver's license. Finally, he hears the wail of sirens as other officers arrive.

Britany Addams has a clean record. On his way back to her, he glances into the white SUV. The two front airbags are deployed along with the driver's-side curtain. A smudge of blood stains the deflated balloon on the passenger side. He catalogues the details, mentally adding to the 523 form in his mind.

"Miss, here's your license. Are you injured?"

Her head moves slowly back and forth, but he can't trust her assessment. He has to evaluate her. She appears uninjured, regardless of the large bloodstain spreading across her right thigh.

Kneeling in front of her, he inventories the contusion above her left eye and checks her exposed skin for injuries. He checks her arms and hands, noting blood in the folds of her fingers and around her fingernails. The blood staining her blue jeans is dark purple. It does not appear to be a bleed through and was likely wiped from her hands.

"Where are you bleeding?" he asks again because there is no visible wound.

Britany's hand rises to her forehead and touches the small contusion. The skin is intact, and she shrugs.

"There's blood on your jeans. Where did it come from?"

She looks down, her face expressionless, and one finger traces the edge. Her shoulders rise and fall with a slight back and forth of her head. She stills and faces forward again.

Cliff leans close, trying to catch the scent of booze, but only the slight hint of a vanilla body spritz overshadows the smell of her fear. "Can you tell me what happened?"

Her eyes close.

"I need you to help me understand what happened here today."

"I looked."

"What was that?"

"I looked. I didn't see that car, but I swear I looked."

"Where were you headed?"

Britany shrugs.

He shifts and looks again down the road. "You sure you were alone today?"

Britany nods and turns to look in the direction of the Honda. "Is she going to be okay?"

Cliff turns to look across the street to where the paramedics are frantically working over Dee. Tommy McSwain is pumping on her chest. Cliff's stomach plummets with dread, remembering the feel of that erratic rhythm and the wound in her neck. She has arrested.

He scans the placement of police cars with flashing lights and the other officers managing the scene. The accident field is clear for observation. The investigation unit has arrived. The scene will be measured and photographed before they remove the red vehicle from the eastbound lane.

"I'm just trying to understand something, Miss Addams. I need you to help me out, okay?" he says, pulling her back from watching the action across the roadway.

Britany nods and looks at him for a second before looking down the road again.

"Why did the passenger airbag deploy? Who was in the car with you?"

She is unresponsive.

The image is sealed in his mind. The blood on the pearlescent finish of the deflated passenger airbag is a wiped-away splotch. He didn't touch anything except the purse when he went to retrieve it, but his mind has rebuilt the interior. Hours of studying crash reports has given him an understanding of how airbags deploy, how they react in the moments after impact. The passenger airbag should not have inflated if Britany was alone in the car.

"Miss Addams, I'm trying to help you." Clifford stands above her, holding his emotions close and tight.

She clutches her purse to her stomach, and trembling courses from her shoulder blades to her toes.

"Was somebody in the car with you at the time of the accident?"

She shakes her head, and her hand slides forward and covers the blood on her jeans. It's oddly protective, that hand.

"Is there somebody you need to call?"

She shakes her head again.

"All right. I'm going to get a paramedic over to check you out."

Chapter 7

It falls to Cliff to notify Dee Martin's parents that she's died. He's no rookie, but of all the things he is asked to do for his job, he dreads notification duty the most. They all hate notification duty. No amount of adrenaline can ease the weight of telling a father, a mother, a brother, a sister, a husband, or a wife that someone important will never come home again.

Dane Shelnutt does the ride along, and he and Cliff sit in silence for several heartbeats before they leave the car, bracing for the telling. Cliff leads the walk up the steps and stands first outside the door. He closes his eyes, swallows, and rings the bell.

"Did you have breakfast today?" Dee's words play inside his head, and in the moment before the door opened, he sees her as she was last Friday, when he pulled through the drive-thru line at Chick-fil-A. She was smiling, friendly. "Good morning, Officer Cliff," she called, recognizing his car and him.

"Good morning, Dee. You look like you could melt out here." It was July in Georgia, so everything looked like it could melt.

"It's a hot one," she agreed, giving that infectious smile and making his day a little better. "Gonna try something different today?"

"Nope."

"All right. I'm proud of you for behaving." She touched the iPad, entering his order, which was the same every time he came through. "They'll take care of your discount at the window."

"Thank you."

"My pleasure, Officer Cliff." She tapped a finger on the ridge of his rolled-down window, and he nodded. He rolled forward with the line, and Dee went on to the next car to ask them how she could serve them, what they would have, and how she could make their day brighter.

The door opens, and Cliff snaps out of his memories. "Mrs. Martin?"

"Yes, I am."

"Is Mr. Martin home?"

"Yes, he's in the study. Is something wrong?"

Cliff opens his wallet, which he has at the ready, and gives his name, rank, and department before asking admittance into her home.

"Of course. Won't you come in?" She steps back, opening the door.

They move past her and into the home, removing their caps and holding them gingerly.

"Ma'am, could you call your husband and have him join us?"

"Of course. Excuse me."

They nod as she leaves. Cliff and Dane catch each other's eyes for a split second and find strength in not being alone. No parent should ever live to see this day, and no cop should have to deliver this news, but it is part of the job—an unwelcome part, but it is their responsibility, regardless of how distasteful it is.

When Mrs. Martin returns with her husband, her brow is furrowed, and her hands twist together in front of her stomach. One hand washes the other, her long fingers catching the light then dipping again to shadow.

Jim Martin steps forward, extending a hand. "Officers, what can we do for you?"

Cliff accepts his hand and asks if he wouldn't like to have a seat. It will be better if they sit, so he won't have to see the crumpling of their knees.

Mrs. Martin sits hard on the sofa at the suggestion, but Mr. Martin remains standing. "What is this about, gentlemen?" he asks, the concern in his voice growing.

"Do you know Deeanne Martin?"

A sharp intake of breath comes from Mrs. Martin as her hand flies to cover her mouth.

"She's our daughter." Mr. Martin reaches toward his wife, who rises to her feet, and they display a united front.

"We regret to inform you that Dee has been involved in an accident."

"Is she all right?" Mr. Martin asks, stoic.

Cliff shakes his head, unable to say *she died*. "I'm very sorry."

Mrs. Martin crumples and misses the couch as her knees give way. She lands with a soft thud on the carpet. Her fingers slip from her husband's hand, and for the split second before he moves to help her onto the sofa, Cliff sees the face of sorrow.

"Where is she?" Mrs. Martin asks.

Cliff braces himself. The words on his tongue are like a living thing. He knows that it's best to be straightforward, but the words grow in his mouth until he thinks they will choke him, and they grow in the air until he thinks they might drown in them. "She died."

"How did it happen?" Mr. Martin asks. His mouth no longer seems to close properly, as if his tongue has grown and no longer fits in its place.

"Car accident," Clifford says, strangled.

"We're still investigating. We'll know more in the coming hours," Dane offers.

It's a precarious dance, saying enough but not saying too much. They can't state the cause of the accident, although it is evident enough, because the official investigation hasn't been completed.

"I'm so sorry." Cliff's voice cracks.

Dane steps forward. "The station chaplain is available to you during this time. Please don't hesitate to reach out."

Mr. Martin reaches for the card Dane offers. Mrs. Martin doesn't move. She's frozen, with an odd clicking coming from her throat as she struggles for air. Cliff glances at her and finds that she is looking at him with clear, unclouded, pleading eyes.

"I'm so sorry," he says again.

She rises from the couch, her eyes diverted, and turns away, listing toward the hallway like a rudderless ship.

"Thank you," Mr. Martin says quietly, his mouth still unable to close. His tongue pulsates behind his teeth as if he's trying to find better words.

"We'll see ourselves out," Dane says.

The flat of his palm touches Cliff's back and angles him away and toward the door. When they're outside in the sun again, away from the photos on the mantel, away from the man and woman and their broken hearts, Dane risks a glance at Cliff.

"You all right, man?"

"Yeah. I just hate notification." Cliff imagines divulging the small conversation he had with Dee before he stepped away to attend to the other driver. He knows better than to second-guess his actions, but still, he thinks he could have kept her alive if he'd stayed and kept her talking.

July 10

Chapter 8

The first day after the accident, Brit stayed in bed. Now, on the second day, she listens as Zack showers, dresses, and leaves for the shop. When she's confident that the garage door has closed and convinced that Zack will not return, she stretches across the precipice between the bed and the nightstand and draws her phone under the blankets, like a child with a stolen treat. She is desperate to call Jason, wanting him to come for her, to rescue her. She wants to check that he's okay. In her mind, she keeps seeing the blood raining through his fingers and the terror in his eyes in that moment.

Brit wonders what he told his wife to cover up his busted nose, where he had been, and who he had been with.

She brings up his number a hundred times. Finally, she texts, *Call me.*

The phone rings, and she answers it before the first trill ends. "Hey," she whispers, still under the covers.

"You okay?"

"Why didn't you call?" she asks.

"I just figured it was best, you know. Considering."

"Considering what?"

"I just figured he'd be around, you know, and you'd be busy." A pause stretches between them. "Did you see the newspaper?"

"No. Is it bad?"

Brit had seen the TV news reports as well as the paper. Zack left it for her. The accident made the front page, but she didn't *read* the article. She skimmed it and saw who the family wanted donations made to, MADD, which she had to google to learn that it was the local Mothers Against Drunk Driving organization. She glanced at the picture of a smiling Dee Martin beside a picture from the crash scene. Then she turned the paper over and dropped it into the trash.

Sweat breaks out on her lip, and suffocating, she pushes the blankets off. She draws a long breath of cool, air-conditioned air.

"Yeah. It's really bad."

"Did they say it was me?" The picture showed the cars, and Brit knows she was just barely out of the photo.

"Yes."

Sighing, she imagines the reactions of her coworkers. She doesn't understand why the article mentioned MADD. Everybody will think she was drunk.

"This sucks," Brit says, but *sucks* is not even remotely a big enough word. "I wish you hadn't left."

"What do you mean?"

"I mean I wish you hadn't left." Brit doesn't know how to say it more clearly than that. She wants him to love her enough, to stand by her, to fight for her.

"We both know that couldn't have happened."

"Why?" Anger wells in her, but she douses it, remembering she told him to leave.

His voice drops to a whisper. "Mary Beth is already suspicious. Wants to know how I broke my nose."

"It's broken?" Guilt washes over her.

"Yeah. You think it will make me look tough?"

She can almost see him striking a pose. "Probably." Silence settles, pooling in the folds of the blanket. "You still love her, don't you?"

"We got a kid, man. It's not that easy to walk away."

"Do you still love her?"

"Come on, Brit. Don't do this."

Jason's exasperation echoes across the line, and she imagines him asking why he's doomed to impossible relationships with impossible, demanding women. He's asked her that question on more than one occasion, as if she were the impossible, demanding woman in his life. She doesn't think she's been impossible and demanding. She just wants him to do what he promised all those years they dated in high school—to be hers, to stand by her.

"I'm not doing anything. I'm just asking. I need to know."

A long pause fills the line, and she bites her tongue to keep from wiping the question away.

"Yeah. I mean, I love her. I don't know if I'm *in* love with her, but we have a kid. I'm stuck. You know that."

"Yeah. That's what I thought."

The silence warps, and Brit feels outside of her body, disconnected.

"You there?" he asks.

She snaps back into herself. "Yeah. Do you ever think about how different things could have been?"

"All the time."

Brit hears the sound of defeat in his voice and recognizes it because it's exactly how she feels. They dated, she and Jason, all through high school. It was good, but then he went to college, and she didn't. He ended it, saying he didn't want to date long distance and needed to focus on school. There, he met Mary Beth, the college girl.

"You know I only started dating Zack to make you jealous." She whispers the words, as if the walls have ears and may not already know.

"I know." His voice changes, and she knows he's no longer alone.

"You gotta go?"

"Yeah. All right, then." His voice is all business, the way it is when he's talking to a customer.

"All right. Bye, Jason." Brit presses the button to end the call, and before she can change her mind, she opens his contact page and scrolls down to Block this Caller.

Are you sure? the phone asks, and she presses Yes. Then she removes his contact information entirely and erases every message they've ever shared. She's made her bed, and now she has to lie in it.

Chapter 9

Brit forces herself from the bed and showers. When she's dressed, she makes her way to the living room and settles in the recliner with her laptop. Dee Martin is all over social media. *Everybody* is talking about the tragedy of the accident. *Everybody* is talking about what a bad intersection it is and saying something needs to be done. For a moment, Brit feels vindicated. It *is* a terrible intersection.

She scrolls, trying to move past Dee Martin, and encounters the obituary. Before she can stop herself, before she is even aware of the tears streaming down her face, she clicks it. If only she could see it like all the other people, as a terrible tragedy, she could get on board with calling for change.

The obituary cuts through her, and she can't set it aside. The computer screen glows, and every time it goes dark, she touches the keyboard to wake it. She knows every word. It is seared into her mind.

Deanne (Dee) Martin, 20, of Peachtree City, GA, was killed Monday, July 8, 2019, in a two-vehicle accident.

Born on August 25, 1998, to parents James and Carrie Martin, also of Peachtree City, Dee was a natural-born athlete. She was looking forward to returning to school in the fall at West Georgia State University, where she was a starter on the JV Volleyball team.

Dee was employed at Chick-fil-A, and Tony Roland, local operator, has earmarked a scholarship fund in Dee's honor. "Dee was a shining person, and people just loved her. She always tried to make everybody's day better." Dee loved her work, her friends, and her family. She is survived by her boyfriend, Christopher; her parents, James and Carrie; her paternal grandparents, Sam and Sandra Martin; her maternal grand-

mother, Marie Coggins; and her best friends, April Downy and Tia Shaw. She is preceded in death by her maternal grandfather, Jerry Coggins.

All are welcome to attend Dee's memorial service at the Holy Trinity Catholic Church in Peachtree City, GA, on July 11 at 4:00 p.m. In lieu of flowers, the family requests that donations be sent to Mothers Against Drunk Driving (MADD).

Brit reads the obituary over and over. Every time, she tries to make it say something different. But every time, it says the exact same thing.

"Stop tormenting yourself."

Zack comes up from behind her on stealthy feet. Brit didn't hear him until he was at her shoulder, peering down at the glowing words on the screen. She doesn't know how long she has sat rereading the words.

Brit wants to scream. She wants to turn and face him and tell him to stop telling her what to do. She wants to cry and beat her fists on the wall.

But she only nods, pushing the button to close the screen. "Why would they do that?"

"What?"

"Donate to Mothers Against Drunk Driving."

"I don't know. Why does it matter?"

"Because it makes it sound like I was drunk," Brit whispers, exasperated that she has to explain.

"But you weren't, so what does it matter?"

He's right. It shouldn't matter. She just didn't see the car. That's all. She just didn't see her—it. She didn't see the car.

"You know red is the hardest color for the human eye to detect." Brit pulls the information from some half-forgotten art class. She looks at him and wants him to agree, to justify the accident for her.

"That so?" He studies her, his hand resting on her shoulder. "You know what I still don't understand?"

He squeezes, and Brit's stomach churns. She shakes her head, turning to look again at the darkened screen.

"Where were you going?"

"I told you. I was going to Senoia." Ten years ago, Senoia was a sleepy little burg, barely a dot on the Coweta County map, but some Hollywood group came and turned a part of it into a set for *The Walking Dead*, and now the town is bustling with zombie tours, restaurants, and even a museum.

"But why?" Zach's lips curl as he looks down at her.

"Just to walk around."

"That's funny."

A strangled laugh squeezes from her. "What does it matter?"

"I went by to check on your car today." He walks away, and she hears him moving into the kitchen.

"Yeah? What did they say?"

The refrigerator opens before he answers, and he screws off the top of a bottle and drops it on the counter. "I reckon they'll total it. Repairs would cost more than it's worth."

"I'm never gonna drive again anyway," she says but not loudly enough that he can hear her.

"Did you hear me? They're gonna total it."

"Yeah. I heard." Tears course down her cheeks, but she barely notices. She's cried more than she hasn't in the past forty-eight hours. Tears are her new norm.

He sits down in the living room, crossing one socked foot over the other on the coffee table.

His eyes are so dark and intense that she can barely look at him. A quake starts in the pit of her stomach—fear.

"So, you were just going to Senoia to check out the zombie shit."

"No. I wasn't going for zombies. There are some cute little shops over there. Craftsy, you know." She strains to remember the name of one of those shops, but *craftsy* is all she has.

"Oh yeah. Cause you're so *craftsy* and shit."

"Can I not just go and walk around somewhere? Is that not okay with you?"

"Hmm." Zack narrows his eyes until she looks away. He lifts the bottle to his lips and takes a long drink. "I reckon you can. You're a free agent."

Brit is frozen, unable to move. He knows. He knows Jason was with her.

"I'm tired. I'm gonna go lie down."

"No, come sit with me. I want to talk to you." He pats the couch beside him, and with an effort of will, she rises to her feet and makes the journey from the recliner to join him. "There you go. You comfortable?"

She nods but can no longer meet his unblinking eyes.

"So, I had a visitor up at the shop."

She nods again. Her mouth is too dry to speak.

"Mary Beth Jenkins came by. You know Mary Beth?"

Of course I know Mary Beth.

"Of course you know Mary Beth," he says as if he can read her mind. "She said she heard you were in an accident. She wanted to check and see how were feeling."

"What did you tell her?" Brit's heart freezes.

"Well, I told her it was right kind of her to check on you." His hand moves up her back, sliding under the curtain of her hair. Goose bumps erupt down her arms at his touch.

"That was nice." Her heart squeezes a beat, and the blood flows.

"You know what else she told me?"

Her heart clamps again, and she shakes her head.

Zack's hand reaches her neck. His fingers touch the skin just above her collar. "She told me that dumbass husband of hers has a busted-up face."

Brit nods.

"Said he told her he got in a fight. Can you believe that shit?"

"I wouldn't know. I don't know anything about him anymore."

His fingers squeeze then release. "Well, I just don't believe he got in a fight. Do you? He's the biggest pussy I ever met. Don't you think?"

She nods. "He never was much of a fighter." She has to say it to pacify him and make him blink again. "I'm really tired. I'm gonna go lie down."

"No, stay." His fingers tighten, circling the back of her neck and pressing into the meat at the base.

"You're hurting me."

Like lightning, his hand turns and twists in her hair before it drops free. "Sorry, baby. I'd never want to *hurt* you."

Zack picks up his phone. She stands and makes an escape toward the bedroom, where she can turn out the lights and pretend to be dead.

Brit is halfway across the room when his phone flies past and clatters to the ground in front of her. She stops walking and looks around at him.

"Tell me what that says."

She kneels to retrieve the phone, and the screen is open to a photo. The image captures the screen of another phone, showing a text chain. She recognizes the back-and-forth as one she deleted from her phone the morning after the accident.

I can't wait to see you.

I can't wait to feel you.

There are several lines more, but Brit doesn't waste time reading. She drops the phone and runs. When she reaches the bedroom, she slams the door, locking the pathetic twist handle. Expecting the impact of Zack's body, she braces against the wood, but nothing comes. She listens through the door but can't hear him moving. The silence is thick and heavy, broken only by the thudding of the blood coursing through her veins.

Then the sound of socked feet comes to her, moving with languid patience. When Zack reaches the other side, he taps lightly. "You in there?" he calls. His voice is almost a whisper.

She doesn't answer.

"I'm gonna leave now, and when I come back in an hour or so, you better be gone. If you're not... I mean, if you're stupid enough to still be here, I'm gonna kill you."

Tap, tap.

"You hear me?"

She nods, and a sob escapes her lungs.

"I'll take that as a yes."

Chapter 10

Brit's mind fills with a red fog. Fear at every sound makes her scurry to the window to see if Zack has returned. She doesn't have delusions that she can convince him to keep her, not after seeing him unblinking. When she saw him angry like that once before, the man who caused it was never quite right again. Maybe he wasn't quite right to begin with, but either way, Zack was a guy who did what he said.

When she scurries like a mouse from the home, where she has lived with Zack for nearly two years, she carries only a backpack and a duffel bag. She has no time to pack anything more, not without a car to load her belongings into. Brit called Kay, whom she works with at a small law firm in Newnan, the only person she could think to call. They're friends, the way people who work together are, but they're at different stages in life so not social. Kay has three kids under the age of ten, and at twenty-four, Brit isn't even sure she likes kids. But she does like Kay, and she likes her even more when she agrees to pick her up at the Waffle House just past the neighborhood where Zack's house sits.

"Are you okay?" Kay asks across the phone line.

"Zack kicked me out. I don't have a car. I need a ride." It seems the most reasonable thing to say.

"Yeah? What happened?"

Brit shakes her head, unable to admit her role in the dissolution. "It's not been good for a while."

"All right. I'm on my way."

Brit stands on the far side of the restaurant, away from the entrance, and watches the cars as they stop at the light and move on.

She feels relief when she sees Kay's car making the turn and is even more grateful to see that the kids are not in tow. As Kay lifts Brit's bags and places them in the back of the SUV, Brit slides into the passenger seat. She busies herself with her seat belt, struggling to get the latch connected with trembling hands.

"You want to talk about it?"

"Which part?" Brit faces forward as the vehicle begins to move, clenching her teeth and keeping her fists at her sides to keep from reaching for the dash or the door to escape.

"Was it about the accident?" Kay almost whispers.

"You know about that?"

It was in the paper, so of course she knows. Brit shakes her head, wondering if they have all been talking about it while she was home, hiding from the world. Shame overwhelms her.

"We've been worried."

The nervous energy bounding from Brit's skin fills the car. "I wasn't drunk. I don't know why they put that in the obituary like that. It made it sound like I was drunk."

"I didn't think that." Her words rush out on a breath. "Do you want to talk about it?"

Brit closes her eyes as they pull out of the parking lot, into traffic, making a slow right-hand turn.

"No," she manages to say.

Kay's next question is lost to Brit in the terror that grips her as she feels the tires rolling, taking them down the road. The sound of other vehicles passing them is overwhelming, and she braces for impact as the car picks up speed.

Her hands scrabble for the door, and Kay, seeing the panic, asks, "Are you okay?"

"Pull over. Pull over. Pull over."

Kay pulls the car to the side of the road, and Brit erupts onto the shoulder like demons are chasing her. She falls, sprawling across the ground.

"Oh my god, Brit. What's wrong?" Kay calls and climbs cautiously from the driver's side.

When she reaches Brit, she kneels, searching her face. Brit imagines Kay's thoughts as if she has said them aloud. Kay doesn't really know Brit. *Maybe she does drink. Maybe she does drugs. Is she high right now?* Brit can *feel* Kay's disgust. In the midst of a panic attack, she can *hear* Kay trying to decide if she's high. If she *is* a druggie, Kay can't have her in her home. She has babies. They can't be exposed to that.

"I can't be in that car." Brit sobs. The panic wells inside of her, her words coming on gasps of captured breaths.

"What do you mean?"

"I can't breathe." The utter terror that gripped her inside the car begins to wane, and Brit realizes she is sitting on the dirty roadside. She pulls herself to her feet.

"Where are you going tonight?"

Brit shakes her head. She doesn't have any place to go. When she called Kay, it had only been to get away from Zack's house before he came home.

"Well, get back in the car. We'll go slow. I'm only a mile down the road. You can sleep on our couch tonight, and tomorrow, we'll talk to Ben, and he'll help us work something out."

It takes some coercing, but finally, Brit forces herself into the seat and manages the mile drive to Kay's house without further incident.

July 11

Chapter 11

After a restless night in a stranger's house, where Brit hears every whispered conversation and every stumble to the bathroom, she gathers her belongings and leaves long before daylight. She walks, alternating the weight of her bags as she makes the slow ten-mile trek toward downtown Newnan.

At seven thirty, she finds the place in her phone that houses blocked numbers and dials the only number listed.

"Hey," Jason says, answering on the second ring.

"Can you talk?"

"I'm driving. Are you okay? You sound strange."

"I'm walking. Look, be careful. Zack knows you were with me."

"Shit. You told him?" The fear in his voice is undeniable.

Brit hears Zack's voice saying he has no fight, implying that he's a coward. "Yeah, I told him. What—you think I'm stupid?" Brit lowers her bags to the ground on the side of the road, and when she rises, she pushes her shoulders back to stretch the kinked muscles.

"How'd he find out?"

"How do you think he found out, Jason? What did you tell your *wife*?"

"I told her I got in a fight."

"Yeah, well, she didn't believe you." Her voice is thin and brittle. The exertion of her walk has made her intolerant.

"Of course she did."

"No, she didn't, and she showed up to tell Zack and sent him a picture of our texts."

"No. That didn't happen," he insists.

"Oh really? It did. I saw the texts she sent to Zack's phone! Do you have any idea what your wife has cost me?" Her voice crescendos.

"Calm down. Come on. You're acting crazy. Settle down."

"Don't tell me to settle down! I don't have a place to live, Jason!" She doesn't care that any person listening will know her business. But nobody is listening. Nobody cares. She's invisible.

"It'll blow over. You'll work it out," Jason says, keeping his voice calm, but she can hear his need to get off the phone, to check with his wife and make sure she's still buying his bullshit.

"He said he'd kill me if he ever saw me again."

"You think he meant it?"

Brit remembers his dark, unblinking eyes. "Yeah, I think he did. So you might want to watch your back." She disconnects the call before he can give her an excuse for why he needs to go when it's obvious he's setting up for damage control.

Brit gathers her bags and starts walking again. When she knows she is going to be late for work, she pulls out her phone to call the office. The screen lights up with Call Failed, so she tries again with the same result. She walks faster, anxious about not being able to get through and worrying that she will be in trouble. Heat rises around her, and rivulets of sweat course down her face.

Brit walks for nearly three and a half hours. She hadn't been able to even think about getting back into Kay's car for a fifteen-minute drive.

As she reaches the front of the office, Kay bursts through the door.

"I've been so worried."

"I figured you would have passed me. I walked thirty-four." She left Kay a note.

"I come in the back way."

Of course she would. Brit remembers her talking about the youngest one getting into the Montessori school over on Jack Dale Street before the square.

Brit shrugs her bags from her shoulders and apologizes.

"Why did you leave?"

Shaking her head, Brit looks away, unable to give a reasonable answer. No reasonable person walks ten miles instead of riding in a car for fifteen minutes. Kay doesn't say that Brit leaving the way she did was crazy, but Brit can read the thoughts in her eyes.

"Are you okay?"

Brit wishes she hadn't called Kay. She wishes she hadn't asked for her help. Now Kay will feel like Brit is her new project. What she wants is for Kay to step off... to go away and stop acting like she's going to fix it.

"I'm fine. I just needed to think."

The office phone rings, and Brit rushes to answer. "Walton and Shrieve. This is Brit. How can I help you?" She needs to show Kay that everything is fine. Yesterday was a glitch. Brit will work everything out, and it will be okay. She converses with the caller as if her entire life hasn't just exploded at the seams.

After Brit settles her bags under her desk, hiding them from view in the reception alcove, she is almost able to believe everything will be okay.

Ben Walton, senior partner, arrives twenty minutes later, unaware that his office has not been fully staffed. He will know soon enough, Brit figures, courtesy of Elise, the office manager, who has probably heard the whole sordid story from Kay.

"I need you to clear my afternoon," Ben says on his way into his office, speaking away from the phone he's holding to his ear.

Brit is confused because he is wearing his blue suit, tie and all, but he was just meeting with clients, not going to court. He never wears a suit unless he's going to court. She can't figure out what she missed.

But she simply nods and pulls open his schedule to start calling clients to set new times. She feels that it's important to be on top of her job today, as she's been gone for three days, and with everything else going so wrong, she can't risk her job.

An hour later, Ben invites Brit into his office. She takes a note pad and pen, trying to be prepared. Without looking up from his computer screen, he motions for her to sit across the desk from him. Brit waits, pen poised, until he finishes and turns to face her.

"You feeling better?" he asks.

Brit called out sick for two days after the accident. Additionally, she called out sick the day of the accident to meet up with Jason.

"I wasn't really sick, you know. I just needed some time." Tears pool in her eyes, and she looks away from him to fight them back.

"I know. Tragic thing, Brit. A real tragedy... for everybody."

"I wasn't drinking, Ben. I know that's what everybody thinks because of that thing about donations, but I swear I wasn't." She doesn't know why it's so important that people know she wasn't drinking. She had still been distracted, had still caused the accident, so it didn't matter. Brit hates herself for the groveling sound of her voice.

"I hadn't heard that you were drinking. I don't think the family thinks that."

The suggestion that he might know what the family thinks hits her like a bolt of lightning. "Do you know them?" She hasn't thought about people knowing the Martins.

"Sure. Jim and I graduated high school together."

In a flash, the pieces make sense to her. He asked her to clear his schedule so he could attend the funeral. His blue suit is a funeral suit.

Brit melts, tears wash down her face. She folds over her knees and tries to pull her features back into order.

"It was an accident," Ben offers, sounding somewhat surprised by the flood erupting before him.

"I looked. I looked. I just didn't even see her." The words bubble and roll from her lips like a torrent.

Brit can feel Ben watching as she sinks into the chair. He dislikes overt displays of emotion, and she feels stuck in the biggest over-display in history. He probably feels disgusted. He likes her fine—at least, she thinks he does. *I'm outgoing, and his clients seem to like the way I talk to them. I do a decent job of putting the schedule together, don't I?*

Brit is disgusted by herself. It's so inappropriate, and she knows how blubbering women make Ben uncomfortable. Brit overheard him talking to his partner, Newt, once, after a particularly emotional client left his office. "What was I supposed to do while she shuddered in my guest chair?"

He doesn't do anything while she tries to find some shape for her face to contain all of her emotions. When she finally looks up, tears still leaking, it's only because she runs out of energy, and she is hyper aware of her surroundings.

"I'm sorry," she whispers, embarrassed, and takes the offered box of tissues to wipe her eyes and nose. She blows her nose, making a vulgar squawk. "I'm sorry."

"You should take the day off, Britany. I don't think you're ready to be back at work," Ben says when the sounds of snuffling and wiping finally die away.

Brit can't argue. She has just dissolved into goo in her boss's office, so she is clearly not ready to be back at work.

"Okay."

"We'll see you tomorrow." He rises from his chair, ready to see her out, to sanitize the chair, open the windows, and let the despair out through the screen.

Brit has already missed three days this week and doesn't know that she has any more time available to take off with pay. She can't take the day without pay, especially now that Zack has kicked her out and she'll have to pull together money for a deposit, rent, and a new phone plan. She needs to pull herself together and get through the day. "Really, I'm okay. I can stay."

"I think it's best if you take the day off. You've been through a lot. Give yourself time to recover."

She nods and nods because that's what she always does, trying to please. As they pass the receptionist's alcove, he hands her the purse she left on her desk. He then walks her to the door.

Only when Brit is down the steps does she remember that all the rest of her belongings are inside the building, stuffed under her desk in the reception alcove. But she can't go back in to grab her stuff. That would be too embarrassing. She has her purse, so she can go have lunch somewhere and figure out what her next steps should be.

Ben is right. She isn't ready to be at work yet.

Chapter 12

Cliff attended the service for Dee Martin in uniform, representing the force, and now his chest feels hollow. The idea of returning to his stark one-bedroom apartment fills him with dread. He's been off duty for an hour, wearing his civvies while driving the familiar streets of Coweta County in his personal vehicle.

Dusk falls late during these summer months, and Cliff drives in the heat, his mind not engaged. The wheels turn, and he travels from the intersection that claimed Dee Martin's life to the edge of the county near Chattahoochee Bend State Park and back again. Finally, the car settles to an idle at the curb in front of the house he and Maggie shared for the three years they were together.

Maggie. He can see her through the window. He has cautioned her numerous times about not pulling the blinds when it starts to get dark. Any creep can look in on her, sitting there with her hair catching the light.

What went wrong?

She wants marriage. The picket fence isn't enough.

He dials her number and watches from the vantage point of his car as she raises her phone to her ear.

"Hey, Cliff," she says, and the sound of her voice takes his breath away.

Why is it so important that we get married? Why does it matter so much to her? "Hey, Mags. Busy?"

"No. Not busy. How are you?"

He watches her set her book aside and push her hair back from her face.

"I'm okay," he says, but he isn't.

"You don't sound okay."

"Yeah, well. I miss you." The silence stretches, and for a moment, he looks away from the window. "Think we could go to dinner?"

"I've already eaten."

"Well, then, another night? I just need to see you." He looks back at the window and is startled to see her standing right up against the windowpane, looking directly at him.

"You *are* seeing me." She smiles sadly and waves.

"Yeah. You need to close those blinds."

"I know." She doesn't move, and he reaches for the door handle, but before he can open the door and remove at least one of the barriers between them, she asks, "Have you changed your mind?"

His hand falls away from the handle, and he shakes his head. *Infuriating woman.* "Not about marriage."

"Have you thought about it?"

"Of course I've thought about it. Why is it so important to you?"

"I never lied to you. I always told you I wanted to get married and have kids."

"And I never lied to you."

"True," she agrees and places her palm on the window. "I just thought you'd change your mind."

"Why do you need a piece of paper saying what we are? Why does it matter?"

"It just does." She sighs and turns away from the window.

Continuing the familiar conversation, he says, "It doesn't matter to me. You know how I feel about you. I would never leave you."

"Then marry me." She settles again on her sofa but doesn't raise her face to look through the window again.

"You know I don't believe in it."

"It exists. You should believe in it."

"Mags. Why are you doing this? Weren't we good together? We were happy. Why do you want to throw it all away?"

"I am not your mother, and you are not your father."

"What is that supposed to mean?" His irritation sparks finally, not just at her words but also at the fact that she has left the sofa and moved out of the living room, out of sight.

"You know what it means."

Maggie returns to the living room, and Cliff lets out a heavy breath. His mind whirls through all the statistics about the marriages that end in divorce, which is a slightly higher percentage among cops. His mouth opens to form the words, but she speaks again before they can escape, and the words die.

"Did you go to the funeral?"

"I did." His voice is strangled.

"Such a tragedy." She's back at the window.

"Can I come in?"

"You can't stay."

"I know."

"Come on." Maggie opens the front door.

When Cliff meets her at the threshold, she steps into his arms just like she always has. She fits there like a piece of him. Tears leak from the corners of his eyes, and a shudder washes over him. He doesn't know how he has lived a single moment without her.

He never lied to her. She knew he didn't want marriage the same way she knew he had been born to the force. He would run into danger to serve his community, and she had accepted it, but she was not able to accept his views on marriage. She knew how his mother left without warning or reason. There was no fight or disagreement that had pushed her out the door—nothing he had seen anyway. His mother was there one day, and the next, the boys got off the bus to a motherless house. Cliff thought she had been abducted or kidnapped and couldn't understand why his father didn't have the police at the house, looking for her. She called later in the week to tell them she was okay but that she would not be coming back. It had rocked the family, particularly Cliff, who began wetting the bed. Their father spoke freely to them about how he hadn't had a clue. Cliff vowed then, as he watched his father in his confusion and loneliness, that he would never marry.

Maggie knows. He has told her about his family, how it disintegrated without warning, and still she believed he would change his mind.

Cliff wipes his thoughts clean, standing with her in his arms, and the shuddering and the tears stop, and soon, they're breathing on the same rhythm. Evening falls beyond the tree line, and the night creatures begin to hum.

July 19

Chapter 13

Eight days after Dee Martin was laid to rest, the preliminary accident report arrives in Cliff's dailies. He prints it before heading out for patrol then parks his car on the shoulder of Fischer Road near the intersection where the accident happened. There were no additional witnesses beyond the involved parties, so the report consists of facts and measurements. Dee Martin was driving a 2011 Honda Fit. Britany Addams was driving a 2009 Nissan Rogue. Dee died at the scene of the accident. The coroner's report, which is included, indicates that the cause of death was a gas embolism that traveled from her severed external jugular to her heart, causing the right ventricle to fill with foam, which caused cessation of function. The external jugular was severed by shrapnel released from the airbag upon inflation.

The airbag was meant to save her life, and it killed her.

Cliff is familiar with the airbag manufacturer, Takata. His personal vehicle, a Honda Civic, was under recall in 2016 for a Takata airbag issue. Maggie took it to the shop for the repair. The sick feeling in the pit of his stomach surges. He put Maggie in a death trap and thought nothing of it. He needs to check whether the 2011 Honda Fit was part of that recall, the largest recall in automotive history.

The vehicle accident report includes the 523 form Cliff filled out at the scene, and the remaining documentation details skid marks, angle of impact, and resting placement of both vehicles. It's exactly what he expected.

Armed with the report, Cliff drives to the address listed for Britany Addams but finds nobody home, so he dials the number he obtained from her the day of the accident.

"The number you have dialed has been disconnected or is no longer in service. If you feel you have reached this message in error, please dial the number again."

Cliff dials the number again and hears the same recorded message. *Odd that she would change her number.*

He puts in a call to the station. "Hey, Sue. This is Cliff. I'm following up on the accident report for case file GA-A-732 and trying to locate Britany Addams. Can you get me her work information?"

"Yeah, give me a second."

Cliff waits, and soon, Sue comes back to say, "She works for Walton and Shrieve. They're located at 26 Jack Dale Street in Newnan. Need a phone number?"

"Yeah, go ahead and give it to me. I think I'll drive over, but it can't hurt to have it." Sue relays the number, and Cliff jots it down on the back of the accident report. "Thanks, Sue. I owe you one."

As he drives, his mind cycles back to the moments he spent with Dee Martin before the paramedics arrived and he turned her over to them. He remembers the clamminess of her skin beneath his fingers and the slight blue tinge just beneath the surface. There was nothing he could do to save her, but he's grateful she wasn't scared in her last moments. She was smiling and asking him if he had breakfast.

The skin of his scalp prickles, and he shakes himself free of the memory, forcing his mind to practical matters. He wonders if Dee received a recall notice and didn't take the risk to heart. Maybe she skipped the repairs, or a previous owner did. She may not have known anything about the danger posed by a defective airbag when she bought the car.

Dee died because the airbag malfunctioned. She would likely have survived if it had operated properly. The coroner's report didn't indicate head trauma, and there were no broken bones. Cliff feels certain she would have lived but for the sliver of debris that exploded from the airbag to sever her vein.

He climbs the steps, enters Walton and Shrieve, and sees Britany Addams behind the reception desk. Her hair is pulled back in a low ponytail, and her face is free of makeup. Dark circles hollow out the area beneath her eyes, which seem too large for her face. He recognizes the evidence of insomnia.

"Ms. Addams, I'm Officer Clifford Rathborn with the Coweta County Sheriff's Department. Do you have a moment?"

He catches the movement of her trachea beneath her skin when she swallows.

Nodding, Britany rises from her seat, then she crosses the hall and leans into the open door. "Ben, the police are here." Her voice wavers. "Can I take a minute?"

Cliff can't quite hear his response, but when Britany responds with "No, I'll be fine. Thank you, though," he understands that Mr. Walton offered to join her in the conference.

Britany comes through the door. Her clothes are rumpled and seem too big, hanging from her shoulders and hips. The back of the shirt has come free, and she absently tucks it into the loose band of her pants. Cliff follows her into the conference room and sits in the chair at the head of the table. She takes the first seat along the edge to his right, and seconds pass while she settles herself.

"Are you here to arrest me?" she asks in a flat voice.

"No, ma'am. I just needed to follow up and get your statement to complete the accident investigation."

She nods, and her teeth close on the insides of her cheeks, which pulls the flesh inward and causes her to look even more skeletal.

"I'd like to hear your version of the accident."

"Didn't we already do this?"

"Yes, but I thought you might remember something away from the moment. You were in shock when we spoke that day."

"I'm still in shock." She catches his eye and holds it for half a second before looking out the window. "I was on Fischer Road, going toward Highway 54, on my way to Senoia to walk around. They have some neat shops over there." Shrugging, she tilts her head as if listening to someone speaking that only she can hear.

"Yes, ma'am."

"I stopped at the stop sign, and I looked. I didn't see anybody coming, so I pulled out onto 54. That's when the other car hit me."

"You're certain you looked?"

"Yes, sir." Britany fixes her wide, watery eyes on him. "I looked. There was nothin' there."

"You were driving a 2009 Nissan Rogue. Is that correct?"

When she nods, he makes a check mark beside the make and year of her vehicle. "Had you ever noticed any blind spots in that car?"

Her bottom lip protrudes, and her head moves back and forth. He becomes aware of an odor surrounding the woman, the funk of unwashed flesh.

Cliff remembers the smear of blood on her pants and the blood on the passenger-side airbag, for which he's unable to discover the source. "Were you alone in the vehicle at the time of the accident?"

She swallows, and her watery eyes shift free of him to rest on her hands. Her chewed nails look angry and red, the only color remaining in her countenance. Her head tilts again, as if listening, and Cliff repeats his question.

"Yes, sir."

"All right." He scans the front page of the document and says, "It seems your phone is out of service. Were you aware?"

She nods. "You can reach me here."

"Okay." He circles the phone number he wrote on the back of the document. "Do you still live at 283 Andrew Bailey Road?"

"No." She shakes her head.

"Can I have your new address?"

"I'm between places right now."

Her watery eyes come back to him, and he almost wants to touch her, to tell her that everything will be okay and explain that the injuries Dee sustained were not solely from the accident, and had the airbag functioned properly, Dee would probably have survived. But he doesn't. He simply nods and rises from his chair.

"Is there anything you need?"

Britany shakes her head, compressing her lips into a thin line.

"All right." He pushes the chair under the table and angles toward the door. "Be sure to get us an address when you get settled." He opens the door.

"What happens next?"

"We'll complete the investigation and file our report."

"So you aren't going to arrest me?" she asks and tilts her head a third time, in that same odd way.

"Do you think I should arrest you?"

She nods, an unfocused expression in her eyes that makes her look very young and very old at the same time.

Cliff sits down. "Ms. Addams, I don't know what the outcome of this investigation will be, and if the district attorney sees cause, then you'll have an opportunity at that time to plead your case. Until such a time, you should go about living your life the best you can."

Again, she nods but still with that vacant expression in her eyes.

"Do you have anybody you can talk with?"

"Sure."

He studies her. "I wouldn't think the DA will be interested in seeking an arrest warrant in this situation."

"What does that mean?"

"You don't have a history of reckless driving. It doesn't appear you were being willfully negligent. Sometimes accidents are just accidents."

"But somebody died. I killed somebody."

Cliff sees the torment in Britany's face and realizes she's the hair-shirt variety of person. She wears her guilt like a penance. Some people live life without recognizing the damage they do, and others, hair-shirt people, stew in the soup of guilt, beating themselves down for every ill-conceived action and every perceived error.

"Somebody died. That doesn't mean you killed her." He wants to tell her about the defective airbag to ease her worry, but it isn't his place to divulge preliminary findings in an ongoing investigation.

Chapter 14

" Somebody died. That doesn't mean you killed her."

The words reach Brit but only after she walks with Officer Rathborn from the room. Somebody died. Dee Martin died. Dee Martin, who worked at Chick-fil-A and played volleyball at West Georgia. Deanne Martin, daughter of James and Carrie Martin, girlfriend of Christopher, granddaughter of Sam and Sandra Martin and Marie Coggins. Preceded in death only by her grandfather, Jerry Coggins. She had friends. She had a future.

And now she doesn't.

After the officer leaves, when Brit finally understands that she's not to be arrested today, she goes back to her desk and tries to finish Ben's stack of dictation.

At five, she shuts down her computer and stands in Ben's doorway. "Is there anything else I can do?"

Ben looks up from his desk and shakes his head. "No, you go on home and get some rest."

She nods, her throat tight. Her heart thuds. She turns back to her desk, gathers her purse, checks her belongings under the desk to ensure they're not visible from the hall, and leaves the office on the heels of Kay.

"You need a ride anywhere?" Kay asks. Brit can tell she feels obligated to offer but hopes Brit will refuse.

"No. I'm good. I'm just going to walk over to the bank. We should have gotten paid today."

"Yeah, payday!" Kay says with mock enthusiasm.

After Brit nods, they part ways at the base of the steps.

Brit spoke with Elise, the office manager, earlier about not having her pay auto-deposited. "Can you just give me a check instead?"

"I can't do that. It's already deposited. You can't just change that the day payroll runs. You have to tell me in advance. There's a form you have to sign." She was annoyed, her flabby jaw quaking with the motion of her gray-haired head.

She was unhelpful, and Brit felt dirty standing at the edge of Elise's desk, aware that her hair was stringy and in need of a good washing. "Okay. Well, can we do that for next time?"

"Yes. You'll have to sign the form." Elise sighed, annoyed.

Brit's stomach churns as she makes her way to the bank. July heat bakes her skin. Lifting each foot is an effort. She ran out of the change from the bottom of her purse two days ago, and last night, she ate half a sleeve of stale Fig Newtons she found forgotten in the kitchen at Walton and Shrieve.

The bank lobby is closed, so Brit waits in line for the ATM. She inserts her card and punches in the access pin then presses the button to view the balance in the account.

The information that spreads across the screen can't be right. Elise said her money had been deposited, so she doesn't understand how the available balance could be zero. Null. Empty. Void.

There should be at least $623.00 in there that belongs to her, but the account is empty. She pushes another button on the screen, requesting to see previous transactions, and slowly, the information breaks through the dark shadows lurking in her mind. The list of transactions goes back two days. Zack's check was deposited yesterday, $1,450.00. The available balance yesterday at close of day was $2,432.76. This morning, Brit's check was deposited. The available balance at eleven was $3,055.76. Just after noon, a withdrawal of the entire amount was made, leaving the account with a zero balance. She stares, not hearing the traffic moving down the street or the man behind her becoming impatient.

Zack. She digs through her purse and pulls out her phone, desperate to call him and demand an answer. But the phone has been disconnected, and even if it hadn't been, it's dead. She didn't bring a charging cord.

Her teeth clench until her jaw aches, and she stares at the ATM screen until a message appears. *Are you still there?*

Apparently not.

The traffic roars, and the man behind her clears his throat. Brit pushes the button to cancel her transaction and retrieves her useless card. When she tries the door for the lobby, she finds it locked. She walks around the building to the drive-through and peers through the window into the empty building.

"Shit." *He stole my money.*

"If I ever see you again, I'll kill you."

Brit spins away from the window, hearing Zack's voice rising above the traffic. She loses her balance with the motion and falls to the pavement.

"If I ever see you again, I'll kill you."

She hears it again, but this time from its rightful place inside her memory.

Tap, tap, tap, his finger went on the door. "You in there?" he called. His voice was so soft, almost a whisper.

She didn't answer.

"I'm gonna leave now, and when I come back in an hour or so, you better be gone. If you're not, I mean, if you're stupid enough to still be here, I'm gonna kill you."

Tap, tap.

"You hear me?"

Brit nodded, and a sob ratcheted from her lungs, the same as it does now.

"I'll take that as a yes."

How could everything go so wrong so fast? She tries to calculate the days until her mother will be back in the country, knowing she'll help her get through this. Her mom will be disappointed, but she'll still help. She doesn't have to tell her about Jason. Her mother made her thoughts about that clear enough when Brit told her they ran into each other every now and then. Brit's father was a cheater, and her mother detested cheaters. She imagines her mother asking what she was doing driving around town on a workday, shirking her responsibilities.

Closing her eyes, she tries to make a conversation with her mother work the way she wants, but every time, her mother sees through her, just like Zack did. She was lying and cheating, no different from her dad. Brit opens her eyes and stops crying. This is her fault. She should have talked to Elise earlier about changing her auto-deposit. She should have known that Zack wouldn't leave her money in the account, which only has his name on it. She should have been at work the day of the accident and not looking for a place to park with a married man. Brit is disgusted with herself, ashamed because she created this whole mess and until now just thought everybody else would fix it for her. Nobody is coming to her rescue. She is the bad guy in her life, and she's all she has.

Brit sits for a long time in the shelter of the building, and her mind churns as she tries to find a path forward. Without her phone, she can't even call her mother to tell her she's okay, let alone ask for help. All her stupid decisions flash through her mind. Brit wrote a series of bad checks two years ago, which resulted in her personal bank account being closed. Instead of taking care of the checks, she just let the bank close her account and pretended it didn't happen. She just started depositing her money into Zack's account and hadn't even asked him to add her name. She was such an idiot. They talked about it one weekend, but she was afraid that trying to add her name would alert the bank, then Zack would know. Brit should have cleared those checks. If she had done the right thing, she would still have her personal account, and Zack wouldn't have been able to take her money. *Karma.* Brit almost laughs in bitterness, but then the series of bad choices rolls to a stop with the accident. It plays out in slow motion, the seven seconds that changed her life.

Zack isn't the problem. He was just one of her bad decisions. She's been irresponsible and selfish, and now she can't unsee it. Understanding squelches her anger. She is only where she is because of the things she did. Zack came to her after the accident. He was sweet and loving. He helped her into bed and held her, kissing her forehead like she was a child. Even the next day, he was kind, offering food and encouraging her to get out of bed.

She's the one who destroyed everything. She snuck away to see Jason, knowing that if they got caught, everything would change—almost like she wanted to get caught.

Brit wanted somebody to tell Mary Beth so she would be done, and she and Jason could be together the way he promised when they were in high school. Mary Beth threatened to leave the last time. Brit wanted to get caught so that Zack would tell Mary Beth. Instead, Mary Beth told Zack.

That's it. She needs to call Jason. He will help her through this. He loves her. She rouses herself and makes her way back to the office. She walks around to the back, feeling better now that she has a plan. The parking lot is empty, and Brit makes her way to the door, unlocks it with her key, and slips inside.

Evening casts the interior of the small house in gold. Brit doesn't dare turn on lights but touches the mouse of her computer, and it wakes. She types Jason's name in the search bar.

When she has his phone number, she calls it from the office phone. After one trill, his voice mail picks up. "This is Jason. Go."

Hearing his voice in an unanswered call is more than she can handle. She thought he loved her, all those years in high school, but when he went to college, he let her go. His voice in the message is so nonchalant, so unconcerned. When they started sleeping together last fall, she and Zack were already struggling. Jason said he'd never stopped thinking about her, that he couldn't get her out of his mind.

Brit drops the handset onto its cradle and stares down at her hand, where the blue veins rise over the bones. Deep inside her soul, she believed he was going to rescue her from her tense relationship with Zack. She thought he was going to leave his wife and their four-year-old son to be with her. He said he loved her, but he left when the accident happened, just turned and walked away. He told his wife he had been in a fight.

He was never going to leave her.

Understanding comes on a wave, wiping clean the thoughts that were scratched in the sand. Jason had not loved her. He had used her. She had used him too. They had used each other to feel alive.

She dials Zack's phone with her heart in her throat.

"Hello?"

"Zack, it's me. Don't hang up."

A long silence stretches between them.

"What do you want?"

"I went to the bank, and the account is empty." The small quake in her voice threatens to give her away, and she bites her lip to keep from crying, to keep from begging him to come get her.

"So?"

"So? I got paid today. I need that money."

"Hmm…" He puffs out a breath of air, almost a laugh. "I don't know what you're talking about."

"My check was deposited today. The account was empty when I got to the ATM. I need that money."

"Seems that money deposited into my account is my money."

"It's *my* money!" she screams, her voice ricocheting off the walls.

"Woah," Zack says, unconcerned. Maybe he's high.

Brit pulls herself together, gritting her teeth. She hisses, "It's my money, Zack. You know that. I need my money. I'm going to the bank tomorrow, and I'd better be able to get my money."

"You don't have an account at the bank." His voice drops low and is muffled as he speaks to someone who laughs.

"Who was that?" Brit asks, even though it's none of her business.

"What do you want?" Zack oversteps her question.

"I want my money."

"Good luck with that."

Her eyes widen, and she forgets how to blink. "What am I supposed to do?"

"I don't care what you do. Call your lover. Maybe you can move in with him and his wife."

She deserves that and says nothing.

"Speaking of Lover Boy, I talked to Mary Beth today."

She can't understand why he would be talking to Mary Beth. They don't even know each other. She wonders if it's Mary Beth in the background of the call.

"Did you hear me?"

"Yeah, but so?" Exasperation makes her pull the phone away from her ear.

"Ha!" he barks. "You don't know."

She puts the phone back to her ear. "Know what?"

"She's pregnant. They're having another kid." He says it with triumph, mocking her and salving his wounded pride with the breaking of her. "He was never gonna leave her for you."

Again, Brit removes the phone from her ear, and his voice grows smaller.

"You there? Brit, did you hear me? They're having another kid. Don't you feel stupid now?"

Brit drops the phone into its cradle.

She does feel stupid—stupid, hopeless, guilty, and dirty. Brit feels trashy. She feels disgusted suddenly by the faint aroma emanating from her skin and the greasiness of her hair.

The computer screen goes black and leaves Brit sitting in darkness, trying to reconcile how it all came to this. Expecting tears, she waits, needing the release to wash away her guilt and sorrow.

Someone died.

Somebody died because of her bad decisions. Nothing else matters.

July 20

Chapter 15

"Hey, Tony," Cliff calls as he climbs out of his car and joins his brother on the sidewalk leading to their father's house.

Both hold shopping bags for the meal they'll cook to celebrate Carla's completion of therapy. Tony waits, shifting his bags to one hand. When they're close, he raises a fist, and Cliff obligingly bumps it.

"Where's Maggie?"

"We're taking a break." He hates the way it sounds, like they're teens. "Where's Trish?"

Tony quirks an eyebrow. "We're taking a break."

"No shit?"

"She wants to get married." Tony knocks on the door then pushes it open.

"Maggie too."

"Go figure." Tony drops a fist on Cliff's shoulder. "You know Maggie isn't Mom."

"Yeah, neither is Trish."

"I know." Tony gives a sad smile. "Impossible relationships."

They both know, but it doesn't make it any easier.

Tony was fifteen when their mother left, and Cliff was eleven. They got off the bus, and their father met them at the end of the drive.

"Where's Mom?" Cliff asked.

"She's gone," Dad answered then ran his tongue over the line of his teeth and sucked air.

"What do you mean?" Tony asked.

"I mean she done left us."

"When will she be home?" Cliff asked, not understanding that when Dad said she was gone, he meant she was *gone*.

He meant that none of them would ever hear from her again. They hadn't, either. Not a birthday card or a *howdy do*—only a single message left on the answering machine ever connected them to her again.

It didn't take long for Dad to remove all vestiges of her from the house. Photos went into a box and disappeared into the attic. The clothes she left behind were gone one day, and the boys never knew where to. Cliff figured he probably donated them to Goodwill, but knowing his dad, he also thought he might have made a bonfire and burned everything. But he would have seen evidence of that, so he always assumed they were donated. Cliff often wondered about his mom, Miriam, but the subject was officially closed in the Rathborn home. Dad never spoke her name after the day he met them coming off the bus. It didn't take long for him to convey to the boys that speaking of her was bad manners. Almost a year passed, and the house took on the appearance of utility. Curtains grew dingy and hung limp at the windows. The boys grew used to the grime, so when Carla moved in and took over the laundry and demanded that the boys clean up after themselves, they both bucked against her.

She was good for them, though, and over time, she filled some of the space left by Miriam's abandonment.

Carla's the one who brings both the boys to visit today. She rang the bell for completing thirteen rounds of chemotherapy after a double mastectomy. They're here to celebrate.

Cliff follows Tony through the foyer and kitchen, where they leave their bags on the table around an arrangement of flowers. They continue through the house until they find their father and Carla sitting side by side on the back deck. Carla's arms are thin, the muscles small and defined by the lack of adipose tissue. A red scarf covers her thinned hair. It seems their father has taken on the excess that the chemo has pulled from Carla, and he's more portly than stout.

"Hey, old man," they say almost in unison, but their attention is for Carla. They lean down to greet her, each in turn.

"How you feeling?" Cliff asks as Tony says, "You're looking good."

Carla smiles, accepting hugs from Tony then Cliff. Her shoulders feel frail beneath Cliff's hands, like the narrow cage of a bird's ribs.

"Where are the girls?" Carla asks when they step away to lean against the railing.

They both take on the air of dragonflies pinned to an examination board, looking away and expecting the other to speak.

"You don't have to tell me. I already know, boys," she says, forcing their attention back to her.

"It just didn't work out," Tony says, as he has said about every relationship he's been in since college.

"I like Trish, Tony, and she's good for you. What happened?"

Tony squints down at her. A small smile plays on her lips. Cliff studies him, contemplating how they both ended up at the same place in life—alone. Tony was old enough when Miriam left to think he didn't need mothering. Old enough to have seen the writing on the wall, he said. He remembers the days when their mother sat catatonic, staring through the wall at something only she could see. That alone should have told them she was a nutcase. He pretended to be relieved when she left. It brought an end to the manic days when she left the house and didn't return until after nightfall, burdened with packages and bundles that would all have to be returned when the bills came due. "She wasn't right," he said more than once when trying to console Cliff. "Something was off in her head." He claimed to feel sorry for his dad and Cliff, who thought they could fix her.

"She wants to get married. I just don't know that I'm ready for that," Tony explains.

Cliff has to turn away, hearing how ridiculous it sounds. Trish and Tony had a good thing. At least Cliff is willing to admit that it's fear keeping him stalling at the marriage altar.

"You was living together, paying bills together. Didn't you buy your car together?"

"Sure." Tony nods.

"You were planning on continuing to do those things, right?" Carla asks.

Again, Tony nods, and his lips spread in a small, chagrined smile.

"Why does a piece of paper from the government saying you plan to continue doing those things together make any difference?"

Tony shrugs. "You aren't married, and you two are happy."

"We aren't married because it isn't important to me."

"Why is it important to her?"

"I don't know, and it doesn't matter. If you love this girl, and I know you do, why not give her what she needs?" Carla lets her hand fall on Rob's knee, and his much larger hand drops over and hides hers like a magic trick.

Tony is silent, not looking at Carla.

"What about you, Cliff? Where's Maggie?"

"We're working on it," he says, holding her eyes. Unlike Tony, Cliff still needed mothering when Miriam left, feeling uprooted and abandoned. He swore he would never trust a girl, would never love anybody, so nobody could ever leave him again.

"I'm glad to hear it. Maggie sent me flowers for ringing the bell. She's a good girl, Cliff. I'd hate to see you lose her."

He nods, compressing his lips into a tight smile. "Me too." The words drift out into the backyard and leave the family on the deck in silence. Cliff remembers the flowers on the kitchen table. Of course Maggie sent flowers.

"Well, brother, we'd best get to cookin'," Tony says, and they move inside to let the man and not-wife sit in the peace and calm of the late-afternoon shade.

July 22

Chapter 16

Brit sets the corporate papers for a new childcare facility into the copier. The owner is coming today to go over the legal documents. Brit has rechecked them three times. She is less confident about the incorporation forms than the estate planning documents because she doesn't really understand how corporations work, how they're structured, and what all the words *mean*. The first series runs through the copier, pausing as each page prepares to feed.

Brit chews on the skin around her fingernail.

"At least she's clean today." The words are whispered, and they sit rolling inside Brit's mind for a few seconds before they make sense. Elise doesn't know she's at the copier, next to the kitchen, or she wouldn't have said it. Her voice traveled through the door and just happened to land at Brit's ears in a moment of quiet.

She *is* clean. After two weeks of washing as best she could in the sink, she took the risk yesterday, the second Sunday she spent in the office, of unpacking the shower stall of its toiletries and reams of paper. After locking the bathroom door, she undressed and stepped into the stream of water. She used the liquid soap from the sink and expected to see a trail of dirt disappearing down the drain, but she didn't. The water felt so good on her skin that she stood under it for a long time, just letting it touch her. It felt like years had passed since she was last touched. It felt like years had passed since her last shower.

After the conversation with Zack on Friday night, in which he told her that Jason and Mary Beth were expecting their second child, she lost her mind a little. She called Jason six times in a row until he picked up the phone.

"What do you want?" he snapped, his voice filled with the residue of sleep.

"Is it true?" she asked. "Is she pregnant?"

Rustling followed, and she imagined him extricating himself from their shared bed. When he spoke again, his voice was no longer filled with sleep. "Yeah. She is." It wasn't an apology to her, but it almost sounded like one.

"Guess what? So am I." Brit wasn't, but she wanted to hurt him. She wanted to shock him, to remind him that she was still alive and that somehow, he *owed* her something.

"What are you and Zack gonna do?"

"It's not Zack's kid," she said, her mind spinning a story as quickly as she spoke. "Zack's sterile. He can't have kids." It may be true. He was in a bad bicycle accident as a child and lost one of his testes. The other could be damaged. She didn't intend to say any of this, and she was as surprised as Jason must have been.

"What are you saying?"

"Won't it be nice? We can share birthday parties. Raise 'em like twins."

"That is not going to happen."

"What do you mean?"

"You're not for real. You're fucking kidding me, right?" His voice rose, cracking.

"No, I'm not joking. I was gonna tell you that day, but then... well, you know."

His voice dropped to a whisper. "You should get an abortion."

"Would you say that to your wife? This is your child. Our baby." Brit almost believed it, that he was asking her to terminate a viable pregnancy. She almost believed she was pregnant and felt hysterical, unable to breathe, until she had to put her head down on the desk to make the lightheaded feeling dissipate.

"Brit..." He said her name like a plea, like an apology.

"You destroyed my life," she whispered, and tears finally rolled over her lashes. "How did this happen?" Her words are stalled and warped.

"What can I do?" he asked, and she thought she had moved him, that he was ready, finally, to leave his wife. "I can't have another kid."

Her hopes deflated, and she drew a shaky breath, understanding. The tears brewing in her eyes dried, and she felt empty and forlorn. "I need money, and I'll take care of it."

True to his word, this morning, he walked into Walton and Shrieve and handed her an envelope with three hundred twenty-five dollars. It's not enough—it won't make up for the lost paycheck—but it will have to do. She felt guilty and almost handed back the money, but then she remembered that she didn't have anybody else, and he owed her.

They did not have a conversation. He entered through the front door, spotted her behind her desk, walked to the counter, and laid the envelope on the ledge of the window that opened above the alcove.

"We're done, right?" he asked quietly.

"Oh yeah. We're through." Her lips quirked, pulled up into a Joker's grin.

She didn't think she had anything left to lose. There was no place lower for her to fall. Then she hears Elise and Kay whispering about her in the kitchen. Her face burns with shame and embarrassment. When she can't stand it any longer, she clears her throat loudly. The whispers stop, and as the printer kicks another sheet through, Kay comes from the kitchen with a mug of steaming coffee.

"Hey," she says. "You're looking good today."

"Hmm," Brit replies, unable to look up. She bites her tongue to keep from snarling "Clean" at her. "Thanks."

"You doin' okay?"

Brit's lips compress, and she nods. She should be angry at hearing them talking about her like that. But Brit doesn't have the bandwidth for angry. All her energy is taken up with shame.

July 27

Chapter 17

On the third Saturday of her homelessness, well before day-break, Brit carries her two bags out of the house that serves as the office to Walton and Shrieve. Today, she will walk to the laundro-mat and doesn't want to risk anybody seeing her lugging the bags out the front door. After settling them out of sight of passersby, she returns to her desk to wait. Weariness flows through her after the small exertion. She's not eating enough, but there's nothing to be done about it until she gets paid again. At her desk, she rests her head on her arms and drifts off.

The sound of a car driving down the alley startles her awake. A glance down the hall toward the parking lot confirms that Newt has pulled in and is climbing out of his car. She doesn't have time to check to make sure she didn't leave a trail or do anything more than scuttle out the front door. Crouching on the front porch, she waits until she's sure Newt has reached his office. She risks looking through the window and sees that she forgot to turn off the small desk light in the alcove, and Newt is looking into the space with a quizzical ex-pression. She drops her head and skitters off the porch into the bush-es. Her heart hammers as she waits for him to open the door and find her.

Brit's getting sloppy. She didn't expect him so early. Last week, he came in, but it was after ten, so she expected him to do the same thing today. Her stomach churns. If he opens the front door, he'll see her. She has no way to explain what she's doing here on a Saturday morning. If she had a legitimate reason for being here, she wouldn't have run out and hidden.

Newt does not come to the front door. Instead, he turns off the light and walks down the hall to his office. Relief washes through her. She doesn't know what would have happened if Newt had discovered she was in the office and isn't sure what she would have done if he had come to the front door and discovered it was unlocked. She only has a key for the back door. It doesn't matter—there was no time to lock it if she'd had a key.

She can't be sloppy like that again.

Brit pulls the duffel strap across her body and the backpack onto her shoulders and walks out of the bushes, away from the small house that Newt and Ben converted into office space. The nearest laundromat is over on Temple Avenue, so she walks down Jack Dale, listening to the morning song of crickets above the whispering of leaves. Brit's mind wanders as she walks, remembering bits of information Zack shared when she first came to live with him. Jack Dale Street is on the Tour of Homes every Christmas. A few of them date to the late 1800s. Newnan was a hospital base during the Civil War, and soldiers from both sides were cared for in the homes, so when devastation fell on many great homes in the South, Newnan was largely spared. She didn't grow up in Newnan but had lived over in Lanett, Alabama, just over the state line. She and Jason both grew up in Lanett. Everything would have been different if they had never left Lanett. They would be married by now, and she would be the one having his kids. But Jason went to college, and that changed everything.

Brit wanted to go to college, but when her parents got divorced at the end of her senior year, nobody had money to help her. She didn't get good-enough grades for a scholarship, although she thought she was plenty smart. Her mother said she could have gotten scholarships if she had just *applied* herself. It seems to be the story of Brit's life. She never quite manages to apply herself the way she should.

After the divorce, her father moved to Colorado and married Lucy, who is only three years older than Brit. That was the last straw, and Brit hasn't spoken to her father since. It creeps her out to think of her dad with somebody Brit is old enough to have gone to high school with. Her mom remarried as well, but at least she stayed within her generation. They moved to Destin two years ago, and they asked Brit if she wanted to move with them, but she was already seeing Zack and had just reconnected with Jason and still thought something in their chemistry was love.

Her mind rolls as she walks left onto Temple, where traffic is already thick. The cricket song is drowned out by the hum of tires on pavement and the roar of engines. Brit's pulse throbs. Heat sits low to the ground, rising from the sidewalk, which is still warm from yesterday.

Crossing at a stop light, Brit adjusts the strap of her duffel, then she makes her way through the parking lot of the laundromat. A woman and her three children are inside. Brit chooses a line of washers away from them. The kids look tired and full of snot, and the mother is rotund in an overfed and undernourished way. Each of the kids has a snack from the vending machine serving as breakfast—powdered donuts, Zingers, and Ho Hos. Brit's stomach grumbles. She is always hungry.

Brit exchanges one of the twenties from the envelope Jason gave her for quarters and sets to sorting her clothes into the washers. When the bags are empty, she purchases single-use soaps from the vending machine and starts the washers, making the clothes churn. Her mind slides to null as the kids begin to push the carts around like they're bumper cars. Brit sits, staying out of the aisles.

Brit's in no hurry for the laundry to finish, as she has nowhere to be. She can't go back to the office until she's sure she won't encounter Ben or Newt. At least here, she can sit like she belongs and stay out of the heat.

After flipping through magazines, she picks up a paperback novel somebody left. She holds it in front of her, but the words shift and slip, and she can't get into the story. So she sits.

The woman and her kids leave as Brit moves her clothes into the dryers. A man comes in and dumps a load into one of the washers and leaves, too busy to watch his wash. Brit pretends not to see him. Then a woman comes in, pushing a wheelchair laden with bags. Brit can't pretend not to see that. The woman has dark hair shot through with gray streaks. She parks the chair in front of a washer and makes her way around the room, checking the change returns on the vending machines before returning to her belongings. Brit keeps her eyes averted, trying not to watch or at least not to be seen watching.

The woman loads clothes into two washers, separating dark and light. Brit thinks she seems familiar, and it bothers her until she puts the pieces together. She's seen this woman before in another life. The woman was walking down Highway 34, pushing her chair. She and Zack spotted her chair late one night, parked and covered in plastic bags, outside Walmart.

"Look at that. Just like it's a car," Brit commented. "You know anything about that woman?"

"Nah. What is there to know? Old crazy woman. I think her name is *I-yam.*"

"That's not a name." Brit remembers laughing and bumping up against him. It was a good day between them.

"I-yam what I yam," Zack mimicked, and he had dropped his arm around Brit's shoulders.

The memory sputters and dissolves, the soft edges going slightly out of focus. He may have loved her, at least in the beginning. Brit lets out a long sigh. It doesn't matter now, whether he loved her. She ruined that. Sure, Zack has issues, but he's not a bad guy. She just doesn't love him the way she loves Jason. *Loved.*

It doesn't matter. She is what she is. Brit watches the old woman and allows her mind to drift, trying to figure out who she is now. Since the accident, everything she thought she understood and everything she did because of the way she felt seems out of balance. Now that Brit can see her series of bad choices, everything ties together, and where she previously thought Mary Beth was the problem—or Zack or her mother—all she can see now is that she was the problem.

When the woman glances her way, not quite making eye contact but making Brit aware that she's been seen, Brit tries to break the ice. "Laundry day?"

The woman doesn't react, as if she hasn't heard.

"I like your chair. I bet that makes things a lot easier." Brit's shoulders still ache from where the straps have dug into her flesh.

The woman looks at her with piercing black eyes, assessing her. "I reckon."

Brit doesn't look away. She meant what she said and feels she has the right to say it. She wasn't insulting the woman or making fun. It's good that the woman has streamlined her life. It was smart. She's found ways to make it easier to walk all day and go nowhere. She found a wheelchair.

Brit's hair falls over her face, a heavy lock of what used to be her best feature but is now brittle and unwieldy without proper care. She always kept it heavily highlighted and hates the way the inch or so of root broadcasts her change in circumstances. At the beginning of July, she was due for a touchup, but then everything happened, and she missed her appointment. She pulls the thick hair back and wraps it into a knot at the back of her head.

"I'm Britany. My friends, when I had any, called me Brit." Her voice creaks, and she clears her throat as the first of her dryers buzzes. She checks the clothes, which aren't dry, and inserts another quarter for more time.

"You have to use the high setting, or they'll never dry," the woman says and slots quarters into her machine. From the bottom of her chair, she withdraws a clear plastic bin with detergent. She sprinkles her two loads and closes the lids.

"Oh. I didn't know that."

"Yeah. They set them that way, so the dummies just keep popping coins in. It'll take ten runs, and they'll still be damp. That's where they make their money."

Brit reaches over and changes the setting on each of the dryers. "Thanks for telling me."

"Yep."

"You ever tried this pizza place next door? I thought I'd get a pizza when it opens."

"I never ate there, but it always smells good."

"Well, let's try it today. I won't be able to eat a whole pizza by myself." It isn't true. Brit could probably eat two whole pizzas. It's been so long since she felt like she could look anybody in the eye that she just keeps talking, and the woman keeps letting her.

Brit is bad off, for sure, but her situation is just temporary. She'll get paid next Friday for two weeks, and this time, Elise will hand her a check. She'll take it to the bank and open her own account, and she'll be able to find a little apartment and start putting her life back together. That is, if they don't come and arrest her before then. At least she's better off than the woman who stores her possessions on a ratty old wheelchair. She'll have her own place by next weekend, and all this will be behind her—a blip.

The second of Brit's dryers runs out of time as the pizza place next door opens. The clothes are still damp, so she adds another quarter and asks, "What do you like on your pizza?"

The woman chuckles. "I like about anything."

"Will you watch my stuff?"

Her black eyes narrow on Brit, really looking at her. Brit feels like she crossed a line, asking if the woman would watch her stuff. She second-guesses herself but doesn't know how to walk it back. Though she doesn't want to carry her bag to the pizza place, she doesn't want it to be gone when she gets back.

"You want me to watch your stuff?" she asks, her eyes relaxing.

"Yeah, so I can go order the pizza. Unless you want to go order, and I'll watch your stuff."

The woman chuckles. "No, girl, that's all right. You go and order that pizza. I'll watch your stuff."

"Will you?"

"Yes." Her voice is barely a whisper, and Brit smiles like she's won the lottery and nearly skips out to order their pie.

When Brit returns, she says the pizza will take fifteen minutes.

Her companion has added more time to her remaining dryer and refuses to accept a coin. "It's all right. It's just a quarter. That's enough for a bite of that pizza. I don't like to owe nobody."

Brit nods in acceptance.

"I kinda like doing laundry like this," she says.

It's true—she likes getting it all done in a chunk. She doesn't have anyplace else to go, so it doesn't matter how long it takes. When she was at Zack's, she sometimes forgot a load in the washer and left it sitting overnight. Then she had to rerun it so that the clothes wouldn't mildew. She never managed to get everything folded and put away, just rotated things in and out of baskets and back into the washer. It will be satisfying to have all of her clothes folded on the table.

"I kind of enjoy the laundromat too. Especially when it's cold out."

"Why is that?"

"'Cause it's warm in here," the woman says.

After fifteen minutes, Brit goes across the lot and retrieves their pizza, and they sit together, neither one talking, just enjoying the hot, melted cheese and the savory sauce. The laundromat is fragrant with the aroma.

When the pizza is eaten and the laundry is done, Brit repacks her bags, and the old woman reloads her chair.

"I never caught your name." Brit needs to know what the woman calls herself, as she doesn't want to see her somewhere later and call out, "I-yam," like she's Popeye, only to discover that it's some derogatory nickname the townies have given her.

"I Am," she says. "My friends call me Am."

"It was nice to meet you. I really enjoyed having pizza with you."

"That was good pizza." She smiles, licking her lips.

Brit hesitates at the door, her bags already digging into her shoulders. "Where you going from here?"

"I just walk."

"Maybe I could walk with you for a bit."

A shadow crosses Am's face. "Ain't you got no place to be?"

"No. Not really. The only place I have to go to is someplace I can't be until later."

"What's that mean?"

"I've been staying where I work, but I'm not supposed to be there after hours. My boss sometimes comes in on Saturdays. I can't go back until evening at least." Shame wells in her for the first time since meeting I Am, and she looks down. "I get paid on Friday. Then I'll be able to get a place."

I Am squares her shoulders and nods. "You can walk with me."

"Thanks."

They set off down Temple Avenue toward Highway 34. When Brit has to stop to switch her duffel from one shoulder to the other, Am says she can sling it across the top of her chair, so she does.

Brit walks all through the long afternoon with Am. They talk when they have something to say and are silent when they don't. They migrate the great distance between Newnan and Peachtree City along Highway 34. In no hurry, they amble, sitting and resting when they're tired.

Am nods toward a clump of trees just past an elementary school and says, "That's a safe place, back in there."

Brit doesn't immediately understand, but then she sees the narrow trail that leads into the underbrush. "Oh. That's good to know."

"You just have to stay away from the fence."

Brit sees the trees that rim the playground and understands what Am means. She wants to ask exactly what's back there but is afraid Am will be offended. It's probably a shanty town. Brit thinks it's strange that she never thought of there being homeless people in Newnan, even when she saw Am walking with her chair. She didn't really understand what it was like to live without a home, without shelter, without a locked front door. It makes her uncomfortable, this new awareness. She's enjoyed Am's company, but she doesn't want to think about homeless people.

When they reach the Walmart in Peachtree City, they leave Am's chair, with Brit's duffel still sitting atop it, in one of the golf cart parking spots alongside the building.

"Will that be okay?"

"Yeah. Nobody will mess with it."

Making their way through the store, they enjoy the cool air. Brit is uncomfortably aware of eyes following them, and she hopes she won't see anybody she knows. She doesn't want anybody to think she's actually homeless. Well, she *is* homeless, but she isn't like Am. She isn't actually living on the streets.

Am doesn't buy anything. Brit picks up a towel and a bar of soap, a tube of toothpaste, a box of saltine crackers, and a jar of peanut butter. Then she chooses a box of hair color that looks like it will match her natural shade. She can't stand the roots, and she certainly can't afford to go see her girl, Jenny, who has always maintained her highlights. She would probably cut her a deal, but Brit is too ashamed to face her. Jenny is from Newnan and probably knows the Martins—and all about the accident. Brit shrugs the shame off her shoulders and puts the box of color in her bag. Spending eight dollars on her hair is an extravagance, but every time she faces a client, she feels embarrassed because her roots are so grown out and dark. Brit is relieved when they leave and she's managed not to speak to anybody except Am.

"Where are you going to look for a place?" Am asks as they walk toward Newnan.

"Somewhere near downtown. Since that's where I work."

"Have you looked at the Lofts?"

"No, not yet."

She's tempted to explain how she finds herself between places, but Am doesn't press for information. Brit relaxes into their walk, even though her feet have blisters and her hips ache. Am is easy to be around, and when just with her, Brit doesn't feel the shame she felt while they were in the store.

They part ways when they reach the clump of trees beside the school. Brit collects her bags, positioning the straps. "Thanks for letting me walk with you today."

"Thanks for the pizza. That was tasty."

It was a good day, the first since Brit started this new life. It was nice just to feel normal, like she wasn't the only person going through a rough patch.

When Brit finally makes it back to the office, she is relieved to see it's dark. Newt's car isn't parked in the lot. She finds her key and unlocks the back door, not turning on lights as she makes her way to her alcove. After choosing clothes to sleep in and to change into for the next day, she stows her bags. Her body is pleasantly weary, and she feels like she may manage to sleep for more than a few hours.

The bathroom is cluttered by the boxes from the shower. The space isn't large, so the boxes make it feel cramped. She sets her towel and the dye on top of a box and turns to the mirror then stands for a long while, looking at herself. All day, she looked at Am's close-cropped hair and thought about how much easier it would be to keep her hair clean if she cut it short. She pulls it back, trying to visualize herself with short hair. But she can't. She has always had long hair.

After closing the door, she takes off her clothes. She works the dye into her hair, careful not to drip any on the carpet, then waits for the color to process.

Brit has clean clothes, a bar of soap, and a shower, and she made a friend today.

Not bad for one day.

She turns on the shower, and the water runs, a small gift at the end of this long day. The soap lathers away the sweat and dye. If only she had a razor, she might feel normal. Shaving is a luxury. But it doesn't matter. She wears long pants for work anyway. A hum slips from her lips, unexpected and surprising. She is coming out of the terrible fog, like her mind is finally clearing.

The police haven't come back to arrest her, and there are moments when she almost forgets that the accident happened—seconds when the worst thing in her life is that her roots are showing, and she's between places. She doesn't miss Zack. Though she isn't necessarily glad he kicked her out, she's relieved not to have to work around his moods anymore.

The water runs until all the residual dye washes down the drain and the water runs clear. She turns off the shower and dries with her new towel then tries to see how her hair is going to look, but it's too wet to know. It looks really dark, but at least the roots blend in with the rest of it.

Brit wipes down the shower, gets dressed, and lifts the first box of copier paper to replace it in the shower. The motion makes her body protest, and she realizes she didn't have to move the boxes out of the shower before getting into it.

She didn't have to empty the shower. She had set her box of hair color on top of one of the boxes as she had worked the color through.

Oh shit.

She didn't have to empty the shower.

She meant to restack the boxes this morning, but she fell asleep with her head on the desk, then Newt surprised her. She left the light on in the alcove.

Newt might have thought the light was left on overnight, but there is no reason the boxes should have been out of the shower. The small pearl of hope that had been forming in Brit's gut shattered and turned to dust.

July 30

Chapter 18

By the end of July, Cliff knows the DA has no interest in filing charges against Britany Addams for her role in the fatal accident that happened on July 8. As the lead investigating officer, Cliff has the dubious duty of informing Dee Martin's parents that there will be no charges. He doesn't know what to expect, but when he and Dane arrive at their house, they walk to the front door just as they did the day they came to do the notification.

Cliff knows seeing them at the door will reopen the wound of their loss, so he prepared them with a phone call before arriving. Protocol didn't warrant the call, but he felt a sense of obligation. He knew Dee. He knows the loss the family suffered because he now finds himself unable to pull into the Chick-fil-A where Dee worked. The memory of her last words haunts him, and he hears her voice every time he drives past. "Did you have breakfast today? I missed you."

He misses her. Everybody does. It's difficult to think that her life ended in such a senseless way. Even now, a cross stands at that intersection, and every day, the county removes small stuffed animals and framed photographs from the site. This morning, he passed on patrol and saw that the flowers were fresh, and a new porcelain angel with arms folded in prayer had been left there.

It makes him feel hollow to be on this porch again. He doesn't know what to expect. Dee's parents may be angry that the DA isn't bringing charges. They may feel that justice is not being served if Britany Addams walks free while their daughter lies cold in the ground.

The door opens as Cliff reaches for the bell. Jim Martin stands within. The gloom of the foyer casts him in darkness.

"Officer Rathborn, it's good to see you again."

Cliff is often amazed by the code of manners that Jim's generation exhibits.

"Yes, Mr. Martin. Thank you for having us," Cliff says, as if this is a social call and they're invited for tea.

"Please come in."

They follow him through the foyer and down the hall to the living room, where Mrs. Martin is setting a pitcher of lemonade and glasses on the coffee table.

Nodding, she offers a pinched smile. She and her husband have both aged in the few weeks since the accident. "Have a seat?"

Dane sits and accepts the proffered glass of lemonade. Cliff declines the beverage and sits only after Mrs. Martin has. He directs his words toward Mrs. Martin, expecting that if either of them is going to demand justice, it will be her.

"We've completed our investigation. I wanted to let you know in person that the DA is not bringing charges against Ms. Addams."

Mrs. Martin looks at her husband, who nods, as if this is what he expected.

"I'm relieved, quite honestly," she says finally. "I'd hate to ruin her life."

Mr. Martin lifts his wife's hand from her knee to his lips and kisses her fingers.

"Yes, ma'am," Cliff says. He's unable to remove his eyes from their point of connection. Longing for Maggie spreads through him in a wave that makes his breath catch in his throat. This is what marriage is supposed to be, raising a family together, going through the good times and the bad times with somebody there to hold a hand. He wishes he knew more about his mother so that he could understand why she left. Their family never went through anything like this. They never lost a child and weren't in constant battle. Maybe it was just his mother who wasn't cut out for marriage. Maybe Maggie is right. He is not his father, and she is not Miriam.

Mrs. Martin leans toward her husband, and they are united in their sorrow.

"What I'd like to know—what we'd like to know," Jim says, "is what caused the airbag to act like that."

Cliff is prepared, having expected some questions about the airbag. "Have you heard anything about a company called Takata?" He waits then looks at Dane, who has done the research on the Takata recall.

Dane sits forward, putting his elbows on his knees and clasping his hands. "Takata is a company out of Japan. They manufacture airbags." He proceeds to give a brief history of the airbag recall that began in 2004 and ultimately included millions of vehicles. In 2017, Takata was ordered to pay 1.3 billion dollars in compensation to victims. In 2018, the company filed chapter 13 bankruptcy. As part of its reorganization, it was purchased by another manufacturer.

"Dee's car was on the recall list," Cliff offers when Dane finishes, and the information hangs like a fog in the air.

"We didn't know anything about a recall," Mrs. Martin says.

"Dee hadn't had the car long. She saved up and bought it last fall. She was so proud to have done it on her own." Mr. Martin squeezes his wife's hand.

Cliff's heart stutters. He imagines Dee feeling proud of such an accomplishment. "She may not have received a recall notice if she bought it from a private seller."

People may not heed recall notices, not understanding the risk, thinking they're too busy to take the time out for the recommended repair. Cliff pulls his eyes from the Martins' hands, thinking again of Maggie. He'll have to check to see if her car is on the list.

It would be just like her to put off repairs. She's a cautious driver, but Dee likely was as well. Maggie's car is a Civic, and all Hondas were on that recall list.

He needs to see Maggie. The room feels too close, with the grief settling in the corners, and their hands, worrying together, making him feel the loss. A bead of sweat erupts on Cliff's lip, and he forcibly pushes Maggie, whom he can't have lost, out of his mind.

"So, she shouldn't have died," Mr. Martin says with resignation in his voice.

"No," Dane admits, although saying so is close to crossing a line. "The impact probably would have left her bruised, but the shrapnel expelled from the airbag damaged a vein in her neck and—"

"She died of an air embolism to her heart," Mr. Martin finishes.

"Yes, sir." Dane nods.

"Of course, you'll already have the autopsy," Cliff says to keep Dane from edging any closer to placing blame.

"So we should get a lawyer," Mr. Martin says, looking at his wife.

"You should probably talk to one. Somebody who specializes in wrongful-death cases," Dane suggests.

"It's not going to bring her back." Mrs. Martin's voice is so soft that Cliff isn't sure she spoke. She catches his eye and asks, "What about the other woman? Was she injured at all?"

"No, ma'am. She was shaken up and a little bruised."

"That's good," Mrs. Martin says with a sigh.

Cliff thinks of the woman he saw at Walton and Shrieve, who wasn't injured by the accident but had clearly been damaged. He considers sharing that but is unsure whether it will bring them peace to know that Britany Addams suffers or if it will bring them greater angst. He holds his tongue.

"I'm glad she's not going to be charged with anything."

"Yes, ma'am. It was just a terrible accident," Cliff agrees.

Rain falls in fat drops against the windshield as Cliff responds to another accident at Highway 54 and Fischer Road in the hours after the visit with the Martins. A 2014 Chevy Tahoe missed the curve, flew off the shoulder, and plowed into a tree. Cliff sees the man to the ambulance, and he's taken to the hospital with non-life-threatening injuries. Cliff is eager to finish at the intersection and get back into his car.

The tall grass at the side of the road is flattened, and water pools in the ruts the Tahoe's tires made. It hasn't rained for weeks, and when Cliff looks down the road, the rainbow patterns of oil pulled up from the asphalt glisten. Had it been a clear day, the driver of the Tahoe would probably have been able to prevent the accident. Cliff contemplates the scene, rebuilding the accident. When the truck crossed the line and missed the curve, the driver reacted by slamming on the brakes and turning the wheel. On a dry day, those actions would have altered his course. He might have overcorrected and had to pull out of a swerve, but he would have gone about his day. He would have made it home without a busted wrist, a busted vehicle, and a citation. But the water on the road, liquifying the residual oil, caused his tires not to grip, and he was unable to correct his error. Unfortunately for the driver, it was not his first vehicular incident. Two speeding tickets and one distracted-driving citation in the past eighteen months mean his license will be suspended pending traffic school.

Cliff hates this intersection. He experiences an increase in heart rate every time his patrol brings him down Fischer Road toward 54. He cannot drive onto the scene and not see that red Honda Fit sitting catawampus in the eastbound lane.

"Did you have breakfast today?" she asked as the embolism that took her life was moving on its fatal journey.

Cliff feels sick. He should have stayed with her and kept her talking.

But talking wouldn't have stopped the embolism.

He could have started CPR if he hadn't been dealing with the blond woman wandering down the middle of the street. He has not made it by to tell Britany Addams the results of the investigation, that she won't be charged with a crime. He needs to do that or have Dane handle it. Cliff has never been one to put off a job, but the thought of seeing Britany Addams and her hollowed-out eyes fills him with dread. He is losing his grip. Many cops suffer from PTSD after they've been involved in violent exchanges or have investigated grisly crimes. Cliff understands that. He has investigated more harrowing things than a straightforward road-accident fatality, and they have never left marks, so he doesn't understand his reaction to this incident. He should have notified Britany even before he spoke with the Martins, but somehow, the obligation slips his mind when he's in the vicinity of downtown Newnan.

Cliff finishes his write-up and decides to put the accident behind him. He drives toward Newnan. He'll arrive after five, but he might still catch her. He must do it so that he can be done with it. As he drives, he sees one of Coweta County's homeless pushing a wheelchair down the shoulder of Highway 34. He does a double take at the woman, trying to figure out what about her is familiar. Of course he knows who she is. She is I Am, a woman who appeared in Newnan about five years ago, pushing that wheelchair. Nobody knows where she came from or why she came here. She has never been brought in for loitering or vagrancy, as she never causes any problems, just walks all day long, pushing that chair.

Seeing the old woman isn't what causes Cliff to stare. Something in her expression seems familiar. It's the slicked-down dark hair and the square set of her shoulders, not even drawn in to protect her from the rain. He sits at the traffic light, pausing with the traffic, and squints at the woman as she makes her slow progress past the intersection at Andrew Bailey.

The traffic light turns, and Clifford rolls forward with the other vehicles. He lets the old homeless woman slip out of his mind and focuses on closing the case on Dee Martin's death.

The law office is still open when he arrives, and he walks through the front door. The receptionist alcove is empty.

"Hello?" he calls out.

Ben Walton appears at the door to his office. "How can I help you, Officer?" He reaches back and turns out the light behind him, preparing for his departure.

"I was hoping to find Ms. Addams here. Has she left for the day?"

"Oh yes. She is out of here one minute past five most days."

"Do you have an address for her?"

"I reckon we do." He turns and calls down the hall, "Elise, you still here? Do we have a home address for Brit?"

A gray-haired woman steps from a side office half a second later with a Post-it note with an address on Andrew Bailey penned there. "That's the last I have."

Cliff accepts the address but remembers that Britany said she was between places. "Maybe I'll just try back. She's here till five usually?"

"Not a minute later," Elise says, and Cliff hears a note of disdain in her voice. She gives a little shake of her head, dismissive, and turns and walks back down the hall.

Chapter 19

About half a block down from Walton and Shrieve, on the opposite side of Jack Dale, is a small used bookstore. For about a week now, Brit has crossed the street after work and walked down to peruse the books on the front porch. It is like the office, a house converted for commercial use. When Brit first started working at the firm, it was a restaurant, and she sometimes walked over to grab a sandwich for lunch. She feels nostalgic for those days, when dropping ten or fifteen dollars for lunch didn't feel like a big deal.

Nobody else is on the porch as Brit climbs the steps, dashing to get out of the rain. Through the front window, she can see the woman who runs the shop sitting behind the counter, her nose buried in a book. She considers going inside, but with her hair dripping, she decides that today is not that day. She doesn't have money to buy anything, so she shouldn't waste the woman's time. The porch has rolling carts filled with books, so she doesn't really need to go inside. A sandwich board reads Last Chance, and Brit peers down at the spines to keep occupied. She picks out a travel guide for Greece. That's where her mother is or was. She isn't sure when she's coming back because she didn't pay much attention to her mother's travel plans. It doesn't matter. It's just a book to hold in her hands so that she can justify sitting on the front porch while she waits for the lights at the law firm to go out.

She has just settled, leaning against the building, book in hand, when a police car drives down the road. She follows its progress with her eyes without changing her stance. The car parks in front of the firm, and that cop she talked to gets out and goes inside. Brit slides down a little, trying to blend in with the books and the building, and her heart jackhammers. Today may be the day they come to arrest her. She should just walk over and take whatever they have to dish out to her, like an adult. At least then she would have a place to be, and she could stop being scared about it all the time.

"Time to pay the piper," Brit whispers. That's what her father used to say before he doled out punishment.

The cop is inside for several minutes, and Brit thumbs the slightly damp pages of the travel guide between glances. The rain continues to fall.

When the cop comes out, he returns to his car and pulls away. Brit missed her chance. She wonders what he said to Ben. *Did Ben tell him what time I'll be in tomorrow? Will the cop be there waiting for me?* Every morning before it's time for work, Brit leaves the office, locking the back door behind her, and walks around the square so that she isn't the first one in the office, which she thinks would look suspicious. She was never early before Zack kicked her out, so she can't start being early now.

Several minutes pass before the lights at Walton and Shrieve start to go out. The last light is the lobby. Ben walks out with Elise, and they part, each going to their separate cars. Brit watches them drive down the road and waits a little longer. Ben has been known to forget his phone in the office and have to return for it. When she's confident that the office is empty for the night, she reshelves the travel guide and scampers, like a rat, across the street.

August 2

Chapter 20

Brit hasn't received her check yet. It's almost the end of the day, and she's still waiting. At lunch, she asked Elise if she remembered that she needed a check. Usually, pay is disbursed early in the day, but since Brit has always had her check auto-deposited, she isn't sure when Elise will hand it over.

"I remembered."

"Can I have it?" Brit asked, needing to feel the paper of the check, see the numbers printed there—and know she was going to be able to find an apartment and start fixing her life.

"I'll have to get it to you later." Elise turned back to her computer as if she was too busy right then to reach into her drawer and hand it over.

Brit stood for a beat too long, like a beggar, and when she finally walked away, she felt confused and dismissed.

It's *her* money. She has earned every penny of it and doesn't understand why Elise is making her wait.

She knows that Elise doesn't like her and not just after overhearing them talking about her being clean, which was really them talking about her being dirty. Something is wrong. She can feel it in the air. Ben has been cold to her all week. When she buzzed in to tell him that a client was on the phone, he was barely capable of more than a grunt in response. She hasn't even seen Newt this week except when he walks past her to get to the conference room, as he does now. He doesn't even look into the alcove as he passes. The door to the conference room closes behind him. Seconds later, Ben's intercom buzzes, and Brit hears Newt say, "Ready?"

Elise comes from her office and takes the same path Newt took. Ben follows her, closing the door behind them.

Something big is going on. Brit can feel it. She wonders if they're letting Elise go. That would explain why she was so distant earlier. Poor Elise. She's been with Walton and Shrieve for years. Brit can't imagine what Elise will do.

She has a full range of sympathy built up for Elise when her intercom buzzes and Newt asks, "Britany, can you join us in the conference room?"

"Yes," she says then again because she forgot to push the intercom button the first time. Her stomach stays behind, and the bones of her legs melt as she walks to the closed door, understanding dawning that Elise isn't the one on the chopping block. Brit's the one who has been sleeping in the office. She's been breaking the rules.

She knocks, as if being told to come is not enough, then enters the room and finds the three of them sitting on one side of the table.

A chair is already pulled out on the other side, and Elise says, "Won't you have a seat?"

Brit swallows. "What's going on?" She doesn't sit. She feels sick and weak.

"Please sit," Ben says, and finally, she does.

She doesn't ask again and feels panic rising.

Newt slides a document across the table toward her, and the heading says: *Notice of Termination of Employment.* It's dated August 2, today.

She reads the form. *On this, the 2nd day of August 2019, Walton and Shrieve terminate their employment of Britany Addams. Britany will receive a two-week paid severance package and will return her office key and remove all of her belongings from the building. Ms. Addams shall not take any intellectual property belonging to Walton and Shrieve.* At the bottom of the page are a set of signatories, a line for Ben, another for Newt, and one for her.

"Why?" She looks up at Ben.

"I think you know why," Newt says.

"No, really, I don't." Tears spring to her eyes, and she swipes them away. She will not cry in front of them.

Ben opens a file and slides two envelopes across the table. Brit reaches for them. Both are addressed to the same client, and Brit remembers doing the dictation for the letters.

"Oookay?"

"Look what's inside," Ben says.

She withdraws the letter from the first envelope and understands. The day she did this dictation, she had several letters, and the letter inside this envelope was intended for a different recipient than the one listed on the envelope. It was the day the policeman came and said they weren't going to arrest her yet.

"I'm sorry, Ben. That won't happen again," Brit says, knowing it's not sufficient.

"It did happen again." Ben inclines his head toward the second envelope. "And these are just the two that I know about."

It is cause enough. Ben was very clear when she was in training about the importance of accuracy. Walton and Shrieve often deal in sensitive matters, and their reputation is built on discretion. With a sinking feeling, Brit reaches for the second envelope. She lifts the flap and withdraws the letter outlining a private support agreement between a local real estate mogul and his mistress, acknowledging paternity of her child.

Brit drops her head into her hands, feeling sick. The silence grows. "I'm so sorry, " Brit whispers.

"I know you are," Ben says, and for a second Brit believes they will relent.

"Have you been staying in the office?" Newt asks.

"No. What do you mean?"

A look passes between Newt and Elise.

"We know you've been sleeping here." Elise opens her own file and slides a photograph of Brit asleep under her desk.

Brit has no defense. "How did you get that?"

"Last week, I came in on Saturday and found the supplies outside the shower stall. I began to think that someone had been in the office overnight, so I asked Elise to set up a time-lapse camera," Newt says.

He didn't think someone was staying here—he thought I *was staying here.* Brit remembers that morning, when she left the light on in her alcove and forgot to put away the supplies.

"And on top of that, money has been missing from the petty cash," Elise says with irritation.

"What?"

"Yes, nearly sixty dollars," Elise says, her lips compressing and deepening the lines of her face.

"I didn't steal any money. I didn't even remember that there *was* petty cash." Had she remembered, she might have risked borrowing a bit, but she would have paid it back.

A look passes between them, and she realizes she hasn't tried to deny that she's been sleeping under her desk.

"Well, say what you will, but money is missing, and you are the most logical suspect," Elise says, judgment thick in her tone.

"Oh my god, are you, like, going to have me arrested?" Brit asks, fighting to keep her tone level.

"Well, not if you sign the termination agreement and leave quietly," Newt says, taking charge again.

"Fine." The ridge of hysteria cracks, and Brit grabs the termination agreement. The page dents with the passage of her pen. "I didn't steal your money." Tears roll down her cheeks, and she swipes them away.

Elise reaches across the table and takes the agreement then places it in the folder, which, Brit now sees, has her name on the tab. Elise extends an envelope. Brit snatches it and stands.

The bell rings on the receptionist desk, and Brit is the first in the hall to see the uniformed officer.

"Oh my god. I signed your fucking agreement," she calls back into the room. She doesn't speak to the cop but leans under the desk in the receptionist's alcove and pulls out her bags.

It's the same cop who came to the office last week, and she wonders if they called him for a consultation on how to handle the trespass and thievery. They've been planning all week to have her arrested and acted like nothing was going on. She doesn't know how they could just walk around her knowing she was sleeping here and never once asking if they could help.

But they didn't act like nothing was wrong. They were cold to her. Newt hasn't so much as spoken a word to her since last week.

The policeman watches her, but she refuses to acknowledge him. She walks through the lobby, her bags bumping against her legs.

She hears Elise welcoming the cop. "Can I help you?"

"No, ma'am. I just need to talk to that woman right there."

Chapter 21

Cliff follows Britany through the door and catches up to her at the end of the sidewalk.

She's a wreck. Her face is splotchy with anger, and rain begins to soak into her hair.

"Ms. Addams, can I have a moment?"

She drops her bags onto the wet pavement and turns to face him, putting her hands out in front of her. "Go ahead. Arrest me. I don't care."

"No, ma'am. I'm not here to arrest you."

"Then why *are* you here?"

Cliff is surprised by the level of hostility but isn't affronted. In his line of work, he often encounters people at their worst. Britany Addams is angry at the world and, he suspects, is definitely at her worst.

"Are you okay?" he asks, because obviously she isn't. Rain pelts down, dripping from the brim of his hat.

"No." She cuts her eyes to the side, making the blotchy red patches on her face become more pronounced. "I just got fired, okay? I screwed up and sent the wrong letter to the wrong person, so they fired me." The water is already streaming from her face, but she seems oblivious to it.

"I see."

"Yeah. I hate this day," she says, defeat in her voice.

"Yes, ma'am. Can I help you with your bags?"

"No. I've got it." She leans down and hefts the duffel then settles it across her body.

"Can I give you a ride?" He inclines his head, indicating his cruiser parked on the street.

She shakes her head and slides her arms through the loops of her backpack and starts to walk away.

He joins her on the sidewalk. "Where are you going?" He keeps pace with her, and they walk away from his car. "You never did get back to me with an address."

"I don't have an address."

"Where are you going, then?"

She stops and looks at him, and her face is a more normal shade. "I'm going to the bank to cash my check. Then I'm going to sit at Leaf and Bean until my friend can pick me up, and I will go home with her. I'll have dinner with her family, then I will sleep on her couch. Tomorrow, I will find an apartment and start looking for a new job. Is that okay with you?"

He doesn't miss the glance away when she speaks of the friend and her couch. "You've had quite a month," he says and holds out his hands to indicate that they can continue their walk.

"No shit," she says, and a look of surprise crosses her face.

He wonders if she's surprised that he mentioned her month or to find that she can curse in front of him.

"Yeah. Well, that's why I came to see you. I wanted to tell you that the DA is *not* filing charges. You can go about living your life. What happened was just an accident."

The woman drops her arms, and for a split second, the angry look on her face melts, and her chin puckers. She's going to lose it. He's prepared and will catch her if she falls. She closes her eyes for a moment, and rain slides over her face, washing away tears, if there are any.

"Really?" A smile twitches her lips but is quickly suppressed. "But somebody died."

Cliff sees that hair shirt again, her pulling it over her shoulders. "Yes. Somebody died, but she didn't die simply because of the accident."

"What does that mean?"

They reach a crosswalk and stand to wait for the walk symbol to appear. A car drives past, splashing water onto their feet.

"When the airbag inflated... " Cliff gives Britany the simplified explanation of the cause of death. "It wasn't the impact from the accident."

Britany's chin dimples, and her face crumples. The light turns, and Britany starts across the street. Cliff jogs to catch up, hesitant to leave as her face is working through the complicated series of expressions.

"Did you hear what I said? It wasn't your fault that she died."

Her face settles, choosing an expression that is just a step more alive than the one she wore the day of the accident. She doesn't look at him as she says, "So I just get to go back to my life like nothing ever happened?"

"Kind of like that." He has never heard anybody express it like that before, and it sounds strange, unhinged.

"Hmm..." She slows and turns to face him, rain sliding down the planes of her cheeks. "I'll let you know how that works out."

"What do you mean?"

"I just got fired from my job because I've been sleeping under my desk. I was sleeping under my desk because my former boyfriend kicked me out and cleaned out my checking account. He kicked me out because he found out that I was with my ex-boyfriend—" She looks like she's said the wrong thing, like she's been caught, but her eyes snap up, and she says, "The day of the accident." She chuckles, a low, fractured sound. "I have no life to go back to."

Britany waves him back as he starts to walk with her again.

"Thank you, Officer, for letting me know." She jogs a few paces, her bags bouncing and banging against her body and her feet causing spray to splash from the pavement.

Cliff stops following and watches as she walks in haste, not looking back. She's going to the bank and has a friend who is going to pick her up. She'll figure things out when the shock of everything eases.

"Good luck, Ms. Addams," he calls after her, and she nods but doesn't look back.

Cliff is glad when she is gone. Something about her made him uncomfortable. Her eyes didn't just seem vacant—they seemed far away. An image forms in his memory of the dark-haired woman who was his mother with that exact same expression in her eyes.

She sat for hours with those empty eyes, seeing something that wasn't there, while young Cliff tried to catch her attention. It was futile, speaking to her when she was like that.

The woman and her bags turn a corner and are out of sight, and Cliff hopes he has seen the last of her. Some people just can't be helped.

Chapter 22

"What do you mean, you 'can't open an account for me'?" Brit asks, accepting the returned payroll check from the woman who sits across the desk.

"You just said you don't have an address. In order to open an account, you have to have an address."

"I'm just between places right now. Once I get settled, I can give you the new address. What's the problem?" Her voice rises, and she hears the hysteria that has threatened since the door closed at Walton and Shrieve.

"It's bank policy." The woman scrunches her nose, as if she, too, thinks residency is a ridiculous requirement.

"Well, that's stupid." Brit looks down at the check. It's so much money, and she can't even use it. "I have all this money. How am I supposed to get access to it if I can't get a bank account?" It feels overwhelmingly stupid, like she is Vivian Ward trying to shop for clothes on Rodeo Drive while dressed like a hooker.

"We can cash it for you, of course, for a fee."

Brit laughs without mirth. The bank is crowded. Brit looks around as a few people glance her way, and she realizes she's on the verge of making a scene. *What would my mother say, seeing me like this, causing a ruckus and acting spoiled?* She would be so disappointed. Her mother warned her to stay away from Jason back when Brit told her he was back in town and they had bumped into each other. She knew he was bad news. But Brit didn't listen. She never listened. Her mother couldn't be more disappointed than Brit is. She draws a long breath and tries to channel her mother—polite, respectful, and pulled together.

"Of course, and what's the fee?"

"Eight dollars."

"So for the privilege of cashing my check, you get eight dollars? Seriously?" She smiles. It's so absurd. The facade she tried to pull together shatters, and now the people in the bank are looking at her without even trying to pretend they aren't.

"Yes, ma'am. Of course, you'll need two forms of identification."

"What?"

"Like a driver's license and a passport."

"Are you freaking kidding me?" She turns to some of the patrons, as if she might rally them to her cause. People look away, like they're embarrassed by her. She turns back to the woman and keeps her voice low. "I don't even have a passport. I just want my money." It takes a lot of restraint to keep from screaming, cursing in true and honest frustration at the infuriating woman.

"Well, I'm sorry, but it's bank policy. You don't have an account with us, and the check isn't drawn on us. If you want to talk to Regions, where the check is drawn, they might be able to assist you."

"Oh my god. Where is the closest Regions?"

"Just across the block on Jefferson. But I don't think they stay open late on Fridays."

"Fuck," Brit says, and the word feels like liberation on her tongue. "This is fucking stupid." After snatching her check and stuffing it into her pocket, she becomes frustrated at the slowdown of having to heft her bags, but finally, she manages to cross the lobby toward the doors. She has been wronged and maltreated, although the woman was only following the rules.

"Walmart might be able to help you, if Regions can't," a woman says quietly as Brit reaches the door.

"They cash checks?"

"Sure. I don't know their rules, but they're friendly about it."

Brit feels vindicated that somebody else thought the teller was mean and rude in her refusal to help.

It seems like a lifeline, and Brit steps from the bank and into the rain, beaten but with a destination. If this bank needs two forms of identification, Regions probably will too. The teller said they don't stay open late on Fridays, but she may not know for sure. Brit stands there, trying to decide whether or not she should walk the block to Jefferson on a chance that they'll help or even be open.

Fuck it. She's not wasting any more time with stupid banks.

The rain begins to slack off as Brit crosses the square, and by the time she makes it to Jack Dale Street, it stops. She doesn't want to walk past the office drenched like a rat, carrying her bags, and looking pathetic and homeless. Shame burns in her gut, and she keeps her face down as the clouds break and the sun sets the sidewalks to steaming. The lights are all still on in the office, and when she glances toward the conference room window, she sees the three of them relaxed and chatting. She turns away and walks past, her feet sloshing in her shoes, then turns right on 34, following the path she took with I Am a couple of weeks ago. Her clothes cling to her.

Brit's body aches from carrying her bags long before she reaches the Walmart, so she places them on the floor as she waits in line for customer service. She wipes a hand down her front as if she can wipe away the wrinkles, the water, the mud that accumulated during her walk, and the shame of being fired and accused of stealing. As the line moves forward, she scoots her bags with her foot.

"I can help whoever is next."

Brit steps up, her check in hand. "I just need to cash this." She picks up a pen and signs her name with shaking hands.

"How would you like it?"

Brit doesn't understand, as she's never been asked that before. She has never cashed a paycheck.

"You want it in twenties, hundreds, or what?"

"Oh, twenties, I guess."

Brit accepts the cash, realizing only at the end that Walmart takes their fee, too, but at least they only take four dollars. She doesn't say anything, grateful to be done and to have cash in hand, like it's a trophy. After tucking the money into her backpack, she pulls it across her shoulders.

Brit is exhausted. She has spent the better part of the evening walking from the square to Walmart, and now her shoulders ache with the weight of her bags. She studies the hotel across the street. She has money, which means she can drop sixty or a hundred dollars and sleep in a bed for the first time in a month if she wants to, but she feels stingy about the cash. She might have a hard time finding a job, and the money from Walton and Shrieve might be the last she'll get for a while. Nobody will want to hire her now that she's been accused of stealing. She wasn't even able to convince a bank to trust her enough to cash a payroll check. Walton and Shrieve might tell potential employers why they let her go. Even if Ben won't, she knows Elise will.

Brit feels lightheaded and looks for a place to sit down for a minute. She needs to think and clear her mind. Then she'll figure out what to do. She walks across the parking lot and drops her duffel bag into one of the abandoned carts, then she pushes it ahead of her and comes to rest at the edge of the blacktop, where she is sheltered from the road by a stretch of bushes. She sits on the curb and lets her head fall forward onto her knees.

Brit wonders when her mother and stepfather are due back from Greece. She tries to remember when they left, but the days blur together, and she can't sort it out. She doesn't know if she could call her mom and ask for help. She would know that Brit was sneaking around with Jason. Even if nobody told her, she would know. But she would probably still help.

Brit unzips her backpack and reaches for her phone, but when she puts her hands on it, she remembers it's dead. It doesn't have service anymore anyway. She'll figure it out tomorrow. Maybe she can send her an email. The library has computers. Maybe she could use one of them. Her mom will check her email, even if she isn't back from Greece yet. She'll send money if Brit asks.

Brit's mind rolls, and she plays out the series of conversations that would reveal her circumstances, and when she returns to the day of the accident, her stomach twists. The cop said it was just an accident, but the further away from that day she gets, the less certain she is that she looked before rolling onto 54. Dee Martin died because Brit was cheating on her boyfriend, and that was all she could think about. Brit is fed up. She caused all of this. She can't call her mother and have her bail her out. She won't. This is what being an adult looks like. It's time for her to stop expecting other people to take care of her mistakes.

Resolved and feeling a strange sense of peace, she promises herself that she will reach out to her mom tomorrow, not to ask for help but just to tell her that she's okay and that she's making some changes. She doesn't want her to worry.

Brit closes her eyes and drifts off to sleep.

August 3

Chapter 23

Brit doesn't move. Sleep fills all the space inside her, but she hears a voice from a very far distance. It is a slow, raspy voice, full of a lifetime of cigarettes.

"You cain't sleep out front like this."

A toe nudges her foot, and she jerks up and away, startled and confused.

"You cain't sleep out front like this. It looks bad for the customers."

The words register, and Brit blinks to clear her mind, checking that her backpack is still secure and pulling at the strap for her duffel. She is confused about why she's sleeping at the edge of the Walmart parking lot, but then the events from yesterday seep back into her mind. Somebody could have stolen her stuff while it sat in the shopping cart or beaten her up or forced her into a car. She launches to her feet, mumbling an apology. It's predawn, and she's slept through the night on the curb.

"If you ain't got no place to be, you should go over to that church there downtown. They got beds for folks." The man is small and wiry and has black-rimmed glasses that he pushes up his nose.

"What church?" Brit worked on Jack Dale Street for years, but she never knew of a church downtown that offered beds to people.

"It's over there on Washington Street. My cousin got in there for a time. They's good people. Helped him get the methadone and get back on his feet."

"I'm just between places," she says, feeling the need to explain her situation and clarify that she's not a drug user. She is not *really* homeless, just in a jam.

"Yep, well, you can't be between places in the front lot. If you got to, you can hang out behind the loading dock, and nobody will say nothing unless you make a mess, but I cain't guarantee that nobody won't bother you." He nods, giving her a look that says he knows what she is whether she does or not.

Brit organizes her bags after he walks away. The man starts collecting the carts from the lot, his blue vest hanging loose over his bony shoulders. The idea that there is a place she can go feels good. She's relieved that she doesn't have to lie to anybody or pretend everything is okay. She doesn't have to answer Ben Walton's phone and try to sound normal.

It feels like freedom.

Brit feels hope as she puts her duffel bag back in the cart and pushes it toward the entrance of the store, grateful it's open all night. If nothing else, she can be inside until the sun comes up so that she won't be walking the streets in the dark, which feels dangerous. She has money and can buy a little something to eat to hold off her hunger. The bright lights inside the building sting her eyes as she pushes through the doors, contemplating her next step.

Brit needs a place to be. She needs a job. First, she needs a shower before she can walk into an apartment complex and ask to live there. Since she has money, that shouldn't be a problem. The severance pay makes the amount seem great, and she's confident that she can put down a deposit and the first month's rent and still have enough to get her by until she can land a job.

Call your mom. The words bound through her head as if someone else has spoken them. Her mom left for Greece a couple of days before the accident. Now that she has rested, her mind is clearer, and she's more certain that she would not be back from her trip yet. She's probably worried about her. Last night, Brit resolved not to ask for help, but this morning, she wants nothing more than for her mother to wire her enough money to get a hotel until she can find a job.

She could ask for help without telling her mom about Jason or the accident. Brit could just say that she and Zack broke up and she lost her job because she screwed up on some dictation. Her mom would help. She would wire her money to help her get back on her feet. But getting a message like that would ruin her trip. She would know Brit wasn't telling the whole truth. She always knew. Brit would have to explain everything at some point.

She plays a variety of conversations in her head. But the explanation of how she ended up in this situation always ends with Jason. She was cheating on Zack and caused the accident because she was distracted by Jason's hand being on her leg. Somebody died.

Brit halts the conversation in her head. She can't have that conversation because the next sentence her mother would say is "You are just like your father," because he was a cheater too.

Anyway, she has money now. It will be better to reach out when she has a new place, a new phone number, and a new job so that her mom doesn't have to worry.

Brit makes her way to the bathrooms and does the best she can with paper towels and soap. She steps into the stall and changes out of her rumpled, still slightly damp clothes. The fresh clothes are creased from being folded into the duffel, and she's glad she chose this bag when she left Zack's. She didn't even know it would be waterproof. She looks better, at least. Combing her fingers through her hair, she wishes for a brush, but a search through her possessions comes up empty. She squats and starts reassembling her belongings, and in a flash of memory, she sees her brush sitting on the edge of her desk as she leaned under it to pull out the bags. The memory causes her stomach to roll, and she pushes the thoughts out of her mind. She pulls out a ten-dollar bill and places it in her pocket. She will buy a brush and something to eat, and she will fix her life.

When Brit stands at the edge of the parking lot, she has to decide on a direction of travel. The old man mentioned a church on Washington Street, but surely she just needs to find an apartment and put herself together. Anyway, Washington Street is all the way back down by the square, and the thought of walking all that way makes her body ache.

Newnan is full of apartments. The townies threw up a fuss a year or so ago because of the glut. They put "Newnan is the City of Homes, not of apartments" on yard signs and flyers plastered all over downtown. From where she stands at the edge of the parking lot, she can count four apartment complexes within easy walking distance.

The sun crests the horizon, and the heat of it feels good on her skin.

The apartment office at the first complex doesn't open until eight, so she sits in the courtyard and enjoys the idea of living here. It's nice but not one of the new complexes, so she hopes she'll be able to afford it.

Brit watches people coming down the steps and walking with purpose toward their cars, and she feels free. Today is hers. Nobody owns her today, and tomorrow, she will get to work finding a job.

When the front office opens, she waits another fifteen minutes to let the office staff get settled. She always hated when clients showed up as the door opened and didn't give her time to boot up the computer before having to make small talk.

"Good morning." A woman is watering plants, stretching up on one plump leg to reach above her head, when Brit walks through the door.

"Hi. I'm looking for an apartment. Do you have anything available?"

"How many bedrooms you want?"

"Just one or even a studio would be fine."

"Do you have any pets?" She finishes her chore and continues talking as she takes the watering can into the bathroom and stows it under the sink.

"No."

"Great. Let's see what we have." She settles behind the desk and taps a few keys.

The nameplate on the desk reads Suze Delong, and Brit thinks she could do a job like this. She would she enjoy working in the front office at an apartment complex. She should ask if they have any jobs open.

"We have three one bedrooms and a three bedroom currently."

"How much is the rent? For the one bedroom?" Brit asks, setting down her bags to relieve the ache in her shoulders.

"Well, one model is eight fifty a month. The other two are eight seventy-five. The ones for eight seventy-five have new appliances this year."

It's higher than Brit hoped, but she smiles as if the cost is what she thought. "Oh, that's nice. New appliances."

"They all have new carpet. We change that with every tenant. You want to go look at them?"

Brit nods and asks if her bags will be safe here.

Suze says, "I'm gonna lock the door."

Brit scoots her duffel to be flush with the desk and shoulders her backpack, needing to keep her money close.

Suze leaves a sign that reads Back in 15 Minutes on the door and locks it.

They walk through the complex, and Brit feels almost happy. She's nearing the end of this ordeal. They enter a building and climb a flight of steps.

"This one is on the second floor, which I always like because I feel safer in an upstairs apartment," Suze says, looking behind her to Brit.

"Yeah, me too," Brit replies.

"Not that we've had any problems with that sort of thing, but I just like the second floor. It makes for a better view from the balcony." She smiles and unlocks the door to apartment 205B.

The apartment smells musty from being closed up, but it does have a little balcony, like Suze said. Brit moves toward the sliding glass doors and opens them to step out. The balcony overlooks the parking lot, which isn't the great view Suze suggested. Still, she can see herself enjoying the evening on it. She doesn't care about the view. She cares about the shower and a door. Fresh vacuum marks cross the carpet.

"You said the carpet is new?" she asks to fill the silence.

"Oh yes. Do you like the color?"

Brit looks down at the tan nap, thinking that it doesn't really qualify as a color. "Sure. Brown is good."

"This here is the bedroom and the bathroom. It has a nice big closet."

"This is perfect." Brit looks at her reflection in the mirror and smiles. *This was just a glitch.*

"Great. Let's go fill out the paperwork."

They leave the apartment, and Suze offers to show her the other floor plan for the ones that have new appliances.

"No. I think that one will work just fine."

Chapter 24

Brit studies the rental agreement. "It says here you require first and last month's rent plus a deposit?"

"Yes, ma'am."

Brit does a quick mental calculation and figures she will be close to that number with her severance. Maybe she can convince Suze to give her a little flexibility. "And what does it mean by *references?*"

"It means we need your last landlord to vouch for you to say that you didn't trash the place or leave them without notice."

"I don't really have that," Brit says, feeling the glow of hope subside. "I've never actually rented on my own. I've been living with my boyfriend for two years, but we broke up."

"We have to have references. They may accept a referral from your employer, since this is your first time renting on your own." Suze smiles.

Brit stares at her, trying to make sense of the words. "Oh."

Would Ben Walton or Newt Shrieve vouch for me? They accused her of stealing money, made her sign a termination agreement, and called the police. Her face burns as she remembers. They didn't actually *call* the police, but the whole day has merged together into a ball that makes her feel guilty and sick.

"Where do you work?" Suze asks.

"I'm between jobs."

"Oh, honey, you have to have a job to rent an apartment." She says it like it's the most common-sense thing in the world.

"I need a place to live to get a job," Brit says. Tears spring to her eyes, and shame burns through her skin.

Suze reaches across the desk to slide the application from under Brit's hands, and when Brit looks up, Suze crinkles her nose and mouths, *I'm sorry*.

Brit lifts her hands from the paper and lets it slide away. She compresses her lips before rising to her feet, gathering her belongings, and marching to the door with a very straight back. As she opens the door, she turns and says, "Thank you for your time. It was nice meeting you." She smiles as if this is no big deal, and she walks out into the heat of the day.

Brit walks across the street and returns to the Walmart. She puts her belongings in a cart, buys a premade turkey sandwich from the deli, and walks toward the back of the store, steering the cart with her elbows, unpeeling the wrapper, and holding her receipt like a shield. She finds a quiet place in the dog food aisle, where she can sit on the bottom shelf and take a load off.

It feels good to be inside. As Brit finishes her sandwich, an old woman in a blue vest passes the end of the aisle. *How old is she?* Brit wonders. She could be anywhere from seventy to a hundred. The woman is bent forward, shuffling, as if she doesn't have the strength to straighten her back or the ability to move any faster. *How much would it suck to still have to be working at that age?* Walmart will hire anybody. She crumples the wrapper and watches from the corner of her eye as the woman finally makes it past the end of the aisle and moves out of sight.

Walmart will hire anybody. The thought rolls through several times before it strikes a chord. She can get a job here. Then she can go back to Suze and ask if they can work something out. It will be super convenient to be able to walk to work. She won't have to worry about getting a new car or finding rides. It wouldn't be terrible to work here. She makes her way through the store and waits in line at the customer service bay.

"Can I help you?"

"I'd like an application. Are you hiring?"

"We're always hiring. It's done online," the woman behind the counter says.

"Oh. I don't really have access to a computer." Brit feels on edge, frustrated by the obstacles in her path.

"You can do it on your phone," the young woman says.

"You don't just have a paper application?" Brit asks, determined.

"No. It's all done online." The woman looks annoyed, and a new person has come up behind Brit.

"Okay. Great. Thanks." Brit turns away with a smile, as if she'll go home and fill out the application on her phone, the way a normal person would—as if she's a normal person who has a phone that hasn't been disconnected by a pissed-off ex-boyfriend. Brit closes her eyes, feeling doors closing in her head. She lowers her face, and when she opens her eyes, she's calm, and she collects her bags from the cart and leaves the cart in the return.

Brit lets her mind roll, feeling unhinged and unhappy. Everything she tries to do is met with doors, locks, and chains, and the small happy feeling she had when the sun came up is burnt out and destroyed.

She's still hungry. But she won't spend any more of her rent money on food. She walks toward downtown, shouldering her bags. Maybe if she begged Ben, he would give her her job back. If she just explained everything, he would understand.

But she isn't sure he would understand. He thinks she stole from him and knows that she caused the accident that killed Dee Martin, and he and Dee's father are friends.

Cars drive past Brit on 34, and she hopes nobody recognizes her. It would be so embarrassing for Zack to drive by. He would have a good laugh, seeing her knocked down a peg or two. Her feet ache. The sun beats down on her skin.

When Brit doesn't think she can walk any farther, she climbs the bank and slips into the shade of the trees. She sits on her duffel and leans against a trunk. I Am said it was safe back in the trees. She doesn't know how far back the brush goes and considers exploring the patch, finding a comfortable spot to hide for a day or a month, but she worries that a homeless person might think she's encroaching if she goes farther into the shade.

Birds flit. Bugs whir. Cars pass and sound like the tide of the ocean. The frustration from the morning begins to ebb. Brit's been in such a hurry to *accomplish something*, but sitting in the shade of the trees makes the tension melt away. It's summer. It isn't like she's going to freeze to death sleeping outside. *Didn't I wake up this morning just fine? Happy, even?* She had felt free. She breathes, looking into the shadows, and the lockdown in her mind begins to ease.

"I just need to relax," she says. "I just need to relax."

When Brit wakes to find the afternoon waning, she feels better. *When was the last time I had time to take a nap in the middle of the day?* She feels refreshed, and her feet are not quite so sore.

"Wish I had Am's wheelchair," she says just to hear a voice. The duffel is heavy, but she isn't ready to let go of any of her possessions. This is just a glitch.

She'll be back on her feet in no time.

August 9

Chapter 25

When Cliff runs Maggie's VIN through the safe-car check, he discovers that her Honda Civic is on the recall list. It hasn't yet had the airbags replaced. His stomach churns at the thought of her being involved in an accident, just something minor, and losing her because of a defect in a safety mechanism. He hasn't slept well for a week, reliving the grief he saw on Mrs. Martin's face and hearing Mr. Martin ask, "What caused the airbag to act like that?" and "So she shouldn't have died?"

It irritated him that Takata continued manufacturing and selling the defective product even after they discovered the defect. They first became aware in 2004. Dee Martin's car was a 2011, made seven years later. That should never have been allowed. Maggie's Civic is a 2012 but still affected by the recall. He cannot remember receiving a notice, but it would have been addressed to Maggie, so maybe he wouldn't have paid attention.

Cliff pulls into her drive and parks beside the Honda. A Nissan Pathfinder is parked at the curb, and he makes a mental note of it, wondering who Maggie might have over. It isn't her mother's car or her sister, Mae's.

He rings the bell and waits to be let into the house they shared until three months ago.

Maggie opens the door, a laugh still on her voice. "Hey, Cliff." She doesn't step out of the way or invite him in. Instead, she stands with the door close to her body, blocking his view into the house, whether with intent or without, he is unsure.

"Is this a bad time?" he asks.

"I have a friend over," she says with a backward glance into the room.

That glance tells him everything he needs to know. The friend is a man, and she's not yet convinced he will only be a friend. Cliff's stomach churns, and he wants to push her out of the way and get his hands on the man.

"You got a man in my house?" Anger and jealousy ignite, and he forgets why he came here in the first place.

"He's just a friend," Maggie says. Her hand lands on his chest, stalling his impulse to force his way in. Her touch brings his eyes back to hers. "I promise."

The anger evaporates, and the jealousy cools.

"You want to meet him?"

"No," he nearly barks.

"Oh, come on. He's new at the school and doesn't know anybody yet. He teaches fifth grade."

Maggie opens the door, and Cliff sees the man sitting on the sofa. She takes his hand and pulls him inside. He regrets that he isn't in uniform. The man rises. He's tall and elegant, unfolding from the sofa like a ladder.

"Cliff, this Sean. He's just moved here from Chicago. Sean, this is my Cliff."

Her words cause him to glance at her, wondering if she even heard what she said. *This is my Cliff.* His heart expands.

Sean extends his hand, and Cliff clasps the narrow fingers with strength but not force. He can put a man to his knees with the power of his grip, but suddenly, he feels magnanimous and friendly toward the stranger. He is *her* Cliff.

"Of course. I would have recognized you." Sean tilts his long neck, and his heavy head bobs toward the fireplace. Cliff looks and sees that the last photo they posed for together is matted and framed, the distressed blue paint artfully chipped, showing the bare wood beneath. She wanted to use the image for an engagement announcement, but he got cold feet and moved out instead.

He was a fool. When he tears his eyes from the picture, Maggie's looking at him.

Her eyes are soft, and a blush rises to her cheeks. "I love that picture." She sighs.

Cliff nods, needing to take her in his arms, to feel her living, breathing body safe against him. But he can't, he wouldn't dare, with this strange man looking on. "We look good together."

"Emma's on her way. We're going through class lists," Maggie explains.

Cliff relaxes, finally understanding Sean's purpose in being here. Emma is another fifth-grade teacher from Thomas Crossroads Elementary.

He saw the school buses running this week, so he should have realized that school has started, but it feels too soon. Summer lasted so long when he was a kid, but now it seems to pass in the blink of an eye. It is indeed the first full week of August, so school is back in session.

Last year, when this meeting had occurred, it included Kim, who's now retired. Sean is Kim's replacement, not Cliff's. The elementary school operates on block rotation, and each of the fifth-grade teachers specializes in one element. Maggie teaches English and Language Arts, and Emma specializes in History and Social Studies. He has spent enough time with Maggie to understand how the system works.

"So, you teach math?" Cliff asks of Sean.

"Yep. I like numbers."

"That's good," Cliff says. They stand awkwardly for a moment, each of them looking to someone else to take the next move.

"What brings you by?" Maggie finally asks.

"Oh. Oh right. I came by for a reason." He smiles, despite feeling undone because he almost forgot that he no longer lives here, only his picture does. "I need to take your car. I want you to drive mine for a while."

"Why?"

He offers a brief explanation about the Takata airbag recall and how her car and possibly Sean's as well, being a Nissan, are due replacements.

"I'll take care of it. You don't have to do that for me," Maggie says.

"No. You're not driving that car." Cliff doesn't want to scare her by mentioning Dee.

"You think it's that big of a deal?"

"Yes. I do."

"Well, you shouldn't drive it either."

He can tell she thinks he's being overprotective, but he also knows she kind of likes it.

"I'm taking it straight to the shop. I'll drive Dad's truck until it's done. He won't care." Cliff has already worked out the details, and the dealership has already put in an order for the replacement parts. He doesn't know how long it will take and doesn't care.

The doorbell rings, and Maggie says, "That'll be Emma." She leaves, and Cliff and Sean turn to watch her answer the door.

Cliff collects her keys and leaves his on the mantel beside the photo of them together. He wants her to have to look at the picture and remember how happy they were. *Why does she have to be married? Why is it so important to her? Why is not getting married so important to me?*

He can't say why, but even now, months after he bought the ring, months after he made the plan, the idea of actually saying "I do" makes his blood run cold. It doesn't even make sense to him. Maggie is the only woman he wants—the only woman he will ever want. *Impossible relationships.*

He greets Emma as Maggie ushers her into the living room. "Have a good meeting," he says.

When Maggie walks him to the door, she finally folds into his arms. He longs to kiss her, to smother her with the love he feels for her, but she withdraws.

"Thanks for taking care of my car."

"I'd do anything for you, Mags. You know that."

Except marry me. She doesn't say the words, but he reads them in her eyes. "I know." She smiles and waves as he steps off the porch.

The door closes, and he turns back to see her walking past the window toward her coworkers.

But she said, "This is my Cliff." That means she's still talking about him. It means she still thinks she's his.

Cliff has missed an entire summer with her, and it feels like too much.

August 10

Chapter 26

Cliff is still thinking about Maggie calling him hers the next morning when he arrives at the precinct for roll call. It's already hot. A public service announcement has been running for two weeks, reminding people to stay hydrated. The heat stews on the sidewalks, and people shutter themselves into their homes and businesses during the hottest hours of the afternoon. It's dry, but clouds are building along the horizon and offer a promise of rain.

At the end of roll call, Dane catches Cliff as he's heading out to his car. "You remember the Dee Martin accident?"

"Sure." Cliff shrugs, not wanting to admit he's still waking up with that accident in his mind.

"I got a missing person's report handed out yesterday. Thought you'd be interested." The sheet of paper flutters in his hand. "Britany Addams?" Dane offers up the name, reading from the report.

"She's missing?" Cliff asks, remembering she said she was going to the coffee shop and home with a friend. He reaches for the report, thinking he should have found out more about the friend. She may just be lying low, but he suddenly feels that something could have happened to her.

"Yeah. Called in by her mother. Said she hasn't been able to get in touch with her for over a month and her phone has been disconnected, so she asked us to do a wellness check."

"What'd you find out?"

"We went by her last known, a house registered to a Zachary Timmons, but there was nobody home. It came in late yesterday, so I didn't get any further than that."

"I don't think she lives there anymore. Mind if I take it over?"

"I was hoping you would." Dane winks, and they continue toward their cars.

A week ago was when he gave her the news that the DA wasn't pursuing a case against her. She'd had a hell of a month, starting with the accident and ending with getting fired for sleeping in her office. *Poor kid. A lot can happen to a person in a week.*

Cliff drives out to the last known address for Britany, the residence belonging to Zachary Timmons, and finds the house empty. Sitting in his car, he calls dispatch. "Hey, Ann. I'm working a wellness check. Can you find out where Zachary Timmons works?" He gives her Timmons's address on Andrew Bailey for clarification and waits, listening as she types into the system.

"He works out at Warren's Quality Car Care on Dividend in Peachtree City," she says.

The public would be appalled to know the amount of information available about them, not just to the police but to anybody willing to pay the fee for the results. Ann would also be able to see Timmons's debt, his history of property ownership, and his voting registration, if she were interested.

"Great. Thanks." Peachtree City is known for its miles of golf cart trails and tree-lined streets. Unlike Newnan, which is growing as fast as the apartments can be erected, Peachtree City creates the illusion of forests. Beyond the main thoroughfares, the residences are hidden behind lush greenery with subtle signage denoting the streets. No billboards or advertisements mar the landscape. Even through the industrial part of the city, the trees rise to shelter the view.

Cliff parks the cruiser and steps into the air-conditioned lobby at Warren's.

"Good morning, Officer." The words reach him before he sees the woman behind the counter. She is petite and has long blond hair.

He suspects she was the leader of the pep squad when she was in high school. The Southern lilt of her greeting suggests she's a local.

"Good morning, ma'am. I need to speak with a man who works here, a Zachary Timmons. Is he around?"

"Yes, sir. I'll go fetch him for you."

She leaves the reception desk, and Cliff watches as she walks behind a glass barrier and through a door into the shop, where she's hidden from view. When Zachary Timmons comes through the door, Cliff recognizes him as the man who arrived at the scene of the accident to pick up Britany.

He turns at the counter and wipes his hands on a cloth before extending his stained appendage to shake. "What can I do for you, Officer?"

"Zachary Timmons?"

"Zack. Yeah."

"I'm following up on a report of a missing person. Are you familiar with a woman named Britany Addams?"

"Yep. I know her." He glances at the woman in the reception area and asks, "Can we take this outside?"

Cliff nods, and they step out into the heat of the front lot. "Have you seen her?"

"Nope."

Cliff explains that her last known address is his house, and Zack shrugs. "Yep. She moved out some time back." He turns his head and spits.

"What day was that?"

"I don't know. Sometime mid-July, I guess." He looks away.

"Any idea where she went from there?"

"Nope. She works for Ben Walton in Newnan. They probably know where she is," Zack says, and Cliff realizes Zack doesn't know that Brit was fired.

"All right. I'll talk to him. Anybody else you can think of who might know where she is?"

"Jason Jenkins might know something."

That gets Cliff's attention. Jason Jenkins is a new name. "Who is he?"

"He's the little prick she was sleeping with. Lives over in Kedron."

A flash of anger ignites behind Zack's eyes, and Cliff adds another piece to Britany's story—volatile relationships.

Cliff writes down the name and asks, "Is that why she moved out?" She said as much the day he walked with her away from Walton and Shrieve. But now he has a name.

"Yep. That little son of a bitch just wouldn't leave her alone."

"Know anybody who would want to harm her?"

Zack swallows and shakes his head. "You seriously don't know where she is?"

Cliff notices the shift of Zack's feet and the rapid sideways movement of his eyes.

"No, sir. I'm sure we'll find her, though." Cliff waits for Zack to make eye contact again. "You've not had any contact with her since she moved?"

"No, sir. I cut ties."

"All right, then. Thanks for your help. If you happen to hear from her, would you let me know?" Cliff hands his card to Zack, who studies it before removing his wallet and sliding it among the credit cards.

"Yep. I sure will." He leans, turns, and strolls toward the open service bay.

Cliff watches him go, paying attention to Zach's body language. His stained fingers push through his hair then squeeze the base of his neck. Cliff has the distinct impression that Zack has not told him the entire truth.

Chapter 27

Since Cliff is already in Peachtree City, he calls Ann for an address for Jason Jenkins as he drives out to the Kedron area. The address she gives is in an apartment complex called the Retreat. Cliff parks his cruiser, makes his way to the designated apartment, and rings the bell.

A woman answers the door. Cliff checks the address before asking if Jason Jenkins lives here.

"He's at work. Can I help you? I'm his wife. Is he in some kind of trouble?"

Wife. Well, that makes this a little more complicated. "No, ma'am. When do you expect him home?"

"Around six. Usually."

"Would you have him give me a call?" He hands her the card, and she looks at it for several moments before looking up at him with understanding.

"Is this about that accident? Is this because he left? He wasn't driving, you know, if that's what she told you."

"What accident would that be?"

Blood rises to her face then drains. "Oh. This isn't about that. Oh. What is this about?"

"I'm just following up on a report of a missing person and thought he may know something."

"Who's missing?"

"A woman named Britany Addams."

The woman's eyes roll up, and her hip cocks out.

"Do you know her?"

"Oh my god. Yes. I know her. What do you mean, she's 'missing'?"

A small boy walks from the living room and wraps his arms around the woman's thigh. She ruffles the boy's hair.

Cliff presents a photograph to confirm that they're speaking of the same person before explaining that a missing person's report was filed three days ago by Ms. Addams's mother, who has been unable to reach her. "Have you or your husband had contact with her?"

"No. Not since the accident."

The toddler begins tugging at her, trying to pull her away from the door.

"Your husband was in the car with Ms. Addams. Is that right?" he asks, putting the pieces together. The blood being on the passenger-side air bag makes sense, and the smear of unexplained blood on the leg of Britany's jeans is no longer a mystery. "Were they involved?" He is cautious not to be too overt with the child standing there.

"Bumbee, go inside. Go on."

She peels the child's hands from her leg, and he waddles into the living room. Cliff watches him plop down in front of the television. In the gentle removal of the child from her, his sight flashed forward, and he imagined Maggie with a child, a blend of the two of them.

"He was ending it," she says. One hand moves over her stomach. "They dated in high school. She wouldn't leave him alone. I think she's a little unstable." She twirls her finger beside her temple.

Cliff takes a breath and stands to his full height. That's the same phrase Zack used about Jason, that he "wouldn't leave her alone." He remembers the last time he saw Britany Addams, the day she was fired and he told her there would be no charges against her. She *had* looked unstable. She may have been unhinged enough to drive somebody to violence. Jason Jenkins may have been the friend she was expecting to meet. She may have made demands on him that he couldn't oblige.

"Was he successful? In ending it?"

"Yes." Her jaw juts forward in defiance.

"Good. Where could I find your husband now?" In light of the situation, Cliff thinks he should speak to him before his wife can tell him what's coming.

"I told you. He's working." She turns and looks into the house.

Cliff catches sight of the little boy, who has his thumb in his mouth. "Where does he work?"

"Best Buy," she says.

"Thanks for your time. I'll stop over there and talk with him."

Chapter 28

Brit visited three more apartment complexes over the course of the week, working her way toward derelict. She did not look at any of the apartments. She asked the important questions and didn't waste anybody's time. She had money. It should have been easy, but it wasn't.

The weather was good with clear skies. Brit got used to sleeping on the ground, sheltering under bushes in yards. As she walked, she looked for I Am but without luck. Maybe Am had moved on or something had happened to her. Brit is tempted to go out to the spot by the elementary school where she said she sometimes stays. It isn't like she can't walk that way and just look for her, but she's afraid that Am won't remember her or, worse, won't want her there.

Brit stops at Walmart and puts her bags in a cart. Again, she buys a sandwich from the deli and walks toward the back of the store. She finds the quiet place in the dog food aisle where she can sit on the bottom shelf and not draw attention. Every day over the last week, she has done the same thing. She has read all the ingredients and packaging of the Old Roy dog foods and is working through the Pedigree. Maybe next week, she'll work her way through the cat food.

It feels good to be inside and out of the heat. When she finishes her sandwich, she gathers her belongings and leaves the store, not wanting to get in trouble for loitering. She doesn't know if they would actually arrest somebody for that. Maybe it wouldn't be so bad, to be arrested. At least she wouldn't have to worry about where to sleep tonight.

Brit is still hungry, but she's getting used to it. She doesn't mind her clothes getting a little loose. She always thought she was too big but never seemed to be able to lose those ten pounds. Maybe Zack wouldn't even recognize her with her hair back to her natural shade and her plump cheeks scooped out. *Even Jason wouldn't recognize me,* she thought, and he knew her when she was at her skinniest.

She climbs the bank and slips into the shade of the trees to sit on her duffel, like she does every afternoon, and watches the traffic flow past, wondering where all those people are going. Everybody seems to be in such a hurry, rushing, rushing, rushing. People should take more naps. Her eyes close as she lets herself be lulled to sleep by the white noise of the passing cars.

An arm reaches from the shadow of the trees and grasps the handle of Brit's backpack, ripping it from her hands with a mighty grunt. The motion pulls her arm back, and a searing pain erupts in her shoulder as her hand releases the pack. She grasps her shoulder and leaps to her feet, turning to face the thief.

"Give it back!" she shouts, pushing her way into the limbs of a tree.

He is already running, leaping through the underbrush like a deer.

"Come back!" she screeches when she loses sight of him. Her foot catches on a root, and she face-plants into the leaf litter.

Brit regains her footing and pushes through the next wall of underbrush. A small clearing opens, and three grubby tents form a rough half circle around a well-established firepit. She stops in her tracks. A man with a shaggy gray beard pokes his head from one of the tents and looks at her with mild curiosity. Another man rights himself in a hammock stretched between two trees and approaches her. She scans the clearing.

A fat middle-aged woman without any teeth peers from inside the third tent. "Henley!" she shouts, panic clear in her voice.

Brit puts her hands up.

"What you want?" the man from the hammock asks. He stands a few feet away from her, but his posture makes her feel small and intimidated.

"A man just stole my backpack. I was sitting back there in the shade, and he just ripped it out of my hands and ran this way."

"I ain't seen nobody run through here. You must be mistaken."

"I need my backpack. Everything I have is in it." Tears spring to her eyes, and she doesn't even try to push them down. Her shoulder is throbbing, all her money is in that backpack, and she realizes now that she ran off and left everything else unprotected at the edge of the trees.

"Well, we ain't got it." The fat woman waddles out of the tent and stands beside the man, and Brit takes an involuntary step back. The woman slides a small blade beneath the ridge of her fingernail, and Brit feels it like a threat. "You best be getting on out of here, college girl. Go ask Daddy. He'll buy you another backpack."

Brit scans the clearing. The bearded man has pulled down his flap and is no longer visible.

"It's all I had," Brit insists, but when the man steps toward her, she steps back and makes her way out of the clearing and to where she left her duffel bag. It's open, and the contents are strewn in a wide arc. Brit screams, turning back into the trees.

When the man pushes a branch down and points his finger at her, like it's a weapon, she hastily gathers her clothes and throws them into the duffel. She refuses to cry, but all the way to the Newnan square, she feels a quiver in her chest. This can't be her life. She didn't think she would need to find the church that has beds for people until the weather turns. She slept at the edge of a parking lot one night, for heaven's sake. But she suddenly feels the danger of being a woman without a door to lock, and her understanding about what kind of place the world is rocks her off the little plateau where she thought she could just wander around and take naps in the shade of trees. Brit isn't on vacation. She feels so stupid, so ill-equipped for this life she's living, and the threats suddenly lurking in every shadow.

Chapter 29

The stone glitters in Cliff's hand, catching the light as it moves. It has been sitting in the box on the shelf in his safe. The ring is beautiful, and even though the center stone is what some women might think of as small, Cliff thinks Maggie will see it as perfect. He keeps remembering what Carla said about it being important to Maggie. That's why it mattered. Being married is important to Maggie. He always knew it was. They talked about it early on in a hypothetical way.

She thought he would change. "I feel we're not moving forward." Those are the words she said the day she asked him to move out.

"What are you talking about?"

"It's been three years. I love you, but I think we need different things."

Cliff sucks in a breath through his nostrils, holds it for a beat, then lets it out. The memory fades, and his thoughts shift to a couple of days ago, when he went to get her car and found a man in her house. *In* our *house.* He was irritated—no, he was angry—when he walked up to her door and realized she wasn't alone. *What did you expect would happen?*

He knows she wants to get married, that she is ready for the next step, and with a low knot in his gut, he knows that if it isn't with him, it will be with somebody else. But she won't be happy with anybody else. She's still in love with him—just like he's still in love with her.

The image of Jim Martin lifting his wife's hand so tenderly to his lips flashes and stalls in his mind like a snapshot. That gesture was more than just the kiss of fingers. It was a promise, a guarantee that she wasn't alone. Mrs. Martin will not have to go through her grief alone.

That's the guarantee Maggie wants. He understands. But Maggie knows he's there for the long haul. She knows he would never leave her.

At least, he thinks she knows. She *should* know.

Impossible relationships. He tilts the ring again, and light glints on one of its facets.

Maggie isn't like his mother. Or he doesn't think she is. His memories of Miriam are more grounded in the bits of information his brother offered than actual memories. He remembers her stories—well, not the stories themselves but rather the emotion of being held captive by her voice as she wove some thread into an adventure. He loved her stories, but even that memory is quixotic, flashing like the refracted light from the ring. It glows then dims as he mulls the memory in his mind.

He wishes he knew why his mother left.

That has always been the question. Theirs wasn't a childhood filled with anger and fights. They had the perfect family, and the four of them often talked about how much more perfect theirs was than everybody else's. Miriam didn't run away to escape a violent husband, and Tony and Cliff were good kids. The boys had many conversations while growing up, trying to put together a puzzle that was missing most of its pieces. It never made sense. They asked their dad why Miriam had left. Cliff never forgot the look that passed over his face. He had moved on, but some piece of him remained locked in the moment of her leaving.

"I have no idea," his father said, and for a second, Cliff was afraid that the sullen expression would stay, but the cloud moved past, and he smiled at him. "I reckon it was just something she needed for her. I don't think we'll ever understand it. Your mama was a little bit gypsy."

Cliff went to school the next day and looked up the word *gypsy* and came away as confused as before. He didn't think his mother was from Romany. She did tell a lot of stories, but he had never seen her reading cards or telling fortunes. True, her stories had sometimes been about mythical creatures and magical beings. He didn't understand and asked Tony because Tony always knew more than he did.

"She had itchy feet," Tony said, and Cliff's brow furrowed even more. Not only was she possibly from Romany, possibly a fortune teller, but she also had a fungus on her feet. Cliff was confused and frustrated. He felt like everybody was talking in riddles, and he had never been good at those. Cliff had experienced itchy feet the summer before when he went into the restroom at the public pool without his flip-flops and come away with the devil of a fungus. It had nearly driven him crazy. Surely she hadn't left for that.

Cliff grew up, and now he understands about itchy feet, wanderlust, and living a nomadic life, but still he doesn't understand why she left. Many of her stories were stories about traveling, so maybe that was what was important to her. He wonders if she thinks of them and misses them. If it hadn't been for that one message, he would believe she was taken, maybe killed, but that message told them she left on her own. He was still confused and frustrated.

The ring sparkles, and Cliff's cell vibrates. The screen blooms with Maggie's face, which is smiling and sun bronzed. He remembers the moment he took that picture on a long weekend in the mountains, making love in the morning, hiking through the afternoons, and relaxing in the hot tub well into the night. The last night of their stay, they were startled by a family of bears who strolled ten feet from the hot tub. They sat motionless, watching the mother and her two cubs as they paused at the trash bins, found the lids tight and unbreachable, and moved on.

They erupted from the hot tub, and in that moment, he had captured her, in the seconds after picking up his phone. She was cast in the glow from the underwater lights, smiling with excitement. They went inside and stood watching from behind the glass as the bears made their slow progression down the road, through all the trash cans.

"Hey, Mags," Cliff says, as if he hasn't been thinking of her, as if she's catching him unawares.

"I missed your call. Is everything okay?" Maggie asks.

"Yeah, yeah. Of course. I'd like to take you out."

"Cliff."

"Just dinner. Come on, Mags. You know you want to."

A breath passes through the line, and he can almost hear the smile. "Of course I want to, but I don't know if it's a good idea."

"Come on, Mags. We can go anywhere you want."

She laughs this time, and Cliff knows he has her. "Seasons 52?"

"If that's what you want." He smiles, looking down at the ring. It's stunning against the black velvet of the box. "But I can cut you some grass from our backyard and go one better than farm to fork."

"Ha-ha." He can still hear the smile. "When?"

"Tomorrow?"

"Okay."

He flips the ring box closed, feeling triumphant.

August 11

Chapter 30

Cliff thinks he's done everything right. The ring is perfect. Maggie will love it. He looks in the mirror again, goes to the closet, and changes from his blue blazer to his gray one. Then he checks himself one last time, nods, and turns out the light. He teased her about her restaurant choice, a trendy farm-to-table place that caters to vegans and foodies, but he would eat from a pig's trough if that was what she wanted.

He closes the door to his tiny apartment. *I won't be needing that much longer.* He'll be able to go home, and they'll get back to their lives. Suddenly, he can't understand why he's been so stubborn. All day, he's thought of her—the way she smiles, the way she laughs, the way she makes him less serious sometimes. He doesn't know what he was thinking in letting her go. Nothing would ever be worth being without her.

If Maggie notices his nervousness on the drive to the restaurant, she doesn't let it show. She talks happily about the events of her day, about how the new school year is shaping up, and about her sister, who is planning to hike the Appalachian Trail.

"She's not going alone, is she?" Cliff manages to ask. Caution is his realm of expertise.

"No, her whole group is going."

"That's good. When are they leaving?" He doesn't care, but it will keep her talking, filling the awkward silence he carries into social situations.

"Spring break, I think. She bought a weight vest, and she's walking through her neighborhood with hiking sticks. Her neighbors probably think she's crazy."

He chuckles, imagining tiny Mae in her weight vest. "She's something else."

"Isn't she, though?"

The pride in Maggie's voice makes Cliff glance over at her, thinking of how she always does that. She always gives people credit for greatness. Mae is a flake, but Maggie builds her up like she's an adventurer.

"She still with that guy?"

A month before Maggie asked Cliff to move out, Mae was dating a weasel of a guy Cliff had on his personal watch list as a small-time drug dealer. He isn't trafficking in enough to warrant a takedown, but they're paying attention to him, trying to discern his supply chain.

"No. She said he's got a temper. That's why she's doing the trail. *Reclaiming her independence.*" Maggie says the last part with an inflection Cliff recognizes as Mae's.

"What happened?"

"I don't know, really. She won't talk about it. But she dumped him and said she was starting over, clean slate."

"Let me know if he bothers her. He's trouble."

"She says he's not been around." Maggie puts her hand on his arm. "Thanks."

Her smile makes Cliff want to pull over and take her in his arms. He's dying to feel her body against him again, to kiss her lips, and sleep with her.

Through the meal, they laugh and talk together the way they always do, and all the while, the ring is heavy in his jacket pocket. He feels like Bilbo Baggins, the way his hand itches to reach into the pocket and touch the box, to know that it's still solidly there. She doesn't seem to notice his nervousness.

When he can stand it no longer, he brings it out and sets the velvet box on the table between them.

Maggie looks at it for a very long time, her face unreadable.

Cliff's heart hammers, and for a split second, he imagines removing the ring from the table. *Marriage.* His body shifts, and he slides from his chair and draws the attention of other diners as he kneels on one knee. He reaches for the box and flips it open like a magic trick, a sleight of hand. The ring blinks from the box's velvet folds, and she stares unbelieving and silent.

"Mags, marry me." The words come easily to his lips, rolling over his tongue, and as he hears them, he knows it's right. Of course they should be married.

Tears pool in Maggie's eyes, and her hand covers her heart. The glistening eyes move from the sparkling gem to Cliff's hopeful, expectant face. She reaches out to touch the velvet of the box. Her fingers withdraw, her eyes lift to meet his, and her hand falls away from her heart.

He doesn't understand the expression on her face. It's not the one he thinks should be there. Maggie doesn't look happy. She isn't smiling. She looks sad. She hasn't said yes and fallen into his arms.

Her head shifts slowly back and forth, and the words that form on her lips are "I can't." She closes the box as if the glittering jewel is too much to witness.

Cliff is still kneeling, frowning with confusion. A few people around them began to cheer, realizing this was a proposal. But the celebration falters when Maggie shakes her head. She reaches out and encourages Cliff back into his seat.

"What do you mean, you 'can't'?" he asks after she says it two more times.

The diners near them make efforts not to get caught looking, but Cliff doesn't miss the sideways glances, and neither does Maggie.

She is quick to clasp his hands to keep him there with her. "It's not what you want. You're just doing it because you think I need it and you don't want to let me go."

"No. I don't want to let you go. You're right. You are the best part of my life, and I want to be with you. So I do want to get married to you. I want to be with you, Mags, and if you need to be married, then I want to marry you."

"You're just lonely."

"Yeah. I am. I miss you. These past three months have been terrible, and it made me realize that I don't want to do any more of my life without you beside me. Don't you understand?"

"I think you're doing it because you don't want to be alone."

"Isn't that what I just said?" His voice rises in frustration. *Impossible relationships.*

"That's my point," she says, as if this is logical and he has made her point for her.

"What is?"

"You're scared to be alone." She keeps her voice low, trying not to share their personal stories with others.

"No. I'm not scared to be alone. That's ridiculous. I don't want to be without *you*. I don't care about being alone. I was fine before I met you, but when I showed up at your house and knew that you had a man there, I realized how empty my life would be forever, without you." It's a lot of words for Cliff to string together, and he's a little exhausted from the effort of finding them. "You make me a better man."

She reaches across the table and forces her fingers inside his clenched hand. The ring box sits untouched on the table.

"I feel like I've forced you into this. I don't want to wake up fifteen years down the road and have you feel like I forced you to do something you didn't want to do."

He laughs, a bark of bitterness. "You forced me to move out of our house, Maggie. That's what you forced me to do." He spreads his hand, enveloping hers, to soften his words with his touch. "All my life, there have only been two things I was good at. Being a cop. I'm a good cop."

His voice stalls, and she leans across the table, trying to catch his eyes. "What's the other thing?"

"You, Maggie. I am good at loving you."

Tears form in her eyes, and when she speaks, her voice trips over her emotion. "Can you ask me again?"

His eyes come back to her, and the room around them dissolves. He asks again without taking his eyes off hers. "Please marry me, Maggie."

"Okay." A tear spills free and rolls down her cheek. Then they are standing, holding each other.

"Does that mean I can come home?" he asks, his breath hot in the thick mane of her hair.

"Yes. Yes!"

He lifts her feet off the ground and holds her close to him. The crowd around them cheers.

Chapter 31

The shelter, when Brit finds it, has filled their beds for the night. "You have to be here between one and four to get in, then it's first come and need. If you got kids, you get in first," a woman says, gathering a trash bag and turning to walk away. She has the look of a street person, the same look Brit feels now belongs to her.

"What are we supposed to do?" she calls after the woman and falls into step behind her.

"Get here earlier tomorrow."

Brit takes another step then another then stops, too weary to move forward. Her duffel slides down her arm and thumps onto the ground as if it contains a dead body instead of clothes.

She tilts her head up and stares into the sky as weakness burns out of her. Brit has had about enough of closed doors and *no* for the rest of her life. *I'm not a bad person!* She wants to scream but squares her shoulders and reaches down to grab her duffel and reposition it on her back.

"What the *fuck* am I supposed to do now?" she asks quietly. She just needs a place to sleep where she won't get robbed, beaten up, or killed. The woman who said she needed to get here earlier turns into an alley, and Brit thinks about following her, but the woman isn't friendly, not the way I Am was.

She can't take somebody else telling her to get lost and thinks about walking over to Walton and Shrieve, where she can sleep behind the building, and maybe nobody would bother her. It feels like a lifeline. She draws a deep breath and marches toward Jack Dale Street. As she starts to step onto the street, she recognizes a car driving toward her. *Fucking Elise.* She drops her head and hopes she won't see her but knows she does by the way the car slows beside her. She shifts her pace, and when Elise and another car drive past, she crosses the street and heads toward Highway 34.

The guy in the Walmart parking lot said she could sleep behind the loading dock as long as she didn't leave a mess. Brit walks away from Jack Dale, remembering the photo they took of her sleeping under the desk. Shame rolls through her followed by anger. She worked there for two years, and she never screwed up before. When she had a bad month, they fired her, just like that. She was a good employee. She worked late when Ben was on vacation or just needed something ready for the next morning and almost never stepped away from her desk, not even for lunch, because she wanted to keep the reception area covered.

Brit stops noticing the forward motion of her feet, stops noticing the pain radiating from her toes and her heels. She shifts the bag to her good shoulder. She stops feeling the evening heat as clouds scud together and block out the sun. Lightning bugs flicker as she walks. Cars pass. When she finally reaches the Walmart, she walks toward the back of the building and finds a place along the edge of a shipping container. She twines her arms through the straps of her bag and leans against the crate. Quickly, darkness lowers around her as the clouds converge. Lightning flashes, and the sound of far-off thunder rumbles through a scorched sky.

Rain comes. Thick, cool drops pepper her hair. She lowers her head, and her shoulders heave. Her voice breaks in a cracked laugh erupting from her throat. What a joke her life has become. She thinks again about her mom. But it feels like it's too late to call her. She has slid too far to be able to face her mother's judgment. Lightning crackles, the hair on her body stands up, and the concussion of the thunder pounds through her chest, forcing her to her feet. She staggers to the front of the store and throws her bag into a cart, standing in the shelter of the entrance, staring out at the deluge. The doors behind her slide open as customers join her in the entrance, releasing the frigid air inside. They stop, staring out at the torrent of water pounding against the pavement. They stand together, chatting as Brit shivers, drenched.

Brit is just one of many, part of the excited conversation about the rise of the storm, about the rain falling in sheets across the parking lot.

"I'm parked right there. I can't even see my car," a man muses.

"Was it supposed to rain?" a woman asks.

"Don't worry. The ark will be along any minute. We'll have to load two by two," another man says, and Brit's head snaps around and catches his face in profile as he leans down and opens an umbrella.

Jason.

Her heart skips a beat, and his name forms on her lips the moment before she sees the woman at his side. Then they walk out the door and into the downpour, Jason holding the umbrella to shelter her and the boy on her hip, not himself. Brit watches until the rain swallows them.

The people near her begin to move away as she emits a small, squeaking moan. She sees them watching her as if she's floating above her body. They all turn toward her, and they see the stringiness of her hair, not just from wet but from dirt and sweat. They see the rumpled state of her clothes and the bag in the cart, which does not contain purchases.

Brit whimpers. She wants her life back. Several moments pass, in which some of the people choose to brave the weather. Lightning crackles, and thunder booms, startling Brit's sobs to silence. Back in her body again, she looks at the faces around her. Three women and a man stare at her the way she would look at a train wreck.

She jerks the cart and moves into the store, pushing the cart toward the back of the store. Then she grabs her belongings and pushes into the bathroom, where she is finally alone. The bag falls to the floor in the largest of the stalls, and she sits, dripping on the toilet, rocking forward, and burying her face between her knees. Without tears, without sound, she sobs, wracked by the unbearable grief trapped inside.

August 15

Chapter 32

"Any luck on that missing person?" Dane asks Cliff when they see each other at morning roll call.

The first news report about the missing woman aired the night before, and Cliff received two calls from the hotline.

"Not much. Seems like nobody has seen her since mid-July. I got one lady who said she thinks she saw her at the bank. I'm going to follow up with her today. But it's a pretty cold trail, so it probably won't end well."

"Probably not," Dane agrees.

Cliff hasn't uncovered Jason Jenkins yet. After speaking with his wife, he went to the Best Buy and was told he was in LaGrange for the day, doing inventory. Cliff left his card and asked that they pass it along.

Cliff's radio beeps, and he presses the button. "I'm here," he says, which is almost the same as asking, *What's up?*

"You still in the building?" The voice comes on a squawk.

"Yeah."

"I got a man up front to see you."

Cliff raises his eyebrows and turns toward the front of the building as Dane continues toward his car. "I'll be right there."

The young man is sitting in one of the chairs with his knees bouncing a mile a minute. He is the only person waiting, so Cliff has no doubt he's his guy.

The young man leaps to his feet at Cliff's approach. "Officer Rathborn?"

"Yes, sir, and you are?"

"Jason Jenkins. I was told I need to see you." Dark circles ring his eyes, and he looks like he's about to jump out of his skin.

"Yes, sir. Thank you for coming down. Let's go find someplace where we can talk."

The man nods and follows Cliff into the station house. Cliff leaves him in one of the interrogation rooms and pauses outside the door to ensure that the recording equipment is operational. He grabs a notepad and a pen and joins Jason. They sit across the table from each other, and Cliff can tell from the small motion in Jason's torso that his knee is bouncing again. "Can I get you anything to drink? Coffee? Water?"

"Naw, I've already had too much coffee." He chuckles, explaining away his bouncing knee and red-rimmed eyes.

"You know why I wanted to see you?"

"Yeah, Brit. I saw it on the news last night. So she's really gone missing? Do you think something happened to her?" Concern is etched across his face.

"That's what I'm trying to find out. Her mother filed a missing person's report. So we're just trying to figure out where she's gone. When did you last see her?"

"I don't know. July, I guess."

"When in July?"

"Middle."

"What was your relationship with Britany Addams?" Cliff asks. Even though he knows, he needs to find out if the man will lie.

"It's complicated. We dated through high school. Broke up when I went to college. Neither of us wanted to do the long-distance thing."

"You went away for college?"

"University of Georgia, up in Athens," he says.

"How about Britany? Did she go to college?" Cliff asks, needing to see the shape of their involvement to discern Jason's culpability.

"No. Her folks kinda screwed her. They got divorced her senior year of high school, and whatever money they meant for Brit's education got eaten in that."

"Did she want to go to college?"

"She had always planned to, I guess. She got accepted to Athens, so we could stay together, but she couldn't afford it. She was gonna work for a year and save up, but I don't know. She got busy with life." Jason's voice sounds brittle, tense.

"So whose idea was it to break up?"

Jason lets out a long breath. "Mine. I had never been with anybody but Brit, and all of a sudden, it was like a buffet of girls."

"How did she take it? When you broke up?"

"I don't know. I didn't really see her until I finished college and moved back home. I met Mary Beth my junior year, and she got pregnant second semester. We got married and moved home. I ran into Brit a couple of years ago, and we reconnected. Kinda."

"Was she dating Zack when you reconnected?"

"No. Not at first. And we were just friends, you know? She didn't start seeing Zack until after that."

"Would you say that at some point you and Ms. Addams became something more than friends?"

Jason glanced up at the camera in the corner. "Is this being recorded?"

"Yes."

"Do I need a lawyer?"

"Did you do something to Britany Addams that you would need counsel for?"

"No." He laughs, a nervous sound that skitters across the table, and leans back. "But we did have a relationship, and now she's missing. I just feel like maybe I need a lawyer."

Cliff releases a long breath. "I'm just trying to find a missing woman. That's all. I don't have any evidence at this time that a crime has been committed. I'm trying to establish her last known whereabouts. If you feel you need an attorney to complete a conversation with me, then you should get one."

Jason jumps forward, banging his elbows on the table, and pushes his hands up through his hair. "We'd been seeing each other for about a year and a half when I ended it in July. I haven't heard from her since."

"Were you in the car with her the day she was involved in the accident at Highway 54 and Fischer Road?" Cliff doesn't take his eyes from Jason and sees the shock of being accused flash in his eyes.

"No. Who said that? Who told you that?" He looks down at his hands.

"So you were not in the car with her that day?" Cliff studies him.

"Okay. So what if I was?"

"So you were in the vehicle at the time of the accident?"

"So what if I was? I wasn't driving. She told me to go. Zack has a temper, man, and we didn't want to cross his path."

Cliff asks again, and Jason confirms he was present at the time of the accident. Cliff thinks back to that day. "Can you tell me what happened?"

"Shit. Man, I think I need to get a lawyer." Jason slings his hips forward and leans hard against the back of the chair.

"I'm not interested in arresting you for being in the car. I'm interested in figuring out what happened to this woman. Do you know if she had friends in the area that she could go to for help?"

Jason springs forward again, cupping his head in his hands and shaking it back and forth. "She couldn't have friends. Not once she got with Zack. He didn't like her knowing people."

"Was Zack abusive? Did you ever know him to hit her?"

"I don't know that he ever did, but I definitely think he's capable. I think he scared her a couple of times." Jason drops his hands to the table.

Cliff feels the nervous energy coming off the young man.

"Do you think he killed her?" Jason asks.

"We don't have evidence that she's been killed, but it's very important that we find her."

"Zack is who you need to be talking to, man. He's unhinged." Jason's level of agitation increases.

"Do you know what happened to Britany?"

"No, man, but he was pretty pissed, and now she's missing. What do you think happened? Have you even talked to him yet?"

Cliff doesn't respond, letting Jason stew for a minute, studying him. "Can I ask you something kind of personal?" When Jason nods, Cliff continues, "Were you gonna leave your wife to be with Britany?"

"No. No. We got a kid. I love my wife, man." He pops back against his chair, and his eyes scan the far side of the room.

"Is there any reason Britany would have thought you were going to?"

"No. No way, man."

"You never told her you were going to leave your wife to be with her?" Cliff presses.

Jason sits forward again. "Look, man, we were fooling around, okay? I may have said I wished we had stayed together, you know, like I'd never met Mary Beth, but you know how it is. We were just fooling around."

Cliff looks at the young man for a long time, thinking about the woman he last saw leaving Walton and Shrieve. She wasn't a bad kid, he didn't think. She'd just trusted the wrong people to help her through life.

"Were you aware that after the accident, Zack found out you were together?"

"Yeah, she told me. Said Mary Beth had figured it out."

"Can you tell me what happened then?"

Jason rubs his face, stretching out his eyelids. "I ended it. Said we were through. Mary Beth is expecting, and I just needed to step up, you know. Put my attention on my family."

"I see." Cliff makes a note in the notebook, stalling as he processes. "Are you aware that Zack kicked her out of their house?"

"Yeah. She told me. Said he stole her money, too, zeroed out their account, you know. He's such an ass."

"Did you worry about what was going to happen to her?"

Jason shrugs.

"You don't know if you worried about what would happen to her?"

"Of course I worried, man. I care about Brit, but she isn't my problem. I have to focus on my family. I have to fix my marriage."

"Did she ask you for help? After Zack kicked her out and zeroed out the bank account?" They sit for several seconds, and Cliff bides his time before he collects his notebook and pen together and prepares to stand. "Mr. Jenkins, I think you might want to seek counsel."

"Yeah, she asked me for help."

Cliff sets the notebook back on the table. "How do you think your wife found out?"

"I had a broken nose and told her I was in a fight. She hacked my phone and saw my texts with Brit, including our plans to meet. She took pictures, I guess, and showed Zack."

"What happened then?"

"I don't know. He's a fucking psycho!" Jason shouts.

"Did you make sure she was safe? After you knew Zack had found out?"

"I talked to her on the phone after that. She told me he kicked her out. She said he told her he would kill her if he ever saw her again."

"She told you that?"

"Yeah." He nods, his hair flying forward.

"Do you think he would be capable of such a thing?" Cliff asks, thinking back to the man he met at Warren's and his oil-stained fingers. He sees again the way he squeezed the back of his neck as he walked away. That might have been a tell, if he strangled Britany Addams and dumped her body somewhere. He replays the moment in his mind with his new perspective.

"Hell yeah. Dude is, like, dangerous."

"What did you do then, after she told you he had threatened her life?" Cliff asks, holding his pen poised.

"What do you mean? I didn't do nothing. Stayed low, man. Stayed real low."

Jason is a coward. He messed around with Britany and led her on, and when they got caught, he ran away like a scared rabbit. Cliff is disgusted and is tempted to read him his rights just to keep him from ever doing this in somebody else's life.

"Where did she go after he kicked her out? Did she say?"

Jason shakes his head.

"Was that the last time you talked to her? The last time you saw her?"

"She called me couple of times a couple of weeks after the accident. After I'd ended it, you know. Told me Zack had cleaned out their account and she needed money. So I went by her office and gave her a little money to get her through. I helped her out." His eyes shift, and his middle finger digs at the meat around his thumbnail.

"How much money did you give her?"

"About three hundred dollars. You know, just to help her out."

He repeats the words as if he thinks he deserves a medal. Cliff wants to shake him.

"That was generous. And she just let you go then? Accepted that you were through?"

"Yeah. I guess so. I figured she and Zack would work things out. He was just trying to punish her."

"Do you remember what day you gave her the money? Did you make a bank withdrawal?"

"I don't remember the day. I took the money from the house. We try to keep cash on hand."

"Does your wife know? About the money?"

"No." Jason shakes his head, pressing his lips into a tight line. "I'd prefer that she not. She's pregnant, you know. I don't really want to upset her."

"Oh. Right." Cliff collects the notebook again. "Anything else you can tell me?"

"No, man. I don't know anything else. But I'm telling you Zack is the guy you should be talking to."

"Good to know." Cliff looks at Jason for a long beat. "Still, I don't think you should plan on leaving town for a while. You know, just in case we need to talk to you again."

"Yeah, sure. I ain't going anywhere."

"If you hear from Britany, please let me know," Cliff reminds him, handing him his card.

"Yeah. Sure. I hope you find her."

"I'm sure we will."

August 18

Chapter 33

Maggie reaches for Cliff's hand from across the console as they drive down the country road that leads to Cliff's childhood home. Carla went for her thirty-day checkup, and they discovered that the cancer has jumped to her lymphatic system. It's in her blood, coursing through her veins like a lethal injection.

They don't speak in the car. Maggie sits in the passenger seat with his hand between both of hers as they pull into the driveway. The house is dark. They make their way through it and find Cliff's parents sitting side by side on the deck, so they move stealthily and quietly, not wanting to disturb them.

A peal of laughter erupts from Carla's narrow frame, and when she turns her face to look at Pop, she's radiant. Her smile is a gift, and Cliff lets out a stalled breath.

"Maggie!" Carla moves with ease from her seat and tugs Maggie from Cliff's side and into an embrace.

Maggie inhales a shuddering breath, and Cliff loves her even more for loving Carla. "I've missed you."

Carla pats her back and closes her eyes. "And I, you." She pushes back. "Let me see this ring."

Cliff's heart surges at seeing the two of them together, at the joy on Maggie's face as she displays the ring, and Carla's smile in admiring it.

His dad joins them, thumping Cliff on the back as if he made the championship goal. "Congratulations, son."

"Thanks, Pop," Cliff says, motioning for his dad to join him in the kitchen. "What are the doctors saying?"

"It's not good." They're safely in the kitchen, still able to see the women through the glass door. "It could be a week or months."

"There's nothing they can do?" If medical science can create a human ear, he doesn't understand how they can't remove cancer.

"Not really. She's tired, son." Strain shows around Pop's eyes.

"I know. We want to get married here, and we want her to be with us when we do." Cliff hasn't spoken with Maggie about it, and they can still do the "wedding" for her family, but he's afraid Carla won't make it until then.

Pop's face creases, and he draws one hand up to cover his eyes. When he pulls it free, he is composed, the threat of breaking behind him. "I think she would really like that."

⎯⎯●⎯⎯

It takes three days to get the wedding license. They hold the ceremony on the back deck, with only Cliff's family in attendance. Tony is there, alone, along with Carla and Pop. It takes all of ten minutes to go through the service. Pop sets up his camera and takes a photo of the five of them for a keepsake. Carla's having a decent day. She isn't in pain, she says, although she looks tired, like a flower wilting along the edges.

After the officiant leaves, they eat a potluck wedding feast. Pop has smoked a brisket, Carla made potato salad, Cliff and Maggie provided quinoa salad and greens, and Tony brought bourbon and a tuxedo cake. When the meal is done, Maggie and Carla leave the men to clean up, and Cliff finds them later, sitting in the living room. Pop and Tony have shooed Cliff away, saying it's his wedding day, so he doesn't have to do cleanup.

He sits on the arm of Carla's chair and indicates the shoebox of old photos sitting on the coffee table. "What's this?"

"I've been sorting through those. I want to make you boys albums."

"Oh. That's sweet." Maggie leans forward and draws the box onto her lap. She riffles through the images, pulling some out. She hands one to Carla. It's of Cliff at five or six, in the pool. Then she takes out another that shows him at ten, holding a Red Rider BB gun. Finally, she holds up one of Cliff as a toddler, sitting on a strange woman's lap.

"Is this...?"

"Miriam." Carla offers a small, sad smile. She takes the picture and holds it gingerly.

"I wonder what happened to her." Maggie looks up at Cliff, and he can see the worry in her eyes. It's a touchy subject.

Carla hands him the photo, and he studies it.

Maggie continues digging through the box, passing photos to Carla, who passes them on to Cliff. They can hear the dishes being cleaned away by Tony and Pop, and their voices crawl under the door in easy conversation. When Cliff finishes looking at each photo, he places them on the coffee table.

"You know who that picture makes me think of?" Carla asks, picking up the photo of Cliff and Miriam. "You know that old homeless woman who walks around Newnan? Every time I see her, I think of Miriam."

"Did you know her?" Maggie asks.

"We went to school together."

"I didn't know that," Cliff says and accepts the photograph again.

"Your dad doesn't like me talking about her." Pop is still in the kitchen, and the conversation feels clandestine.

"What was she like?" Cliff asks, still trying to put the puzzle of his mother together.

"She was always a little troubled. Kind of quiet. Kept to herself. She was odd." Carla's words don't come out as critical, just factual.

"She used to be in the middle of doing something, and she'd just stop and stare at something that wasn't there. Nothing I could do would make her notice me or bring her back when she was like that. She could tell a story, though, when she was in the mood." Cliff heaves a sigh and reaches out to hold Carla's hand. "Thanks for being part of our wedding."

Maggie continues picking through the box of photos while Cliff sits and holds Carla's hand.

He slides the picture of him on his mother's lap into his shirt pocket, claiming this one today.

August 22

Chapter 34

Though Brit gets to the shelter early, she still has to stand at the end of a long line. The rain that came through the night did nothing but make today more humid. Standing on the sidewalk, she feels like she will melt.

At one o'clock, the door opens, and a worker steps out. "Any children?"

A woman and two small boys move out of line behind Brit and go to the door. The woman is rotund and clean, and Brit doesn't believe she's homeless. Nobody else in the line is dressed in clean clothes. Nobody else looks overfed. The woman and her children are admitted into the building along with the two people at the front. The line inches forward three at a time.

When Brit is five back, the sun is beating down on her scalp, and she thinks she might faint, the woman at the door says, "We're full for tonight. I do have a sack lunch for everybody, and if you need a shower, we can make that happen."

Another woman steps out and starts passing bagged lunches to the remaining twelve people. Brit accepts her sack and looks directly into the woman's eyes.

"I'd love a shower." Hot tears spring over her lashes, and her face crumples. She steps back and trips over her duffel. As she lands on the hard sidewalk, she yelps in pain. Those who have already received their sacks begin to move away but stop to gawk at her.

"Oh dear. Let me help you." The woman offers her hand.

When Brit reaches up, blood drips from her elbow onto the hot pavement. She is on her feet, and the woman moves her toward the door.

"My stuff," Brit sobs.

"Lisa, grab her bag, won't you?"

The building isn't air conditioned, but fans blow the stale air from pillar to post. Brit is unable to take it in as they rush past the reception and down a hall.

"Miss Clary, we have a young lady who fell. Busted up her elbow. I think we're going to have to find her a bed tonight. You think?" She says the last to Brit, who nods and gives a hiccupping sob.

"There you go." She helps her to sit on the chair in the small office, which functions as a nurse's station. "Can you tell me your name?"

"Bee," Brit says. She gave up her name the night she saw Jason, Mary Beth, and their kid at Walmart. She doesn't want to be Britany Addams anymore.

"Bee as in buzz, buzz?" The woman smiles at her little joke.

Brit nods but doesn't smile, too overwhelmed to recognize humor.

"Do you have a last name, dear?"

Brit shakes her head.

"All right, Miss Bee. You took a tumble out there, but Clary will have you right as rain in no time. Now, I'm Joy, and I'll be back to check on you in just a few minutes, okay? Oh look, here's Lisa with your bag." She stands the bag in the corner and looks at Brit. "Is that good?"

Brit nods and tries to smile, but the nod takes more energy than she has left, and her face drops forward until her chin nearly rests on her bony chest. Only then does she realize she lost her sack lunch somewhere along the way.

<hr>

After Brit's arm is bandaged, she's taken down a corridor to a large room that serves as a cafeteria. The scent of meat and vegetables makes her mouth water. Joy takes her to the line and gives her the key to the locker where they stashed her bag.

"You're lucky. It's meatloaf day," Joy says.

Brit does feel lucky, even though she never much cared for meatloaf as a child and hasn't eaten it since before her parents divorced.

"Thank you," Brit says, gritting her teeth to try to keep from crying again.

Joy picks up a tray and places a napkin and a plastic spork wrapped together on it. "You just tell them what you want, and they'll put it on your plate, okay?"

Brit nods. Joy offers the tray. Brit's hands shake when she tries to take it, and Joy smiles.

"I'll just help you through this line today. How long you been out there?"

Brit shrugs. She has been out there forever.

Joy walks the line, asking Brit what she would like. Brit wants everything, and when the plate is full, Joy escorts her to a seat at one of the tables. They sit across from each other.

"Okay, Bee? You good if I go and see what arrangements I can make for you tonight?"

Brit nods and unwraps the spork with trembling fingers. She tries to remember the last time she sat down to eat a real meal but can't even recall the last time she ate or what it was. Probably crackers or the last fingerful from the jar of peanut butter she bought with Am that day so long ago, when she still believed this was a glitch and not her life.

"Thank you," Brit says, again clenching her teeth.

She's so filled with shame and gratitude that she's unable to look Joy in the eyes. Joy has been so nice, and Brit feels like she will start crying again if she tries to say anything else. She doesn't understand how she got here, how her life tumbled off the rails, how one bad decision sent her down the slope into this new life. Brit doesn't even feel like the same person. Her mother has been sitting in the back of her mind all this time, and suddenly, she realizes she'll never be able to face her again. She dreams of her in the stolen moments of sleep, and every dream ends with her mother's disappointment and sometimes anger. Her mother will never forgive her for being like her father, the cheater. He broke her heart and destroyed her pretty picture of their happy family. She would have helped her—Brit knows she still would—but she would know, and she would never forget. Her mother would never like her again. Brit would rather die than let her mother know who she's become.

Joy leaves, and Brit eats. When her stomach feels full and distended, she takes one last bite to clean the plate before setting down the spork. The cafeteria is mostly cleared out, and she pushes the tray aside and drops her head onto her arms and falls asleep.

August 29

Chapter 35

Brit didn't get a bed that first night, but they moved the cot out of the nurse's office and gave her a place in the women's dormitory. She showered, and they explained that the dining hall is available three times a week even if she doesn't get in for a bed.

"We have laundry facilities on Tuesday and Wednesday to help keep your clothes clean, and the showers are open all day on Monday and Tuesday," Joy explained.

For a week, Brit is first in line to get a bed, and she eats as much as she can hold. Toward the end of the week, the cobwebs that have filled her mind begin to clear, and she begins to think again about how to get out of her situation. Every day, she has to collect her possessions and stand in the line again. This morning, Joy meets her there.

"You can't stay tonight. We have a seven-day limit. I'm sure I explained that."

"Oh…" Brit nods, trying to remember if anybody told her there was a limit. Joy said a lot of things that first day. "I forgot that. Has it been seven days?"

"Yes. I'm afraid it has."

"When can I come back?"

"In three weeks. If you still need a bed in three weeks, you come back and see me. Okay?"

"Okay. I really just need a job," Brit says and turns away, shouldering her duffel onto her back.

"I got a job for ya, baby," a man says with a sneer, exposing rotted teeth and swollen gums. He thrusts his hips forward and backward, and the men around him guffaw.

Brit gives them a cold glare and walks away with her back straight. She has strength, as she's eaten well for a week, so she goes past the square and out to Highway 34 toward Peachtree City, past the overpass where the interstate traffic flows. She looks toward the dark crevices where the overpass and concrete meet. At the shelter, she talked with a woman who said she usually slept there, but she was run off by a man who came in and threatened her. Brit narrows her eyes at the gloom and thinks she sees movement. She hurries through the shadow and into the light.

It wouldn't be a bad place, in a pinch, except for the noise. It would be out of the weather and cool, as shaded as it is. She tries to think of other overpasses in the area but draws a blank. When she looks again toward the shadows, a man steps into the sun on the other side of the freeway. They lock eyes, and she turns away swiftly, walking faster.

Brit's shoulders ache by the time she passes Shenandoah Road. Blisters form on her freshly healed feet. She imagines the skin angry and raw and wishes she packed tennis shoes when Zack threw her out, but she only took her work shoes. It was such a shock, and she wasn't thinking clearly.

Brit doesn't remember it being so hard to keep her feet moving forward the day she walked for hours with I Am and can't understand why it's so much harder today than on that hot Saturday. She repositions her bag then remembers that Am allowed her to put her heavy duffel on the wheelchair. That made all the difference. She'll have to ask her where she got the chair. Having one would make everything easier.

Even though she was turned away from the shelter, she feels hopeful. She can get through anything for three weeks, and now that she knows the ropes a little better, maybe she can start figuring out how to get back into the workforce.

Brit reaches the elementary school. The sun slants through the trees and creates deep shadows. She stands at the edge of the woods, remembering the three people she encountered the day the man stole her backpack, and isn't certain this is the spot where Am entered. Fear grips her heart and squeezes. I Am said it was safe, but Brit never spent time in the woods. A whirring insect flies at her ear, and she flips her hair to send it away. She just needs someplace where she can be invisible for a while.

It feels dangerous to step into the company of trees. She picks her way carefully, ducking away from the overhanging limbs. The trees whisper, and the shadows hide the path. Overwhelmed by the unknown, she starts to turn back.

She will just keep walking.

Till when?

Until I can go back to the shelter? Three weeks stretches like an eternity.

Brit is footsore and weary. She needs a place to be, away from downtown, where the alleys are all claimed, and the men look at her like they want to fuck her or kill her.

"Am," she calls out in an almost-shout.

The trees heave and sigh.

"Am!" she shouts again, louder this time. She begins picking a path through the trees, calling out every few feet. *Will she even remember me?* It's been a long time since they did laundry together and Brit bought a pizza to share. "Am?"

"Hush that shouting. People is trying to rest back in here."

Brit spins and sees a man standing to the right of her. He's leaning on a tree. She walked right past him and didn't see him. "I'm looking for I Am. Is she here?"

"That depends on who's looking."

"Bee," she says then remembers she met Am before she decided to give up her name. "Brit. She knows me. We did laundry together about a month ago." They may turn her away, and Brit hears the warble in her voice, the threat of tears. She doesn't have a backup plan if they tell her to leave.

The man snorts and spits into the leaf litter. "You the pizza girl?"

Brit is confused, not sure whether he thinks she's delivering pizza and uncertain about how to respond.

He smiles mockingly, then he clarifies. "You bought a pizza and shared a bit."

"Yeah. That's me."

"She told us about you. Come on. I'll take you to her. Watch your step here. Come on."

Brit follows him, feeling like she's being led to see the queen.

Am is squatting at a small fire and looks up when Brit and the man break through the underbrush.

"Hey, girl. Where you been keeping yourself?" She smiles, and Brit returns it like they're old friends.

"I just spent a week up at the outreach on Washington Street. Did you know you can do laundry there for free every Tuesday and Wednesday? They have hot showers Monday and Tuesday, even if you don't get a bed."

"Yep. I've eaten up there a couple of times. How is it staying there?"

"It was good. They put you to work, though. You can't just stay. You have to give back."

"Ain't nothin' free," Am says.

"That's okay, though. It was nice. You should go with me next time."

"Nah. I like being outside." She wraps her hand in a rag and reaches to pull the coffee pot from the flames. "Coffee?"

"Yes." Back when Brit had a real life, she wouldn't drink caffeine after noon, believing it would keep her awake, but here in this new life, she doesn't think anything could keep her awake.

With a camping mug in her hands, she gazes around the woods and takes in the two hammocks stretched between the trees. "You've got a nice setup here."

"Yeah. It's not bad. Jed sleeps in that one, when he's here." She nods toward the direction Brit entered from. "Pudge has a tent over that way, but you don't really want to mess with her. She doesn't like new folks."

Brit strains to see a tent but can't find it in the trees' shadows.

"This is really nice," Brit says when a breeze blows through her hair.

"It's okay. You changed your hair."

"Yeah. Figured I couldn't keep up with the roots."

"That's why I keep mine short. It's easier to keep clean." They sit for a moment, staring into the flames. "How you been?"

"It's been rough. Somebody stole my backpack a couple of weeks ago, so I've not had any money since then. I thought I was gonna die. I think I would have if they hadn't let me into the shelter last week. How do people live like this?"

"You get a job."

"How do you get a job without an address?" Brit had tried to get employment at several places in the first weeks after she was dismissed from Walton and Shrieve and gave up when she kept running into the same roadblocks. "How do you get an address without a job?" The cycle spins in her head, the endless loop of frustration.

"Under the table. You got to do stuff off the books."

Brit is appalled, thinking about the dirty man outside the outreach offering to give her work. She doesn't think she could she have sex with somebody for money. Surely that's not what Am means. She cannot imagine Am standing on a corner, offering herself to the highest bidder. Not just because she's old, either, but Am doesn't seem like a person who would do anything she doesn't want to do. "Like what?"

"I stock shelves a couple of nights a week over at the Dollar Store. Make twenty or thirty bucks a night. Keeps me in coffee."

"Oh. Do you think they'd let me stock shelves?" It isn't going to solve the problem of getting an apartment, but it might keep her from starving to death until she can find something better.

"Maybe. One way to find out."

August 30

Chapter 36

Brit and Am work through the night, and the manager, Grant, gives them each twenty dollars as they leave. The sun is not yet up.

He locks the door behind them, saying, "Got a truck Thursday. See you then."

Am nods but doesn't look back as Brit turns to follow, smiling and feeling alive for the first time in a long while.

"I want waffles," Brit says when the glow of the yellow sign of the Waffle House comes into view.

"Yeah?" Am laughs. "Got a little cash burning a hole in your pocket?"

"I barely have pockets." Brit laughs, feeling exuberant. "Thank you for letting me come."

"You should go to the Goodwill later and see if you can find a big sheet, and we'll make you a hammock. I got some rope, so you can get off the ground."

It feels like an invitation, like Am is inviting her to stay in the small outcrop of trees with her, Jed, and Pudge.

They sit by the window and watch the early-morning traffic as it begins to flow on Highway 34. They splurge on a waffle each, and the waitress brings coffee and creams even though they didn't order any.

"We didn't ask for coffee," Am says, moving the mug to the edge of the table.

"I know. It's slow. I'm going to have to toss that pot anyway. Somebody might as well enjoy it. It's on the house."

The waitress sets the plates on the table, and the aroma is intoxicating.

"That was nice," Brit says, smiling up at the waitress. "Thanks." She wraps her hands around the mug and brings it close to her face, allowing the steam to rise around her.

Am nods but does not lift the mug. "Nothing is free," she whispers.

"This coffee is." Brit smiles and sips. "What's Pudge's story? She won't even look at me."

"She's a little odd. I told you she don't like new people. Just leave her alone, and she'll get used to you." Syrup drips into the squares of the waffle, and Am cuts a wedge free.

"She's got an accent. Where is she from?"

Am shakes her head and shrugs. "Does she? I never noticed. We been traveling together for a long time, but I never asked about where she came from. Nobody wants to talk about how they got here."

A cloud crosses Am's face, and her expression slides to vacant, her eyes focusing somewhere behind and beyond Brit. A breath passes, and Brit watches Am's face, thinking that maybe Am is a little odd too.

Am's eyes refocus, and her expression rebalances. "What did you say?"

"I was just asking about Pudge's accent, but you said you never noticed." Brit cuts a bit of waffle and pops it into her mouth. She wants to ask more questions to understand these people who have nothing but offered help when almost nobody else did, but she bites back her words. Am is right. Brit doesn't want to talk about what landed her on the streets, and she shouldn't expect anybody else to want to either.

"I guess it just happens," Brit says, glad to be eating waffles bought with money she earned with a friend who isn't judging her for her mistakes.

"That's how it goes. That slippery slope," Am offers.

"I guess it is. But you know what? I think everything is going to be okay."

"Of course it is. It's gonna be what it's going to be."

They finish their waffles, and Brit enjoys a second cup of coffee. Am's sits cooling on the edge of the table. When they're done, they pay the waitress, and Am goes back to leave a tip on the table. Brit is ashamed. She didn't even think of leaving a tip, even though the waitress gave them free coffee. The good feeling she had through the night ebbs. She feels like she never quite manages to do the right thing. Am turns to her and smiles, as if it's nothing, as if her leaving a tip is not any form of admonition.

They walk through the parking lot, down past the veterinarian's, through the empty parking spaces of the strip mall next to the elementary school, and toward their little outcrop of trees.

"Sometimes, I feel invisible," Brit says.

Am nods. "We are."

"I know, right? People try not to see us. It's like they don't have to do anything if they don't acknowledge us."

"Yep, pretty much. What do you want them to do? It's not their problem. They ain't on the slope, so they don't have to do anything," Am says, scanning the cars passing down the street. They wait for a break in the traffic before slipping into the trees.

"What time do you think Goodwill opens?"

"Nine. Maybe ten."

Brit never thought of shopping at Goodwill. She doesn't know what to expect, but she's excited at the idea of shopping for anything. She's excited to have even a few dollars in her pocket. Jed is asleep in his hammock as they come through the shrubs into the small clearing.

Brit left her bag propped next to a tree, beside Am's wheelchair, and is confused when she doesn't see it.

"Where's my bag?" Brit asks, rushing the last few feet, and looks around the back of the tree. She sees it several feet away, open, the contents flung out and hanging from several branches. In the middle of the mess is Pudge, wearing a striped button-down shirt and a skirt that Brit doesn't even know why she packed.

"Oh my god!" Brit shouts.

The woman wearing her clothes begins to laugh, a loud, cackling, hysterical sound. Brit rips her clothes from the tree limbs and stuffs them into the duffel.

"Pudge," Am says, standing back, waiting for the laughter to abate. "Take off her clothes."

The woman rocks, laughing in small spurts and snorting.

Brit drops the duffel and rushes at the laughing woman, pushing her over like a Weeble. The laughter turns to shrieking. Am grabs Brit's arms and pulls her back. Brit comes away in a fury, spittle flying from her lips and her eyes burning with unshed tears.

Jed, wakened by the commotion, rushes to Pudge. He helps her up and guides her away, toward the tent. Am stands like a guardian, her palms raised against Brit.

Brit spins away. "What the fuck!" She isn't the one in the wrong here. Those are her clothes. They're all she has. She squats, wrapping her hands in her hair and pulling. Without warning, she vomits onto the dirt.

"I told you she wasn't right," Am says, as if that explains everything.

Brit wipes her mouth and stands up to face Am. "None of us are right. Maybe somebody should tell her not to mess with other people's shit. That's all I have. That is all I have!" Her voice breaks and echoes on the trees.

Am looks at her sadly. "That's just stuff. You think it matters?"

The fire of Brit's fury burns out, and she pushes the heels of her hands into her eyes, pressing down the tears. "Everything matters."

"Only if you let it." Am touches Brit's arm, and Brit doesn't pull away. "I told you she isn't right."

Brit nods, and she cries, overwhelmed by the emotions that have passed through her in the past half hour. She was genuinely happy when they left the Dollar Store. Brit was hopeful when they stopped for breakfast like normal people. She was peaceful when they talked about buying a sheet at the Goodwill to make into a hammock.

"I just want my life back," Brit whispers.

"Yep, and you'll probably get it back. You're a smart girl. What is this? What was the word you used?"

"Glitch," Brit offers, hearing herself in memory, saying, "This is just a glitch."

"That's right. This is just a glitch for you. Not for Pudge. Not for Jed. This is it. There is no life to get back."

Am's voice is soothing, and the blood pounding in Brit's temples begins to ease. The protective way Jed rushed to Pudge, the way Am pulled Brit off her, the way Jed was standing up by the path the first time Brit arrived—it all begins to come together and make sense. They're a family of sorts.

Brit is embarrassed that she lost her temper. She sees Pudge and Jed through the trees. Pudge is squatting on the ground, rocking back and forth, one hand thumping the side of her head—not hard but on a rhythm. It's obvious that she isn't right, and Brit is ashamed of herself. She steps around Am and makes her way toward Pudge and Jed. He sees her and shakes his head to tell her to stop. But Brit crouches and crab walks the last few feet toward them.

"Hey," she says, keeping her voice small.

Pudge refuses to look at her. Her mouth is open in a silent moan.

"Pudge," Brit tries again, glancing back at Am, who is standing behind her with her arms crossed over her stomach. "I'm sorry."

It feels strange to apologize when it was Pudge's fault. She shouldn't have been in her stuff, but Brit shouldn't have pushed her. Her wild eyes touch on Brit and roll away.

"I'm sorry. I shouldn't have pushed you. That skirt looks better on you than it ever did on me."

The rhythmic thumping of the hand slows, and the rolling eyes calm. The lips close. She still rocks but with less intensity. Jed sits back on his heels and watches.

"Are you okay?" Brit swipes at her face, irritated that she's crying.

Pudge nods and looks toward Brit, not making eye contact but focusing somewhere on Brit's cheek.

"You can just keep that outfit, okay? I want to be friends. I'm sorry I scared you."

Pudge pushes a lip out, and a hand flies out and grabs Brit's in a strong grip. She nods, and her face swivels toward the ground.

"Well, looky there, Pudge. You got a new friend," Jed says.

Pudge releases Brit's hand and pats it.

"Friends." Pudge smiles and stands. She moves toward her tent, her hips swaying. She twirls, and the skirt rises in the air. "Pretty, pretty, pretty."

Her voice comes back to them in song. The skirt sways, and Pudge's hands flutter in the fabric. Jed, Brit, and Am watch her go, and when Am reaches a hand down to Brit, she accepts it.

"That was kind of you." Am smiles and pats Brit on the back.

Brit doesn't feel kind, but she nods. She starts collecting the remaining clothes, refolds them, and places them in her duffel. She figures that Am will expect her to move on now, after the disruption. She's the outsider. This is their group.

"Goodwill is probably open by now. I'll walk over with ya," Am offers.

Brit recognizes it as an invitation to stay.

Chapter 37

" Yes, ma'am. I understand you're worried," Cliff says, reassuring Britany Addams's mother as best as he can. "I appreciate you coming up to speak with us." Charlotte Loukis doesn't look old enough to have a grown daughter. She flew from Florida to Atlanta, finally, when the police were unable to locate Britany or assure her that she was safe.

Between them sits a collection of photographs Charlotte brought. Cliff sorts through the collection, selecting two that most closely resemble the girl he met.

"You lost contact with her when?" Cliff opens a folder and removes a sheet of paper. He draws a long line down the middle of the page and adds a hatch mark at the beginning of the line.

"I spoke to her early in July, before we went out of the country. On July 7. She was fine." Charlotte watches as he marks the paper with the date and the note *Call with mom.*

"At what point did you realize you were unable to reach your daughter?" Cliff asks.

"When we got home. I tried to call her on August 8, and her phone was disconnected."

Cliff makes another mark at the end of the line, dates it, and writes, *Missing.*

"You left for Greece after talking to her." He makes another hatch mark close to the first. "Okay. So that's what *you* know. Let me fill in what *we* know. On July 8, your daughter was involved in a two-vehicle accident in which a person died of injuries sustained at the scene."

Charlotte's hand rises to cover a gasp.

"On July 10, your daughter's live-in boyfriend asked her to move out."

"Oh my god."

"She spent that night with the family of a coworker, Kay Garcia, and returned to work the following day. She was in some distress, and her boss, Ben Walton, asked her to take the day off. That was July 11. On July 19, I spoke with your daughter about the preliminary findings from the accident, and on August 2, I spoke with her again at her place of employment. I told her at that time that the DA completed his investigation into the accident and declined to file a case against her in the death of Dee Martin. She didn't die because of the trauma caused by the accident but rather from a faulty safety mechanism in her vehicle. I notified your daughter at that time that she was not going to be charged." He marks over the hatch mark for August 2, draws a line under the notation he has just made, and writes, *Fired.* "On that same day, your daughter was let go by her employer. She said she was going to the bank to cash her check, then she was meeting a friend." He marks the timeline.

Charlotte's face is a mask of horror. "This can't be right."

"Do you know if she had anybody she would have reached out to, since you were out of the country? Her father? A family friend?"

"No. She didn't reach out to her father." Charlotte lowers her face into her hands.

Cliff doesn't move, just watches her reaction.

"Well, where did she go? After she got fired. Where did she go?" Charlotte asks, her concern written in the fine lines of her face.

"We have no way of knowing."

"So you just let her walk away? Why would you just let her walk away, not knowing if she had someplace to be?"

"Ma'am, I need you to think about who she may know in the area."

"I wouldn't know who she knows here. She grew up in Lanett. I don't know any of her friends here. Except Zack. I know her boyfriend. Where is he? Have you talked with him at least?"

"Britany doesn't talk to you about her friends?"

"No. She's kind of a private person. She's mad at me. Us. Her father and me. She's been mad since the divorce. Didn't speak to either of us for three months after we told her."

"When was that?"

"Her senior year of high school. She packed her bags and moved in with some friends after her father moved to Colorado."

"That's a long time to hold a grudge," Cliff says, remembering that Jason Jenkins mentioned that Britany had not taken her parents' divorce well. "So this isn't the first time she's gone radio silent?"

"No. I knew where she was then. Of course, I wanted her to come home, but she was mad. It wasn't like this." Charlotte sits up straighter.

"How often do you speak with your daughter?"

"We talk all the time."

"Daily?"

"No, weekly, sometimes more," Charlotte says. "Maybe every other week. I don't know. She's busy. We're busy. But we stay in touch."

"Do you believe she would let you know if she was in trouble?"

"Yes! Of course she would."

An expression of doubt clouds her eyes, and Cliff stores it away. Britany didn't have a support system. He suspected as much, but seeing the doubt in Charlotte's face confirms it.

"But she didn't reach out?" Cliff asks, even though he believes she hasn't heard from Britany.

Charlotte shakes her head. "No, but she knew I was going out of the country. She wouldn't have wanted to trouble me. I know something bad has happened to her."

"Well, I think our next step is to get the community involved. We can get some flyers put together and make the rounds," Cliff says.

"Can we do a press conference?" Charlotte asks, and Cliff can see that she's ready to take action.

"Yeah, we can do that. I think we just need to let Britany know that people are concerned and encourage her to reach out."

Charlotte nods.

"Look, we'll find her," Cliff says.

Charlotte's phone vibrates. The name *Asshole* scrolls across it. She turns slightly to the side and lifts the phone to her ear. "What?"

Cliff can see the irritation arcing through her. Apparently, holding a grudge is a family trait.

"Have you heard from her?" Cliff can hear the voice on the other end because Charlotte doesn't put the phone to her ear but holds it out, away from her head.

"No, Paul. I haven't. That's why I'm here."

"Do I need to come?"

"I don't care what you do. You're a big boy. I'm worried about my daughter, so I'm here to look for her."

"I'm worried about her, too, Charlotte."

"Really, Paul? Really? If I hadn't called you, would you even know she was missing?"

He doesn't respond, and she looks at Cliff like she expects him to confirm her accusation.

"I'm sure she's fine. She's just punishing us. Probably got in a fight with Zack and is hiding somewhere," Charlotte says, toning down her hostility.

"I've never liked that guy," Paul says.

"You never even met Zack. Anyway, she's a grown-up. You don't get a say in who she dates." Charlotte breathes a heavy sigh and puts the phone to her ear. "When did you talk to her last?"

Cliff can no longer hear his responses, but he doesn't excuse himself from the room. Understanding the family dynamic feels important.

"Oh my god, Paul. That was over a month ago. Yeah, I know she's still mad at you. She's mad at me, too, but didn't you think something may be up when you didn't hear from her for *a month?* Shit, Paul."

Cliff considers the family drama—mother who puts her ex-husband's name in her phone as *Asshole*, new spouses—and sees how Britany could have felt that she had to figure it out on her own. Britany is not the only one in the family with a lot of balls in the air.

She passes another exasperated look toward Cliff and says, "I have to go. I'm at the police station." Her face crumples, and her tone changes. "Oh my god, Paul, what if something happened to her?" The phone separates from her head once again.

"I'm sure she's fine. You know Brit."

"I'll never forgive myself if something happened to her." Hysteria causes her voice to crack.

"Come on, Charlotte. I'm sure she's fine."

"I'm not so sure. I have to go. I've got to go." She sits for several moments after she disconnects the call.

"I'm sure we'll find her," Cliff says.

Charlotte looks up at him like she's broken.

Cliff collects his notes and the two pictures he chose and stands. "I'm going to go get them working on the flyer and see what I can do about getting a press conference set. Do you have a place to stay in town?"

"Yes, I'm at the Marriott."

"Okay. I'll give you a call when we get things going."

Charlotte begins gathering her photographs, and a single tear slips down her cheek.

Cliff slides back into his seat and catches her eye. "Britany seems like a resilient woman. I need you to stay strong for her. Go to your

room and try to think about what you might be able to say to encourage her to reconnect."

Charlotte nods and swipes away her tear.

"We're gonna find her," Cliff says. Then he holds the door open
and walks Charlotte through the station to the exit.

Chapter 38

Cliff meets with Captain Rojas and gives him the details of the timeline and one of the flyers the team created. "This the woman from the Martin accident?" Rojas asks.

"Yes."

Rojas studies the pictures, the flyer, and the notes for about a minute before sliding them into a folder. "Looks like a hell of a month. What do you think happened?"

"I don't know. She has some complicated relationships, so there might be something there. Or she may have just fallen through the cracks and be lying low until she can get back on her feet."

"All right. Go get the mother."

At four, Cliff called the Marriott and told Charlotte the plans for the press conference, which will be held in the front of the police station at five and air on the evening news. When she arrived, she was led to an interrogation room to wait.

Cliff knocks on the door and opens it. Charlotte holds a small mirror in front of her face and is touching up her makeup. It strikes him as odd that she would be worried about how she looks at a time like this, but he understands that people sometimes respond to stress in surprising ways. Touching up her makeup may be a sign of a need to have control over something, or it may just be an indication of vanity. There is a strong family resemblance between Charlotte and Britany. They have the same jawline and the same arch of eyebrow. Cliff wonders if her concern over appearances could have kept Britany from reaching out. He can't quite determine how Charlotte would have responded to the news that Britany needed help. Nothing he has seen indicates she would have withheld support.

"We're almost ready." He studies her. "I have to ask one thing. You mentioned that Britany wouldn't have wanted to worry you while you were on your trip to Greece. Do you really think she wouldn't have gotten in touch with you if she was in a desperate situation?"

Charlotte looks at him over her compact and considers. "Brit is very stubborn and very private. I don't always know what's going on with her, so honestly, I don't know if she would have called me if I wasn't in Greece. I just don't know."

It feels like the most honest thing Cliff has heard from her all day. Britany *is* stubborn. Cliff knows that from the times he offered her a ride and she refused. Most people, he thinks, are private. "All right. Well, let's go talk to the reporters."

Cliff and Charlotte reach Rojas's office, and Cliff leans in past the open door. "We're ready."

Rojas joins them, folder in hand, and Cliff makes introductions.

Rojas leads the way to the parking lot, and Cliff and Charlotte follow. At the lectern that's been brought out, Rojas takes center and indicates that Charlotte should stand to his left so that she can speak when he's through. Cliff and another officer stand two steps behind.

Several news vans are parked in the lot, and about five crews have come out to cover the press conference. The crew from Fox Five Atlanta claims a spot in the center as the biggest of the news organizations in attendance.

Rojas checks the mic, and the gaggle of reporters quiets down. "Thank you for coming," Rojas says and clears his throat. "On August 2, Britany Addams walked away from her place of work, Walton and Shrieve, located at Twenty-Eight Jack Dale Avenue at around five o'clock in the evening. At that time, she indicated that she was going to the bank to cash a check then wait at the Leaf and Bean coffee shop for a friend who was going to pick her up. She planned to spend the night with her friend. She was dressed in blue slacks and a white top. At this time, we do not suspect foul play. However, we would like to speak with the friend or anybody else who has knowledge of her whereabouts. I'll take a few questions, then Mrs. Loukis will make a plea to her daughter."

"Is it true that she was one of the drivers in the fatal accident on July 8 on Fischer Road and 54?" the reporter from the local newspaper calls out.

"Yes, that is correct," Captain Rojas replies.

"Were you going to arrest her? Would she have taken off to avoid arrest?" another reporter asks.

"We do not believe she thought she was going to be arrested. She was in some distress about the accident, but our findings did not suggest she caused the death of the other driver." His words cause a stir, and the reporters talk among themselves for a moment before the next question rises above the din.

"Do we know who the friend was?"

"Not at this time."

Questions about Britany's height and weight are answered before Chief Rojas turns the microphone over to Charlotte.

She grips the microphone with trembling hands, and her red-rimmed eyes scan the cameras. "Brit, please come home. I'm here. I am looking for you. We have to know you're okay. I am so sorry I wasn't here when you needed me. But if you'll just let us know you're okay, we can bring you home and help you through this time. Please come home. We all love you." Tears stream down her face, and the beautiful work with her makeup is ruined. She steps to the side, blotting her eyes, and Rojas takes the lectern again.

"We've established a hotline and will be accepting information leading to the whereabouts of Ms. Addams," Captain Rojas says then gives the number and repeats it.

August 31

Chapter 39

"Is Mr. Walton available?" Cliff asks, standing at the counter that overlooks the receptionist alcove. He spent the morning working through the tip line, and Ben Walton left a message asking for someone to come by.

"Officer Rathborn." Ben steps from his office and greets Cliff with a handshake. They aren't familiar with each other, but Ben is clearly a hand clasper, a mannered man. "Thank you for coming."

"Thank you for calling in. Do you have information?"

"No, no. I don't know where she is, but we saw the press conference and wanted to put up a reward. We can offer our office space, too, if you need to coordinate a search."

"That's very generous. How much are you thinking?"

"We'll start at five thousand. She's a good kid. I just hate that all this happened." Ben motions toward the conference room and allows Cliff to enter first. "Sit anywhere. Would you like coffee? A water?"

"No, sir. I'm fine. That's a generous reward. Maybe it will encourage someone to come forward." Cliff has worked diligently to dispel his Southern accent, but here in the presence of this very Southern gentleman, whose great-great-great-granddaddy was likely a founding member of the town, it creeps back.

"I sure hope so." He slides a sheet of paper across the conference table. It's a document indicating that the firm pledges the reward, which will be held in the firm's escrow account until Britany is found.

"I would never have let her go if I thought she was going to come to harm."

"Yes, sir." Cliff feels the same way.

"She probably just thinks she's going to be arrested because of the accident and is keeping her nose down, hoping it will blow over," Ben says.

"No, sir. She was cleared in the accident. I notified her of that as she was leaving the office that day. She's not in any trouble, Mr. Walton. She understood when I saw her that the DA was not interested in bringing charges against her and that she could close that chapter of her life." Cliff feels obliged to explain that Dee's death was because of the faulty airbag, and Ben writes *Takata* on a notepad. The pattern of Cliff's speech causes him to clear his throat, as if the accent, the drawing forth of a bygone era, is nothing more than phlegm.

"Oh, well, I hadn't heard they'd finished the investigation." Ben picks up a thin folder and opens it. "I don't know if this will be of any help, but it's everything I have on Brit." He hands the folder to Cliff.

Cliff flips through the file. It includes a resume, an application, and several blurry pictures of Brit sleeping. She doesn't look comfortable, scrunched with her knees up so that she's entirely under the desk.

He looks at Ben with a raised eyebrow. "Mr. Walton, I have to ask. Why would you think somebody would sleep like this if they had someplace else to be?"

Ben, to his credit, doesn't answer.

"Why was she terminated?"

"She made several mistakes. Mistakes that caused our clients to be more at risk than we like to put them," Ben says, but his voice is thin, as though he wonders if he could have handled the situation better. "We pride ourselves on being circumspect, Officer Rathborn. Our clients depend upon our discretion. Surely you understand." Ben regains a note of arrogance.

"I do. You keep secrets." The annoying accent drops out of his voice as quickly as it came.

"Yes, sir."

"Had this been a problem? Was she indiscreet?"

"No. It was never a problem before. But that last month or so, she couldn't keep her head on straight. She just got messy."

"When would you say she began to be *messy*?"

Ben thinks for a moment before he says, "I reckon it was back in July. She was never quite right after that accident. Never pulled herself back together."

"Is that so?"

"Yeah. She moved herself in here. Started sleeping under the desk. If she had just asked, I would have been happy to help her get on her feet. I understand that folks can get down on their luck, but then we came up with money missing from petty cash."

"She stole money from you?" Cliff's brow furrows.

"No. Well, we thought she did, but it turns out Elise just hadn't input a couple of receipts. Honest mistake, you know?"

"Of course. Mistakes are made." Cliff remembers the day he came into the office and walked out with Britany. He should have kept her in his sights. She was distraught. He should have been more persistent about where she was going. If she's come to harm, he feels he must shoulder some of the blame along with Ben Walton.

Cliff flips through the rest of the file—the termination agreement, the sparse resume, a day-off request form from July 8, and another from November for two days off around Thanksgiving. "She worked for you for two years?"

"Yes."

"It's a pretty thin file. Was she a good employee?" Cliff expected more issues regarding her employment—late days, failures to make it into the office, mistakes on the job—to explain her dismissal.

"She was. I'd say she was." The arrogance falters. "We should probably have handled all that differently. But she couldn't have gone far."

"Why do you say that?" Cliff asks.

"She didn't have a car. She was on foot," Ben explains.

"She could have taken a ride with somebody."

"I think that's doubtful. My paralegal tried to give her a ride once, and she had a panic attack or somethin'. Kay said she could barely sit in a moving car."

That did narrow the search zone.

Cliff replays that day and considers that she probably lied about having a friend. A pattern of deceit is forming. She was lying to her boyfriend about her affair with Jason. She was keeping her living situation to herself up to the day she got terminated. It seems in character not to call her mother. Britany wouldn't have wanted to explain that she was fooling around. She wouldn't want to tell her mother that she caused an accident, especially when she thought she might be charged with vehicular manslaughter. He wonders what other lies of omission and otherwise she may have told over the last month. Cliff is certain that there was no friend coming to pick her up, unless it was one of those two men, Jason or Zack. If either of them was the friend, Cliff feels confident that they won't find Britany alive.

He turns his attention back to Ben. "Can I keep this for the time being?" Cliff asks, holding up Britany's employee file.

Ben waves a hand as if he's happy to see it out of the office.

"Thank you for putting up a reward. That will encourage people to look for her. I'll get you a copy of the flyer." Cliff rises and extends his hand to Ben.

They shake, and Cliff is pleased to see concern clouding Ben's eyes. Cliff suspects that Ben is a decent man who feels at least partially responsible for Britany's disappearance. He will be a good ally in the search. "If you think of anything else, I hope you'll give me a call."

"I will."

September 4

Chapter 40

Cliff continues to monitor the tip line. Over the next several days, tips come in from around the county. Someone spotted Britany Addams hitchhiking on 85 going toward Atlanta. Another person saw her with an old homeless woman at the Goodwill. One of the volunteers at one of the homeless shelters in the area called and said a girl that may have been Britany had come in. They failed to leave the name of the specific outreach. Somebody saw her at a sports bar in Peachtree City, and somebody else saw her being sucked into a spaceship and transported.

Diligently, Cliff follows up on the leads—except the one that included the spaceship. He figures that one would have taken her clear out of his jurisdiction. As he makes the rounds, talking to locals, showing her photograph, and handing out flyers to be placed in store windows, he answers texts from Maggie, who is doing her best not to let her mother know they're already married. He's surprised at the change in his attitude about being married over the past few weeks. The dread and anxiety the idea filled him with before have evaporated entirely. He still doesn't really *believe* in marriage, but maybe he believes enough in *them*. When Maggie said yes, when she married him on the quiet for Carla, when she continued putting together the wedding her mother needs for her, Cliff saw how happy she is, and that has made him better. She has always made him better. Carla was right. Making Maggie happy is the most important thing he will ever do.

Without a body, Cliff has no evidence of a crime. Jason's assertion that Zack made a threat against Britany is hearsay. Even if he did make a threat against her, she was alive on August 2, several weeks after the alleged threat occurred. After a phone conversation with a woman named Jill Lindsey, Cliff feels that he's beginning to put together her movements. Ms. Lindsey called the hotline, and he interviewed her on her front porch. She witnessed a woman matching Britany's description attempting to open a bank account.

"I heard her say she was between places. I felt really bad for her. She just wanted to open an account. They wouldn't do it because she said she didn't have an address or enough identification or some stupid bank rule."

"What did she do then?"

"She picked up her stuff—she had one of those military duffel bags, you know, the big green ones—and a backpack and started to leave. I kind of whispered that Walmart cashes checks. You know. I didn't want to get involved, but she just seemed like she could use a little help."

"When she left the bank, did you see where she went?"

"No. I didn't want to stare at her, you know. She was having a bad day."

"It sounds like it." Cliff nods. "Do you have anything else you'd like to add?"

The woman shakes her head.

"Okay. Well, thank you for coming forward."

"I hope you find her."

"Me too." He tilts his head in respect and leaves the woman's porch.

Britany was alive on August 2. She's an adult and is free to disappear if she wants to. Still, when Cliff's patrol takes him down Dividend in Peachtree City, he turns into the drive at Warren's Quality Car Care and sees Zack Timmons coming out of the service bay, walking across the lot, and climbing into an SUV. He pulls it into the bay. Cliff parks and steps out, staying within the sight line of the SUV, and waits to see whether Zack will come out or if he will have to go in to ask for him.

Cliff is rewarded for his patience when Zack climbs out of the SUV and makes eye contact. They nod at each other.

Zack calls out, "Hey, Joe, I'll be right back."

"Did she show up?" he asks when he's still several feet away.

"I'm afraid not," Cliff says. He keeps his eyes on the man, looking for reaction or subterfuge. "You've not heard from her?"

Zack shakes his head.

"You told me she moved out in mid-July. Can you tell me what the circumstances of her leaving were? Was your split amicable? Was it just time to move on?"

"Something like that," Zack says.

"Walk me through it," Cliff insists. Britany was seen after that. She slept at Ben Walton's office until the date of her termination, nearly a full month after she moved out of Zack's house. But he's looking for threads.

"I came home and told her she needed to get out. Her boyfriend's wife had been by to see me earlier that day and told me they were together. Showed me some text messages she found on his phone. I told Brit she needed to pack her shit and get out. I left the house, and when I came back, she was gone."

Cliff flips open a small spiral notebook and refers to it. "Did you have any contact with her after that?"

"I talked to her once, about a week after she left."

"Can you tell me about that conversation?" Cliff raises his eyebrows in expectation.

"Look, man, I don't remember. I'd closed the bank account, so she called thinking I owed her something."

"Did you?"

Zack shrugs. "I really got to get back to work."

"Of course. I understand. We all got a job to do. Just one more question."

Zack pauses, half turned away, and waits.

"Did you threaten to *kill* Britany the day you told her to move out?" Cliff studies him, paying attention to the smallest detail of his body language.

"What? No. Of course not. Who said that?" The flicker of anger flares in his eyes, chased by fear, and Cliff knows he's lying.

"I've been told by a source that Britany said you told her that you would 'kill her if you ever saw her again.' Do you recall saying anything of that nature?" Cliff asks without taking his eyes off of Zack.

"That's bullshit. I never laid a hand on her." He clamps his lips together and crosses his arms.

"So you did not threaten her the night she moved out?"

"No. I just told her she needed to get the fuck out. That's all. I left, and when I came back, she was gone."

"Yeah. That makes sense. You told her to go. She went. Okay. One more thing, though. You said you closed the account? Did Britany have any money in that account?"

"Man, I don't know. I was just cutting ties. She still had a debit card, and I didn't want her emptying it out."

"So you emptied it before she could?" Cliff clarifies.

"Something like that." Tension sits around his lips and jaw, and his fist is tight at his side.

"Were you concerned about how she would find a new place to live after you closed the account?"

"No. Not really. She wanted Jason so bad that I figured he could pick up her slack."

"Yeah. I hear that. You were pretty mad about that, weren't you? I'm with you, man. Nobody likes to be lied to. God knows I don't."

Cliff intimates that they have this in common, that they have both been cuckolded and belong to the same club.

"I was mad, but I didn't do anything to her," Zack insists.

"Okay. If you hear from her, don't forget to call."

Zack turns away and lopes toward the service bay. Cliff watches until he's inside then sits in his car for a good five minutes before inching out of the lot.

September 6

Chapter 41

On Friday, Cliff begins to work his way through the outreach programs in the area. He works the missing persons case between other business, including traffic stops, a domestic disturbance, and a shoplifter at the Academy Sports in Newnan. At One Roof, Bridging the Gap, and Angel's House, he's met with concerned expressions but no recognition. When he finally makes his way toward downtown Newnan, he parks on the curb and enters Washington Street Outreach.

"Hello, Officer. How can I help you?" a woman asks as she comes out from behind a desk.

"I'm following up on a missing person. Have you seen this woman?" He produces a snapshot of Britany Addams, her blond hair glowing.

"She doesn't look familiar to me. But we help a lot of people. I can't say I remember everybody."

"Is there anybody else I could ask?"

"Sure. Joy is probably down in the cafeteria. She works a lot of intake, so she may have seen her."

The woman gives Cliff directions, and he makes his way toward the cafeteria.

"I'm looking for Joy," he says to one of the women working at the buffet.

"I'm Joy," someone calls, and Cliff turns to see her walking purposefully toward him. "How can I help you?"

Cliff explains his search and hands her the photograph.

"Yeah, that's Bee. She was in here a week or so ago."

"You've seen this girl?"

Joy nods. "I called the tip line. Said I thought she'd been here."

Cliff smiles at the solved mystery but doesn't explain to the woman that she failed to mention which program she was with.

"Is there somewhere we could talk?"

Joy leads him to an office, and they sit across from each other at a desk. "Her hair wasn't blond, but I'm sure that's her."

"What color was it?"

"Brown." Joy opens a file cabinet and withdraws a binder. She flips several sheets until she comes to the one she wants. "She came in on the eleventh, stayed the week, then headed out. Said her name was Bee. Declined to give a last name." She slides the binder in front of Cliff, and he looks at the three letters that mean that Britany was here. "What'd you say her real name was?"

"Britany Addams." Cliff taps the photo. "How confident are you that this is that girl?"

"I'm positive. I never forget a face. She was having a bad day when she showed up here, nearly starved to death, from the looks of it. We didn't really have a bed for her that night, but she tripped over her bag and banged up her arm, so we found her a cot." She explains how Bee stayed for the allowed week before they sent her away.

"Any idea where she was going to go?"

"Said she just needed to get a job. Maybe she found one. Britany Addams." Joy rolls the name on her tongue. "Why does that name sound familiar? I feel like I know that name."

"May have heard it on the news. We've been looking for her for a couple of weeks. So you say she was here until what? The seventeenth?"

Joy flips the pages in the binder and confirms that Bee is not listed on roll call for the eighteenth. "That's right."

"You've been very helpful. If she comes back, I hope you'll call me. Her family is worried about her."

"Absolutely." She accepts his card and walks with him to the front. "What happens if you don't find her?"

"Nothing. She's just another missing girl." Cliff figures she'll end up a loose thread, one of many unsolved missing persons cases. At least now he knows she was alive up to the seventeenth of August, and that's more than they knew before. She wasn't murdered the night he let her walk away from him. "Ms. Addams is under no legal obligation to keep in touch with her family. She's an adult, free to move away without telling anybody, even her mother. The most logical explanation is that she left the area to start fresh in a new place, or at least it was. Now it looks like she's just run into a stretch of back luck. Maybe she'll come in on her own and put her family at ease."

"Do you believe that?" Joy asks as they reach the door.

Cliff holds her eyes for several moments, assessing. "No. But I'm hopeful." If Britany was going to ask for help, she would have done it already.

He pushes through the door, and it falls shut behind him.

Cliff settles in his cruiser, trying to decide where else he can search. He has covered all the bases, and at this point, it's a waiting game for something to turn up. Cliff has other cases to attend to. He feels less certain that she's dead after speaking with Joy, since she was alive August 17, the last day she stayed at Washington Street Outreach. In his gut, Cliff still feels that he should have handled things differently, and maybe he could have helped her get back on her feet at the beginning of August. Though it's not his job to fix everybody else's life, he could have done something. He isn't any better than Ben Walton. He watched her walk away and was glad when she was gone.

There isn't much more he can do. Either she'll show up, or she'll stay missing, or a body will turn up, and they'll have something to work with.

Chief Rojas sees Cliff as he enters the station and calls out for him to come to his office. He sits when the chief invites him to.

"I got your time-off approval today," he says and slides the form across the desk.

"Great."

"You ready?" he asks.

Everyone, including the chief, knows Cliff's opinions on marriage. He and Maggie didn't spread the word of their wedding at his father's house. Maggie felt that her mother would be hurt that she wasn't invited, and Cliff was willing to respect her wishes.

"Ready to get married?" Cliff asks. "Yeah. I am." He smiles, feeling at ease, which he would never have expected. Before, it was such a weight, the idea of getting married. Now he can't understand what his hesitation was about. Seeing Maggie so happy is a glorious thing.

"Where are you doing it?" The chief was sent an invitation, but he wasn't the one paying attention to the details.

"Over in Carrolton."

"Where to after that?" Chief Rojas asks.

"Florida."

"Great. Florida's a great honeymoon spot."

They smile and nod.

The chief says, "Tell me where you are on the Britany Addams file."

"I had a bit of luck today. One of the shelters had her in from August 11 until August 17."

"So she may not be dead," Rojas offers.

"Maybe not. Just having a bad couple of months, I guess," Cliff says.

"She'll show up when she wants to be found, I reckon," Rojas says.

"Probably."

The chief nods. "All right. Call her mother and give her an update."

"Yes, sir."

September 12

Chapter 42

Brit wears a hole in her shoe as she walks with Am to the Dollar Store to stock shelves. She's never literally worn out a pair of shoes before. It's somewhere in the middle of September. Brit has long since lost track of days and only knows it's Thursday because Am asked her if she's stocking shelves tonight.

"Look at that," Brit says, bending over and lifting her foot to look at her shoe while waiting for Grant to unlock the door.

"Yep. You done wore through."

A light drizzle began as they walked from the trees, and now they both have the look of drowned rats. "I'm glad we'll be inside tonight."

"Yep."

Brit looks at Am, curious about her short answers—her reluctance to have a conversation. "You all right?" she asks as the lock on the door turns and bright light spills from inside the building to cover them.

Am greets Grant but doesn't answer Brit's question. Brit worries she's done something wrong. For two days, Am has been distracted and distant, staring off into the distance like she didn't even hear the rest of them talking to her. Brit wonders if maybe she has stayed too long in the copse of trees with them. But she doesn't think that's it, because she's being distant with Pudge and Jed, too, and they aren't acting like something's wrong.

They make their way inside, and Grant sets them to work stocking from the pallets that came in on the truck today. Brit is loading a new display rack with canvas sneakers.

"Heya, Grant, could I buy a pair of these shoes?" She raises her foot so that he can see the hole worn in her sole.

"Yeah, you can buy a pair. I'll give 'em to you at cost, you know, because I like you." He winks, and Brit blushes.

Am huffs and walks past her to work on a display of trinkets and knickknacks.

Brit and Grant look at each other, both noticing Am's attitude. For a second, Brit feels a small thrill at his holding her eyes. Maybe he likes her. Just because she's homeless doesn't mean she suddenly got homely. For the first time in weeks, she thinks that somebody might actually find her attractive. She has felt invisible, and his catching her eye like that suddenly makes her feel seen.

"Let's get you some shoes. Get out of those old ones. Don't they hurt your feet?"

"They do. They are the worst shoes I've ever had. I don't know why I took them when I left."

"Where'd you leave from?"

"Nowhere. I had a boyfriend. We broke up. He kicked me out, and I didn't have time to get all my stuff."

"That's pretty shitty."

"Yeah. He had his reasons. I'm no angel."

"I bet you're not." He smiles and hands her a pair of gray size-seven sneakers. "What about these?"

Grant is standing too close. Brit can smell his cologne and feel the electricity coming off him.

"Perfect," she says, accepting the shoes. "How much?"

"Don't worry about it."

"No, I'll pay for them. Seriously, you can take it out of what I do tonight."

"Consider them a gift." He winks, and when she starts to protest, he says, "I'd do more if I could." He lifts his hand and touches her gently on the shoulder.

Tears spring to her eyes at his kindness. "Thank you." She tries to infuse the depth of her appreciation into her voice.

He smiles and steps away from her, leaving her to get her work done while he goes behind the counter and finishes the day's accounting.

It's raining full force when Brit and Am finish stocking and Grant opens the back door to see them out into the world.

"Thanks," Am says, pocketing her night's wages and stepping out into the rain.

"Thanks. I mean, really, thanks." Brit indicates her new shoes as she pockets her money.

"Yeah." He leans against the door, and she hesitates for a split second. He looks like he wants to say something more.

"See you next week," Brit says and finally steps into the rain.

"Can't wait."

The block of light holds until she jogs to catch up to Am and the door closes.

Brit hunches her shoulders and lowers her face against the rain. They walk in silence through the strip mall parking lot and past the Waffle House.

"You shouldn't let him give you stuff," Am says, breaking the uncomfortable silence.

"I told him I'd pay him for them," Brit says, feeling attacked.

"It's not about the money. Now you owe him. You think he isn't going to try to collect somewhere down the road?"

"What is there to collect? I haven't got anything. He's just a nice guy."

Am's black eyes swing to look at Brit, and she's shocked by the level of disgust in them. "There are no nice guys."

"That's very cynical."

"It's very true."

"What's the difference? He lets us come in and work. Isn't that him giving us something? Isn't that the same 'cause he gives us a place to be out of the weather?"

"No. It's not the same. We do something he doesn't want to do, and he pays us to do it. It's a job. You took those shoes, and he's going to expect something in return."

"Oh my god, Am. They're like five-dollar shoes."

"Yep," Am says and clamps her mouth closed.

"I think you're wrong," Brit says as all the good feelings she had about the small bit of chemistry she felt with Grant evaporates.

They make their way into the shelter of the trees, and Brit's new shoes are soaked through and muddy when they finally reach the clearing. Maybe she was wrong to let him give them to her. She doesn't want Am to be mad at her, and even if she isn't mad, she is definitely annoyed. No, she's disappointed, and Brit feels the same churning in her stomach she used to feel when her mother told her she was doing something wrong. Am is probably right. She should have just waited until the Goodwill opened and gone to pick up something from there. She feels ashamed, with Am looking down at her. Accepting the shoes as a gift suddenly feels like being cheap and dishonest.

Am walks to her hammock without another word, climbs in, and pulls the tarp over herself.

Maybe she's just jealous because Grant has never offered to give her anything. Brit's hammock is soaked, so she squats with her head on her knees in a sheltered spot under a low-hanging tree branch. Water still drips on her but not with the regularity it would if she were on her hammock. She doesn't have a tarp. She wishes she'd bought one along the way, but she didn't find one at Goodwill and wasn't comfortable spending so much at Walmart. She really wants a tent and almost picked one up a week ago, but it was too big for one person, and she decided against it.

September 19

Chapter 43

“What do you mean, you're 'moving on'?" Brit asks.

Temperatures have started to drop with the change of season, especially at night. The four of them huddle around the fire. Brit wears her clothes in layers, those she didn't give away to Pudge, who really likes what Brit used to wear for work. Brit doesn't care. She has shifted most of her wardrobe by visiting Goodwill and buying jeans and flannel shirts, which are so much warmer than the silk tops Pudge loves. She holds her hands toward the fire.

"We're heading to Florida," Jed explains.

"Winter home," Pudge says, rocking and saying it several times on a rhythm.

"Why?"

"It's too cold here," Am says.

As if on cue, the wind blows through the trees, and the dry leaves fly free, skittering. The flames warp before settling. When Brit first set up her hammock, they couldn't even see the school from the clearing, but now the security light glows through the empty branches, and they had to hang a green sleeping bag, another Goodwill find, between two trees to shield the camp.

"We can go to the outreach," Brit says, confused by their sudden announcement of plans.

"No," Am says with finality.

"Why not?"

"Am doesn't sleep inside. Ever," Jed says with a smile.

"We travel south in the winter," Am says, poking the fire with a stick. Sparks shoot toward the sky.

"How do you even get there?"

"We walk-a, walk-a, walk-a," Pudge says.

Brit didn't think she was still listening. "Dang. You walk all the way to Florida?"

"You should come with us, since you have people in Florida. You could see them," Am suggests.

Brit stares into the fire and imagines showing up at her mother's door like this. "Will you come back?"

Am nods and pulls the blanket closer around her shoulders. "In the spring."

"Why? Why not just stay in Florida?"

"Because I have people here," Am answers in a quiet voice.

"You have people here? Where?" Brit is incredulous. She stares at Am, trying to make sense of her words. She understands that Pudge and Jed travel with Am, that they take care of one another, that they're her people. Brit never asked about Am's past. It's a closed subject. Everybody's past is. "Who?"

Am gets that distant look on her face and is apparently done with the conversation. She stares into the fire for another minute before announcing that she's going to bed.

"It's Thursday. Aren't we going to the store?" Grant doesn't always have a lot for them to stock, but they always go, and he always lets them in to work. He pays them the same for the night whether it's a full truck or a partial one.

"Nah, gonna get an early start."

"Wait. What? You're leaving tomorrow?" Brit is annoyed that she wasn't included in the plan. Yes, they invited her but not like they want her around, more like she was just present when the subject came up.

No, she doesn't want to *walk* to Florida. No, she doesn't want to *see* her people. A small pang of guilt washes through her at the thought. She wonders if her mother has even noticed she's gone. She would have gotten back from her trip in August. Brit should call her to let her know she's okay... but she isn't okay. It's been too long now for a casual phone call. Calling now would require explanations about where she's been, and that conversation still always ends in her mother being disappointed that Brit was cheating on Zack. It still ends with her mother never being able to forget that Brit is just like her dad, a cheater. She probably already knows. The thought nearly takes her breath away as she imagines Zack telling her mother the worst things about her. It would be just like him to screw her over one more time.

She'll call her when she gets back on her feet, then she'll be able to talk about it without needing her mother to rescue her. If she isn't asking for anything, she won't owe her an explanation. She just can't ask for help. Then her mother will never stop punishing her, the same way they're both still punishing her father. If she can call when she's back on her feet and doesn't need anything, she won't have to have the conversation. She can just say, "Sorry, Mom. I know I should have called, but I was just working through some stuff. I needed some space. I'm sorry if I worried you." Brit likes the way that imagined conversation goes, almost like she and her mother are peers, two adults, not a parent and a child.

"Yep. It's gonna start getting cold up here. I can feel it in my bones." Am unfolds her body and walks out of the glow of the fire.

Brit turns to gape at Jed. "People?" She widens her eyes at the ludicrous idea. Brit has lived in the shelter of the trees with them for weeks, and never once did Am mention that she has people.

Jed is quiet for a long time, watching Am settle in her hammock.

"Her family is still around here. She comes back to see her boys."

"Oh my god." Brit is stunned. "She has kids? Where? Won't they help her? Why does she live like this if she has kids?" The absurdity of her statement isn't lost on her. She could call her mother and not have to live like this. Maybe Am did something bad and is too ashamed to face her family, just like Brit.

"She's living exactly the way she wants to live. Make no mistake."

"When does she see them?"

"All over. She walks. She sees them."

"How could I not know this?" Brit walked with Am from New-nan to Peachtree City and all around the areas in between, and she never saw Am stop to talk to someone who might have been a son.

"Just because she sees them doesn't mean they see her."

"What does that even mean?" Brit is flabbergasted. She thought she knew Am—thought she knew them all—but now she feels like she's been an outsider in their midst all this time. Then she hears what he said, the meaning behind the words, and understanding dawns. "They don't see her because we're invisible."

Jed raises an eyebrow, and they sit for a long while, staring into the fire.

Finally, Pudge yawns, and Jed says, "I reckon we should turn in. It's gonna be a long day tomorrow."

Brit nods but doesn't speak, still processing not being *wanted*. After Pudge and Jed leave her, she sits for another half hour, staring into the fire before she pulls her mind free. If she's going to keep stocking shelves, she needs to go.

Chapter 44

"Where is Am?" Grant asks, allowing Brit to enter the back door of the Dollar Store as she has every Thursday and occasional Sunday in September.

"She isn't coming. Can I still work?" Brit asks, stepping out of the dark night and into the lit interior of the closed store.

"Sure." He locks the door behind her and follows her toward the stockroom.

Midnight passes, and Brit breaks down boxes as she fills the shelves.

"Is there anything else?" she asks when the last of the boxes is flattened and stacked.

"Come sit with me while I finish this up."

Brit joins Grant behind the counter, where he's entering information into his accounting program. She's careful to position herself so she cannot see the screen. When he's done, he closes the laptop and moves it aside. He leans back in his chair and gives her an assessing look.

Brit blushes and smiles. "What?" It's been a long time since anybody looked at her like that.

"What's your story?"

"What do you mean?"

"You're a smart girl. At least, you seem like it. You don't seem like you're on drugs. Do you drink?"

"No, I don't drink. Who has money for drugs?" She laughs. But she has encountered several people who drink or buy drugs on trade or by using money they collected up by the interstate. She doesn't judge. If Brit hadn't met up with Am again, she isn't sure that she wouldn't have gotten into that scene just to forget herself for a little while.

"Why are you living like this? You a runaway? How old are you?" Grant lights a cigarette, even though the sign on the door says no smoking. He flips a button on an ashtray, and a small motor whirs, pulling the smoke into it.

"I'm old enough not to be a runaway. I'm just... between places, between jobs, between the past and the future."

"Why?"

"Did you know you can't get an apartment without a job? And you can't get a job if you don't have a place to get clean. You can't even open a bank account if you don't have an address."

"I didn't know that." Grant draws on the cigarette, and Brit is mesmerized by the tip, watching it glow and pulse. He holds the smoke in his lungs for a long beat and squints as he studies her. Then he blows out a long stream of smoke toward the ashtray, and they both watch as the smoke is eaten by the fan. "So what do you need?"

"I guess I need an apartment or at least a room in somebody's house. But nobody is going to let me move into their house without a job. See how it goes? My life is just a big circle of no."

"What if I told you I know of an apartment you could rent?"

"I'd tell you I don't have enough money for rent. And I don't have references." Brit is annoyed that he's dangling a carrot in front of her to see if she'll jump. "Thirty or forty dollars a week doesn't go far. Not to say that I don't appreciate it, 'cause without it, I'd probably be dead." The truth of the words causes her lips to quiver. He doesn't understand. "I had money but no references and no job, then some asshole stole my money. Now I have nothing."

Grant leans forward and writes an address on a piece of paper then slides it across the desk. "It's only four units, but we've got one open. I'm putting in new carpet this week."

"I don't have any money." Brit enunciates her words and pushes the paper back across the desk without looking.

"We'll work it out. I'd rather have someone in it than leave it sitting empty."

The gears in her mind click, and she says, "Are you for real? You, like, own it?"

He nods, and a small smile plays on his lips. "It's nothing fancy, but if you need a place, I can help you out."

"Really?" Brit is scared to believe him. But he nods, and she looks down at the piece of paper. "Okay. I'll think about it. Thank you."

"Yeah. Now, you'd better get on out of here before the morning team comes."

"Thank you, Grant. I mean, seriously, thank you."

"It will take me a week to get it ready. Talk to me about it next time you come."

Brit is ecstatic. She hopes Am is still there. Maybe if they have an apartment to go to, Am, Jed, and Pudge will stay.

But when she reaches the small clearing beside the school, she finds it empty. Pudge's tent is gone, and the two hammocks where Am and Jed slept are gone. Only the sleeping bag stretched between the trees, Brit's bag, and her hammock remain. Brit stands for several moments, looking around at the vacated camp. Emotions tangle and warp as she processes her changed circumstances. This morning, she felt hopeful walking back to the woods. She secured the promise of an apartment. They could all go, then they wouldn't have to live outside like animals. They wouldn't have to move on with the weather.

Anger flares, and Brit swipes at her eyes. She won't cry, dammit. If nobody cares about her enough to even say goodbye, then to hell with them. She wishes the apartment was ready today, but it isn't. She climbs into her makeshift hammock and stares up through the trees to the bright sky. The loneliness nearly overwhelms her. When she hears the kids out in the playground, she moves stealthily toward the sound of them, keeping to the shadows and staying sheltered by the underbrush. She squats in the dirt and watches as a group of three girls, probably third graders, walk toward the fence. When she was little, she had friends. She was just like everybody else.

"See? It's honeysuckle," one of the girls says, reaching up to a vine on Brit's side of the fence.

"That's a weed," another girl says.

"Try it." The first one plucks a flower and tucks it into her mouth. She smiles at her friends' appalled reactions and laughs.

Brit smiles, too, her spirits rising. Oh, to be little again. Her mother's face floats into her mind. She should call. The thought has been hovering for days, but she refuses to acknowledge it. They aren't close. Maybe her mom hasn't even called. Perhaps she decided to stay in Greece. Brit was pissed when her parents got divorced and ruined her life. She still hasn't forgiven them. If they hadn't gotten divorced, she would have been able to go to college, she and Jason wouldn't have broken up, she wouldn't have met Zack, and she would have married Jason. Brit wouldn't have snuck around to see him or been distracted by his touch. She wouldn't have been driving toward Senoia that day, and Dee Martin would still be alive. Maybe she is punishing them for messing up her future.

The third girl tries the honeysuckle, and they squeal. The bell rings, and Brit watches them running away from the fence and tries to remember who she was when she was a kid.

She should call her mother.

When all the kids were back inside, Brit returns to her hammock and folds into it. Maybe she'll call her mother the next time she gets to a phone. She closes her eyes and tries to sleep.

September 20

Chapter 45

Cliff feels the weight in the chords as the music moves into the processional. He blinks several times when the door from the vestibule opens, and he sees Maggie. She is stunning. His knees are locked, and he releases them, shifting his weight to a wider stance. They're already married. She was beautiful that day, like she always is, but she was not dressed like a queen.

The dress has simple lines, and he's mesmerized by the movement of her hips and legs as she walks toward him. Tony's hand falls on Cliff's shoulder, and he remembers to breathe. She stops three feet away, and her smile spreads. Maggie is the most beautiful woman in the world.

"Who gives this woman in marriage?" Pastor Stewart asks.

"Her mother and I." Her father, Harmon, reaches out a hand, and Cliff clasps it, promising in the strength of his handshake that he will never let harm come to Maggie.

Harmon leans in and kisses Maggie on the cheek before handing her up to Cliff on the riser.

After Harmon sits, the preacher starts. "Friends and family, we are gathered here today to celebrate the very special love between Maggie and Cliff by joining them in marriage."

Cliff's breath catches in his throat, and he swallows around it. She is so damned beautiful. Maggie squeezes his fingers, and he takes in her face—her smile and her warm brown eyes. He raises her hand to his lips.

"Maggie and Cliff, your marriage will allow you a new environment to share your lives together, standing together to face life and the world hand in hand. To be successful, you will need strength, courage, patience, and a really good sense of humor."

The friends and family laugh, and Cliff and Maggie's smiles broaden.

"If you find humor, have patience, and protect your relationship from outside influence, you will have a lifetime of waking each morning and falling in love."

Everything blurs until Cliff is given the right to kiss her. He lifts the veil, aware of the coarse fabric between his fingers, the translucent quality of her skin, and the sheen of balm on her lips. The moment he worried about, the public kiss, is upon him, and he forgets entirely that others are present. He cups her head, they come together, and the world stops its rotation.

"I am honored to present for the first time Mr. and Mrs. Rathborn."

Cliff lifts Maggie from the riser and places her feet on the aisle. Her fingers twine in his, and they proceed past their friends and family, including his father and Carla, who made it to the wedding after all. They pass into the daylight. His cop eye takes in the surroundings—the cars moving down Highway 16 and the group of three people standing around a wheelchair on the opposite side of the street, watching.

Birdseed is tossed as Cliff and Maggie duck and dash out to their waiting car to drive to the reception.

They drive toward the road. Maggie turns back to wave at the family and guests as Cliff steers toward the street. The woman standing behind the wheelchair is bone thin but stands tall and doesn't turn away. Their eyes connect through the glass, and a small smile spreads across her face. She nods at him before he breaks the connection and turns onto the street.

September 21

Chapter 46

In his dream, Cliff is in the pool, a child but not. He looks up at the woman who was his mother as she stands on the deck. Her hair glistens from the water. She's stuck, like she sometimes was, staring out at something that isn't there. He reaches for her, but the air around her warps, and she's standing on the roadside behind a laden wheelchair.

Cliff startles awake, gasping and pawing at the blanket to get free.

"Hey? Did I wake you?" Maggie is pouring water into the coffeepot in the little kitchenette of their honeymoon suite. She is sexy, dressed in boy shorts and a tank.

"No. I just had a dream." He doesn't want to tell her about it. It's already fading. His penis jerks when she moves, and the curve of her breast is visible through the armhole of her tank.

"Was it about me?" she asks, teasing.

"All of 'em are." He reaches for her, and she allows him to draw her into the bed. "How are you this morning, Mrs. Rathborn?" His lips touch her collarbone, and he slides his hand under her tank.

Maggie sighs and lets her head fall back, pressing her body into him. He exposes her nipple and breathes on it, enjoying the moment when it contracts before he takes it in his mouth.

The coffeepot drips as her toes catch the waistband of his briefs and slide them down his legs. It drips again as his lips move down to her stomach, as he rises to his knees to draw down her shorts. They kick the remnants of their clothing free, and he kisses his way back up her body until they're face to face.

"Thank you for marrying me," Cliff whispers, kissing her.

"Again," she says on a sigh.

"Again."

"Thank you for asking." Maggie runs her hand through his hair and arches her back to accommodate his penis as it seeks admittance. She wraps her legs around his hips and lifts her body into his. With a moan, he slides in.

They rock, unable to be closer than one, until they are satisfied. When they uncouple, he rolls to lie beside her on the bed, staring up at the ceiling as their breathing returns to normal.

"See what we have to look forward to?" she asks, and he nods, turning to look at her.

They don't move for a long time as the scent of perked coffee fills the air. He thinks she's asleep, but then she speaks.

"Did you see that homeless woman across from the church?"

"I did." His breath stalls, and he waits.

"Wasn't that the woman from Newnan?"

"Was it?" He remembers Carla saying she thought of Miriam every time she saw the old homeless woman, but he doesn't want to think about it. The haunting moment from his dream slips through his mind, and he feels like he has almost caught hold of the story behind his mother leaving.

"I think so. One of the janitors at the school had coffee with her at the Waffle House one time. Said she was really nice but didn't want help. She said her name was I Am. Isn't that odd?" Maggie pushes off the bed, searching through the sheets for her shorts.

"What does I Am mean?"

"I don't know. Do you think it was her?"

Cliff avoids the true question—*Is she Miriam?*—because finding her doesn't answer any of his questions. "I thought she looked like her, but I don't know what she'd be doing in Carrollton or Newnan, for that matter." Cliff connected with her, though. He held her eyes for a moment before she smiled at him.

"Seems like she came to see us get married." Mags smiles, stepping into her shorts.

Cliff chuckles. "That's quite a walk."

"Coffee?" she offers.

"Yes." He finds his briefs and pulls them on then accepts the cup. "I'm starving."

"I bet you are." She smiles, and his penis twitches with desire at the rumble in her throat. *Damn.*

September 27

Chapter 47

Brit takes in the carpet. It's new, just like Grant promised, and the same neutral color that was in the first apartment she looked at months ago. The windows are sealed by layers of paint, and the apartment smells only of new carpet. Brit doesn't have any furniture, but she has a key, a door, and a shower. She has a refrigerator without food and cabinets without dishes.

A knock on the door startles her, and she rushes to look through the peephole. Flinging the door open, she smiles broadly.

"Grant!" She didn't see him when she arrived, but the woman who lives in the first-floor apartment below hers had the key, and Grant told her Brit would be coming.

"I see you got in," Grant says as she spins in the middle of the floor as if she's on stage. "I brought you some things." He holds out a plastic bag.

"What's this?" she asks as she reaches for it.

"Just stuff you probably need. Consider it a housewarming."

She looks down at bottles of shampoo and conditioner, a bar of soap, a tube of toothpaste, a new toothbrush, a clear plastic shower curtain and rings, and a small container of dish soap. Tears spring to her eyes, and she closes the bag. "Wow. That's so nice of you."

"What do you think of the apartment? It needs to be aired out." He wrinkles his nose and goes to the window. With force, he breaks the window free of the paint, and it slides up, letting in a blast of cool, fresh air.

"It's great. I mean really. I don't know how I'll ever make it up to you."

Grant waves a hand and goes to the bedroom, where he forces open the second window. "If you want to ride with me over to my storage unit, I might have some stuff you could use."

"Seriously?"

"Sure. People come and go, and sometimes they leave stuff behind," he says and puts his arm around her shoulder to guide her into the hall.

"Will my bag be okay?"

He shrugs. "Yeah. Lock the door. You have the key."

Brit laughs, feeling giddy. "Oh yeah, I have a key." Her hand trembles as she places the key in the lock and secures the apartment. *I'll never take anything for granted again.*

She follows him down the stairs and out into the beautiful fall day. He opens the door to a truck, and she has to reach up for the handle to climb in. He walks around to the driver's side.

When he gets in, Brit says, "I don't know how I'll ever thank you." She can't remember ever being happier than she is right now.

"I didn't do anything, Bee. I needed a tenant, and you needed a place."

"I know. But seriously, thank you for trusting me. I'll get a job real quick, and I'll pay the rent before I do anything else."

"Don't worry about it. You can pay rent next month. Just get yourself a job and find your feet. Okay?"

Her hand lands on his arm, and he shifts until he takes her hand in his. "Why are you being so nice to me?"

"I like you. Okay? I just think you're a good person who fell on hard times."

"I am. I am a good person." She squeezes his hand and feels comforted by his touch. "I don't even know how this happened."

"Nobody ever does." He drops her hand to shift gears.

They drive until they turn into the storage yard, which consists of three rows of steel buildings with fourteen units in each. They pull in front of the middle building and park at the tenth unit. Before he can come around to her side, she opens her door and jumps out of the truck. They aren't dating, and even though she's grateful and even held his hand, she isn't ready to be interested in anybody. She walks around the truck and joins him at the door as he removes the lock and slides the garage-style door up. Daylight shines into the gloom, revealing a bounty of furniture.

"You need a bed. I have a frame but no mattress. Hmm..." Grant flips the switch to illuminate the room.

She follows. "What about this futon?" Brit asks. She feels self-conscious about suggesting it and trails her fingers along the wood frame.

"To sleep on? It wouldn't be very comfortable."

She laughs. "I've been sleeping in a hammock for a long time. I think a futon would be plenty comfortable."

"Well, I guess it might, then. What about this dresser? You'll need a mirror."

They paw through the unit until the truck is filled, then they drive back and carry everything up the stairs and into the apartment. Brit is exhausted from the effort and feels dizzy with fatigue and hunger when they take up the last two pieces, two chairs for the kitchen table.

They sit together on the futon, Brit panting, sweat beading on her face. "Well, that took some effort."

The door is ajar, and a woman walks past, turning to look.

"Hey, Grant. You got a new girl," she calls, pausing on the other side of the threshold.

"Yeah. This is Bee. She's just getting moved in."

He motions for her to come in, and Brit feels dirty because she hasn't showered yet. She knows she stinks. A person can only get *so* clean in a gas station bathroom.

"This is Chloe."

The girl smiles and doesn't seem to notice how dirty Brit is. She extends her hand. Chloe has beautiful hands with manicured nails and soft skin.

"Good to meet you," Brit says.

"You too." The smile that splits her face makes the whole room seem brighter. "Well, hey, I was gonna order a pizza, but you know, then I'd eat the whole thing." She laughs, putting her hand on her tiny waist. "We could split one."

"Well, you girls should do that. I got to get on home. But I'm glad you came by. Maybe you can help Bee get settled, you know… feel like she's not so alone in the world." Grant pushes himself up and leans in to give the girl a small side hug.

"Well, yeah, I can do that. We'll order pizza and watch a movie. You can come down to my place. I'm just down the hall."

Brit feels caught in a cyclone as plans are made. "I'd like to take a shower."

"Well, yeah. Take a shower and get yourself pretty, then just come down. What do you like on your pizza?"

Brit chuckles. "I like about anything."

The phrase pings in her mind, and she remembers the first time she met Am at the laundromat. She offered to buy a pizza and asked Am what toppings she liked. "I like about anything," Am said. Brit thought she wasn't like Am and that she would be back on her feet in a week.

"Except anchovies. I don't really care for little fish," Brit says, clarifying.

"Ugh. Does anybody? That's just gross." She walks back toward the door. "All right, I'll order it up." She waves and steps back from the door. "Just come on down when you're ready."

"Okay," Brit says, but the girl is already moving down the hall.

Brit and Grant stand for a second, letting the air settle around them.

"She's exciting."

"Oh yeah. Chloe is always on. She'll be a good friend to you. She's not had an easy road, either, but she's taking some classes and is doing good."

October 10

Chapter 48

The day after Brit moved into the apartment, she secured a job at the gas station on the corner of Newnan Crossing Boulevard and Lower Fayetteville Road. Her responsibility is to keep all the food stocked. She puts sausage biscuits together and places them, wrapped, in the warmers, brews coffee, and keeps cups and lids stocked. When she has stocked all the self-serve items, she straightens shelves. The hours slip by from four a.m. until ten a.m., and the last hour slows down. She washes pots and makes fresh coffee before starting the hot dog roller.

"Doug, do you need anything else before I clock out?" she asks every day before she leaves.

"Did you get the hot dogs in?" he asks every day.

"I did. Got you twelve already made and another dozen in the roller," she answers.

"All right. See you tomorrow."

Brit clocks out and walks across the dangerous intersection and up to her apartment to shower for the second time in the day. It is a brainless job, but she doesn't care. The rest of the day is hers. She only has one uniform, so after she showers, she gathers it, her towel, and yesterday's clothes to put in the wash. The fourplex shares two washers and two dryers, and Brit is happy to see that Chloe is sitting in the small laundry room, flipping through an old People magazine.

"Hey, girl." Brit opens the available washer and scans the interior for discoloration. The last time she washed, she came after Kelly, who used the washer after dyeing a pair of jeans black. The dye left residue, and some of Brit's clothes were mottled. The tub looks clean today.

"Hey." Chloe glances up from her magazine. "How's the job going?"

"It sucks." She laughs. "No, just kidding. It's not bad. I'm glad to have it. What are you wearing?" The tiny velveteen strap on her dress reveals a sequined bralette.

"It's definitely laundry day." She gives her dazzling smile with those screwed-in teeth.

After Chloe told Brit how Grant found her dancing in a sleazy joint with her teeth mostly rotted out from meth, Brit felt less embarrassed about her own history. She didn't get hooked on drugs and lose her teeth. She stayed sober all the way through her homeless experience, as she now thinks of it, even though it would have been much easier to be numb. Brit didn't tell Chloe about Dee Martin when it was her turn to share. She only said that her boyfriend kicked her out because she was still hung up on her ex. It wasn't untrue, but it wasn't the whole story.

"No classes today?" Brit asks, reveling in the convenience of having an apartment with laundry facilities just downstairs.

"Nope. I'm free till seven."

"Got a date?"

Chloe was often out during the evenings. Brit sometimes heard her coming up the stairs and making her way toward her door in the darkest hour of the night.

"Yeah. Freddie," she says. "But he may have to cancel."

"Why?" Brit hops onto the washer once it's running and looks down from her perch at Chloe.

"He's got a friend in town and doesn't want to go if he doesn't have a date too." She glances back at the magazine.

"Oh." The machine shifts and rocks beneath Brit.

"Stephie was always my go-to girl when I needed a double."

"What happened to her?"

"I don't know. Just left, I guess. She used to have your apartment. Probably got fed up with Grant. He had a thing for her, you know?"

Brit didn't know. She hadn't asked why the apartment was empty or who was there before her. It hadn't mattered, and it still doesn't.

"What about Mavis? Or Kelly?" Brit met the other two girls who lived in the building, and Mavis, who gave her the key to the apartment that first day, is her least favorite. She's abrasive. She's *pointy.*

"I asked Mavis, but she's already got plans. I haven't seen Kelly in a couple of days. I think she's out of town."

Brit nods and reaches for a magazine.

"I don't know what I'm going to do. I really want to see him, but if his friend doesn't have a date, he's gonna cancel." She pouts. She looks up, and her eyes grow wide. "You could come. You could be his date."

"I don't know about that."

"It'll be fun. They'll take us out for a good meal. We'll just hang out."

"I don't know." Brit was looking forward to a quiet night in her apartment. She lets her mind run with the idea of going out with a man, of having a date. "I guess I could." She hasn't eaten out in a restaurant in months, and she begins to feel excited about the prospect.

"Really. It'll be fun. Freddie's a good guy," Chloe says and places her magazine aside.

"I don't have anything to wear, though."

"Girl, I have date clothes. You can wear something of mine." She stands and tugs Brit's hand to bring her off the washer. "You're about my size. Except for in the boobs, and that won't matter. They'll fit." Chloe straightens her shoulders, and her ample breasts stretch the fabric. "Let's go see what you like."

Brit allows Chloe to draw her out of the laundry room with re-assurances that nobody is going to steal her shitty clothes, and Brit follows her up the stairs and down the hall to Chloe's apartment.

The place is nicer than Brit's. It has faux hardwood floors and is *decorated*. A print of a perplexed-looking Marilyn Monroe in a black dress adorns the wall facing the door.

"Hello, Marilyn," Chloe calls, and Brit follows to Chloe's bedroom.

The bedroom is appointed with a wrought-iron canopy bed draped in a sheer burgundy fabric, and a small pang to have nicer things stirs in Brit's stomach.

"I love your bed."

"Rooms To Go, baby."

"How do you afford all this?" Brit hasn't seen her going to work.

"It wasn't expensive." Chloe opens the closet and paws through hangers, picking out several dresses and handing them to Brit for consideration. "What size shoes do you wear?"

"Seven," Brit says, looking down at her dirty shoes. She bought these at Goodwill when the five-dollar sneakers Grant gave her fell apart. They weren't made for tramping. They were made to look cute for sassy teens.

Brit holds up dresses, and Chloe leaves her alone to try on a few. She removes her T-shirt and pulls one of the dresses over her head then takes in the vision in the mirror. She pulls her hair up and really looks at herself, surprised at how thin she is. Her neck looks long and sinuous. Her arms are narrow, and the ridge of her collarbone is in full view. Tears sting her eyes, and she steps closer to the mirror until her breath creates a small fog on the glass. Brit looks at her reflection and blinks, trying to figure out who she has become. She doesn't know how to just leave the past behind. She isn't sure she can close the door on that part of her life and go out on a date with Chloe and her friends.

"I think that's the one," Chloe says, having stepped into the room without being heard. "I have shoes."

Brit turns away from her reflection, and a tear slips down her face.

Chloe puckers her lips and rushes to wrap her arms around her. "You're going to be okay."

Brit nods and sniffs. "I forgot I was pretty."

"Oh my god, Bee, you're beautiful." She draws back, holding Brit's hands. "Except your hands. How are your feet?"

"They're feet."

"Well, you can't have nasty feet in strappy heels."

"Where'd you get these?" Brit accepts the offered heels, which are a full size or so smaller than the row of shoes lining the back of the closet. Chloe has long, narrow feet. She's at least a size eight.

"I went down and borrowed them from Mavis. She's a seven too."

"Really? She doesn't mind me wearing them?"

"She doesn't care. They're just shoes. Let's see how they look."

Brit obliges and straps on the shoes.

"Definitely have to do something about those feet, but the shoes fit."

"I don't know." Brit is dubious.

"We'll take care of that. We've got time. I need a fill anyway." Chloe holds up a hand, studying her beautiful nails. "You can't let your hands look bad. Men notice them."

Brit nods but says, "I can't afford to get my nails done."

"I'll take care of it, since you are helping me out. It'll be fine. You buy pizza next time." Chloe walks toward the door, telling Brit to get changed. "We've got a lot to do before seven."

Chapter 49

Chloe and Brit drive almost to Tyrone and park on the street in front of a small house. Chloe has talked the whole way, and Brit didn't have time to feel the road under the wheels and freak out. She hopes she's over that. The front door opens as they walk up the sidewalk, and Chloe, taking short steps because of her heels, runs the last few feet into Freddie's arms. She greets him with a firm kiss. His hand slides down the curve of her back to squeeze the meat of her butt. He is not at all what Brit expected. Freddie is pudgy and nearly bald. He doesn't seem like the type of guy Chloe would go for. And he's old. He has to be forty.

Chloe giggles when they break apart. "Freddie, I've missed you. It wasn't nice of you to make me think you weren't going to see me tonight. I look forward to seeing you." She simpers.

Brit cocks an eyebrow and wonders who the hell Chloe is.

Chloe nestles her body into Freddie and turns her eyes to the tall man behind Freddie. "Who's your friend?"

"This is Aaron. My old college buddy."

"Nice to meet you, college buddy." Chloe smiles, flashing those beautiful implants. "This is my friend Bee. Isn't she gorgeous?"

"Oh my god," Brit says, embarrassed as all eyes turn to her.

"Hi, Bee," Aaron says and bobs his head.

Freddie raises a rakish eyebrow, and his eyes travel from Brit's freshly painted toes to her breasts.

"Nice to meet you," Brit says, extending a hand and feeling awkward.

"Shall we take my car?" Freddie holds up keys.

He leads them around the house to the open garage, which is clean. One side holds a black SUV, and the other houses a lawnmower. Aaron opens the back door and gestures for Brit to climb in. She slides across the leather seat, and Aaron folds his tall body to join her. Freddie opens Chloe's door, and before she gets in, she kisses him with enthusiasm. The vehicle's interior is pristine, gleaming with newness.

Chloe claims the radio, and the beat of the music eliminates the threat of conversation. Brit feels a sense of dread and wishes she hadn't agreed to come. Aaron seems like a nice-enough guy, but she's nervous about being in the car, so she's still not quite over that. She feels the wave of panic rising and releases a shuddering breath.

Aaron leans toward her. "You okay?"

Brit faces him. He has kind eyes, deep and expressive. He touches her lightly on her thigh, and the feel of his hand coupled with the concern in his eyes breaks the panic cycle. She draws a long breath and nods. "I'm not very good in cars," she says then again, louder, closer to his ear.

"What does that mean?"

"I had an accident a while ago, and I just don't like cars anymore." It may be the first time she's spoken of the accident to anybody as if it was no big deal.

"Oh. That sucks. Well, this thing is a tank. We'll be okay." He folds his fingers between hers, and she lets him. It helps. She squeezes, appreciating the kind gesture, and lets him hold her hand all the way to the restaurant.

They tumble out of the car, and Aaron places his hand on the small of her back as they walk through the parking lot. Chloe looks back and winks. She hasn't missed his holding her hand, and Brit knows she's going to get teased for it.

They are led to a booth, and Brit slides toward the wall, allowing Aaron and his long legs to have the outside seat. Chloe sits across from her.

"So what do you do?" Chloe asks Aaron.

"I'm a data analyst."

"Oh." Chloe widens her eyes. "How exciting."

Aaron laughs, a low chuckle that seems to start somewhere near his knees. Freddie drops his arm around Chloe and pulls her closer.

"I know it's not very exciting," Aaron says. "But I like numbers. I like to see trends and look for things that are out of place."

"So you're kind of like an investigator?" Brit asks.

"Kind of."

A flutter in her stomach surprises her. She likes him. She imagines herself dating a data analyst and wonders what kind of money he makes. He's a little scrawny, but he has good hair and kind eyes. He has a wide smile. She could like a guy like that.

Chloe fills the table with conversation and only lets the words fall when the food arrives and they're consumed by consuming.

During a lull, Aaron leans in. "How is it?"

"It's really good. You want to try some?" Brit ordered the salmon. He nods and opens his mouth.

"Oh." She laughs, spears a flake on her fork, and allows him to take it from the tines. It feels intimate to share food in such a way, and heat radiates through her. It has been so long since she felt attractive around a man. She has never placed food inside another human's mouth before, and it feels almost sexual.

"Mmm. That is good." He gives a beautiful smile, and Brit's cheeks flush. "You're cute." He leans into her, and she lets her shoulder stay pressed against him.

After dinner, Freddie drives them back to his house and offers wine. Brit accepts a glass then a second. She isn't even aware when

Chloe and Freddie disappear into a room. The wine has warmed her, and when Aaron leads the way into a bedroom, she doesn't stop him.

She wobbles when he steps away to close the door.

"You okay?" he asks.

"That wine hit me hard."

"Yeah, me too." He leans down and kisses her, holding her upright as they move toward the bed.

Aaron is a good kisser, his mouth moving slowly on hers, and she lets herself fall onto the bed beneath him. They kiss until the heat envelopes them, and the dress Chloe gave her is peeled free. When their clothes are piled on the floor and their skin is pressed together, Brit almost forgets that she barely knows him or that it has been a long time since she's been with a man.

He bites her nipple, and it hurts, but she doesn't pull away. He reaches across her to the bedside table and opens the drawer. In the dim light, she sees a square package, and her stomach flutters. She didn't plan to have sex with him. At this point, it seems ridiculous to think that she isn't, with her nipples exposed and erect and their clothes piled on the floor.

Aaron rises to his knees, and his member stands out straight. He offers her the condom, and she takes it. If she doesn't want to go forward, it's too late now. He bought her dinner, she came back to the house with him, and she let him take off her clothes piece by piece. Brit doesn't know how not to move forward. She accepts the condom and opens the package.

After she rolls it down his shaft, he folds down onto her and smashes his mouth against hers. He pulls the sheet over them and settles with his legs between hers, and without pause, he reaches down and guides himself into her. She gasps, and he pushes.

"Damn, you're tight."

Brit tenses then forces herself to relax. There's no going back. It isn't like she doesn't like him. She just didn't think they were going to have sex, and she isn't quite sure how it happened. She shouldn't have drunk the wine or let the men bring them back to Freddie's house. She shouldn't have agreed to go on a date with a man she didn't know.

It doesn't take long. He pumps inside of her and rolls her on top so she's straddling him. She lifts herself up and down as he grabs at her breasts. When he comes, he grasps her hips and holds her hard against his body, and she puts her head back and looks up at the ceiling as if she, too, is feeling the contractions of orgasm.

Brit slides off him and lies down on her back beside him.

"That was good." Aaron pulls his arm from under her head and climbs out of the bed. He removes the condom and collects his clothes from the floor. "Thank you."

He drops her clothes on the bed, and she watches him walk out of the room. Then she hears the shower start in the bathroom next door and feels confused.

Brit pulls her clothes on and steps out into the hall.

"Ready?" Chloe asks, smiling and carrying her shoes by the straps.

"Yeah. I guess. Should I wait to tell him goodbye?" They didn't even exchange numbers.

"Nah. Freddie will tell him." Chloe leans in. "Was he good?"

Brit is flustered and confused, but she smiles and nods. "Yeah, he was fine."

They walk out to the car, and Freddie waves from the front door. Chloe blows him an air kiss. As they drive to the apartment, the feeling of panic sits in Brit's stomach. They arrive safely, seeing very little traffic.

As they walk up the sidewalk to their fourplex, Chloe links arms with Brit and whispers, "Did he have a big dick? Tall men usually have big dicks."

"I guess so." Brit has never been with a particularly tall man before.

When they reach Brit's door, Chloe pulls out a wad of cash. She peels off five twenties and holds them out to Brit.

"What's that?"

"Your cut."

Brit looks at the money for several seconds as the alcohol evaporates from her blood. Chloe is giving her a hundred dollars for going out with her and her friends. It doesn't make sense.

Then it does. Chloe isn't giving her a hundred dollars for going out. Aaron gave her a hundred dollars for fucking him.

Suddenly, his rapid departure from the bed makes sense.

"Take it. You earned it."

Brit takes the money and turns into her apartment as her salmon begins to swim upstream.

October 13

Chapter 50

At the end of Brit's shift, Doug calls her over.

"I don't think you can work here anymore," he says and hands her the check for her last two weeks.

"What? Why?" She's a good employee, coming in on time and doing everything he asks of her.

"We checked your references. You never worked at the Dollar Store like you said."

"Oh my god, did you talk to Grant?" Brit made it very clear that they only needed to talk to Grant. He told her she could put him down as a reference.

"I don't know who I talked to, but they said they had no record of you working there."

"You were supposed to talk to Grant. It was kinda off the books."

"Look, Bee, I don't know what you're playing at, but if I can't trust you to be honest about where you've worked, I can't trust you in my store."

"I need this job."

"I don't care. I don't like liars. You need to leave."

Brit stands for several moments, staring at him with her jaw jutted forward, rage washing through her. She wants to scream. She just needs a fucking break.

You killed someone.

The understanding hits her like a punch.

The check flutters in Doug's hand. Brit looks down at it, reaches for it, then turns and walks out of the station without looking back. She deserves this. She killed somebody because she wanted to get laid. Somebody died because of her.

She walks across the street to the apartment without even checking for traffic as the rain turns to sleet.

Chapter 51

After looking through the peephole to find Grant on the other side, Brit opens her apartment door.

"I hear you had a date," he says, leaning against the doorjamb.

"What?" It's been three days since she went out with Chloe, and she hasn't seen her around the building. Brit doesn't understand why Grant is here or how he knows that she went on a date with Chloe and her friends. She doesn't know why Chloe would tell him something like that, like it's his business.

Brit is dressed in sweatpants and a sweatshirt, both Goodwill finds when she was on the streets. She returned to the apartment after being fired, ripped off her work clothes, and stood in the hot shower until the water ran cold. Nothing could warm the frozen core inside of her. She wrapped her hair in a towel and climbed into her flattened futon, hoping to sleep and wake up in a different life. Then Grant knocked, and she was jerked out of the futon. The towel unwound from her head, leaving her damp hair in disarray.

"You had a date. Chloe told me."

"Oh yeah. Why are you here?" It comes out harsher than she means it. Grant has been kind to her. She doesn't want him to think she doesn't appreciate the apartment, but she's upset that he didn't give the promised reference.

Grant pushes past her as if her question is an invitation. He brings with him the cold air from outdoors. It's sleeting, and his jacket is speckled and dripping cold water onto the floor.

"You look upset. You been crying?" he asks, looking from her to the futon.

"No," Brit says and swipes at her face. She *was* crying.

"You look like you've been crying."

"I just got fired. You told me you would vouch for me if they called for references."

"Oh. They must have called when I wasn't there," he says.

"You promised you would vouch for me," she insists, and she feels the edge of hysteria rising again.

"And I would have, if I had gotten the call," he says with precise enunciation. He pulls his jacket from his shoulders and drapes it across the railing that separates the kitchen from the living room. "It's not my fault you didn't have any references you could put down."

"Fuck." It comes out of her mouth like a sigh. He's right. It's not his fault she has burned every bridge in her life. Grant is a good guy. He gave her this apartment. She glances toward the window as the sleet hits.

"We've got to talk about the rent."

"Oh yeah. Of course." Brit's stomach drops. She has the hundred dollars Chloe gave her, and her first and only paycheck from the gas station is about two hundred fifty. She worked forty hours in two weeks at minimum wage, then they took out taxes. It feels like she was robbed. "How much is it?"

"Six hundred."

"What?"

"Yeah. Didn't I tell you that?" He sits down on the futon, where she sleeps, and his hand spreads out flat against the sheet that covers the coarse fabric of the cushion.

"No. You said we'd work it out."

"Hmm." Grant looks around the apartment. "It sure is cold out there." He shivers as if he just felt a draft. "The thing is I was gonna give you this month to get on your feet, you know, but my business partner doesn't think we can do that."

"But the apartment was empty. You said you'd rather have somebody in it." She feels spun by the trajectory of the day.

"Yeah, it was, but now he's got somebody willing to pay good money for it. So he told me I had to get this settled." He frowns. "I'm not happy about it, but there's nothing I can do."

Tears spring to her eyes. "Oh my god, Grant. I don't have six hundred dollars." She covers her eyes when she can't hold back the tears.

"How much do you have?" He reaches out and pulls her to sit on the futon beside him.

"About three hundred. Three fifty if I don't eat for the rest of the month."

"Well, you can't not eat." He tugs her close and rests his arm across her shoulders. "So you have about three hundred?"

Brit nods.

"That's not enough." His arm falls away.

Brit's stomach roils. "You said we'd work it out."

"Man. I'd hate to put you back on the streets. I mean, that would suck. That weather is turning cold. Shit, Bee. What am I supposed to do?" He leans forward and rests his chin on his hands.

"Can't you talk your partner into giving me a little time? I'll get another job."

"You could see if Chloe has another couple of dates for you," he says, quietly, as if he's just pondering her options.

"What?" Brit asks, ice moving through her veins. She wonders what, exactly, Chloe told him.

Grant turns his head to look at her, scanning her face. "Or you could just fuck me, and I'll make up the difference."

Brit's mouth drops open, and she tries to look away, but his eyes are locked on hers, and she cannot move.

"It's really your choice. You can fuck me, or you can pack your duffel and move on."

"But I can get the money," she whispers.

"I don't think you're understanding me." He leans back and props his hands behind him. "I think I'd like for you to fuck me."

Brit stands up and paces to the door. He follows her with his eyes. She can *feel* him watching her.

She turns and looks out the window. She can almost feel the cold. Being outside in the summer and even the fall was okay. Even when it rained, it wasn't completely terrible. But the idea of being out in the slurry of ice makes her shiver. Brit could load all her shit together and trudge through the sleet and rain to find someplace to shelter. She could walk up to the square and see if she can get another week at the outreach. But it's too late in the day, almost evening, for them to still have openings, especially on a day like today. She doesn't think she could sleep outside on a night like tonight. She could beg Chloe to let her stay over, but she feels wrong about what happened with Aaron, and now she feels like Chloe betrayed her by telling Grant about the date.

Grant knew Aaron had paid her to have sex with him. Chloe told him that.

"What's it gonna be?"

Brit wants to tell him to go to hell and demand that he leave. She wants to slam the door with force behind him.

She doesn't want to pack her possessions back into her duffel bag and have to go out into the nasty weather without a suitable coat or footwear. Brit doesn't want to have to lug her stuff all over creation, looking for a place to stop. She doesn't want to sleep huddled and freezing under somebody's bush.

"Shall I help you pack?" he asks with feigned innocence.

Brit turns and looks at him. This was his plan all along. In a flash, she understands. She was a fool to think he was just going to help her out. People don't ever give something for nothing. She suddenly remembers sitting with Am at the Waffle House the first morning after she worked at the store. The waitress brought them both coffee, even though they hadn't ordered it. She said it was an old pot, and she was going to have to dump it anyway. Brit was grateful, thought it was nice, but Am refused to acknowledge the cup or touch it. *Nothing is free.*

"No, I don't want to pack my stuff." Brit says and lowers her head. Nothing is free.

October 20

Chapter 52

Brit joins Chloe, Mavis, and Kelly in Chloe's apartment on Sunday afternoon to watch football. Brit watched a little football with Zack but wasn't very interested.

"You gotta have something to talk to them about," Mavis says. "It can't just be wham, bam, thank you, ma'am."

Brit isn't used to the way the girls talk about *prostitution* as if it's no big deal.

"It's not like you never had sex with somebody you didn't love," Chloe insisted when Brit said she didn't think she could go on the next date.

But that wasn't true. Brit only had sex with two men before Aaron—Jason and Zack. She had been in love with them both—or so she thought. Then she had sex with Aaron, and she didn't love him, but she had thought maybe she could. Then she had sex with Grant, and she knew she didn't love him.

"Oh my god, you're so naive," Chloe said, annoyed.

Brit relented.

She's had three more dates since Grant visited, and she would rather sleep with strangers than have sex with him again. She almost has half of November covered already. Grant had her sign over her paycheck, and he let her keep sixty dollars for food, since he couldn't break a twenty. She didn't dare argue with him when the whole thing was done. He wasn't the same guy who gave her shoes at the Dollar Store. He was rough and held his hand around her throat when he orgasmed. She thought he was going to kill her. She never wanted to have to let him "make up the difference" in her rent again, so she agreed to the next date and the two after. Next week, Brit will agree to some more, and she'll do what the other girls are doing, setting their sights on the future. The guys Chloe introduced her to were awkward and clumsy but kind. She went out with Mavis once last week, and her guy that night was a bit of a jerk. He had a really small penis, so he probably felt like he had to make up for it. A regular girl might have laughed at him but not Brit. She put on a show for him, telling him how he was just right inside of her.

A regular girl. Brit almost laughs when she realizes she's not a regular girl. She is a prostitute. Three more dates, and she will have her rent for November covered. Her mind rolls as her blood becomes diluted by the drink Chloe gave her when she arrived. It helps if she stays numb, that the other girls are all doing the same thing, and that they all have plans for when they can't get paid to have sex anymore.

The girls sit around Chloe's living room with drinks and chips as the players take the field.

"Why do I have to care about football again?" Brit asks Kelly, who is sitting closest to her.

"Because the wives don't," Kelly says, rolling her eyes at all those women who are too stupid to keep their men satisfied. "They're thinking about babies and bills, and the man just wants a warm hole that can talk to them about the stuff he cares about."

It is crass, and Brit doesn't like thinking of herself as *a warm hole*, but it does kind of make sense. The third guy she was with, after Aaron and Grant, told her about his new baby and even showed her a picture of his wife and little girl. It was bizarre that he then wanted to have sex with her.

Brit starts to think about taking a class, but she has to make rent first. She has put in a few applications around town but has no references so doesn't get called back.

The tone from the television shifts to a commercial followed by a bulletin for the evening news. "In breaking news, the body found yesterday near downtown Newnan has been identified as that of missing teen Stephanie Colliers, a runaway from St. John's County, Florida. If anybody has information about Stephanie Colliers, we are asking that you notify the police."

A picture of a dark-haired girl fills the upper corner of the screen. Kelly and Brit are in front of the TV when the bulletin airs, but Mavis and Chloe are by the window, blowing smoke through the slit at the bottom.

"What did they say?" Chloe asks, walking over and bringing her cigarette out of the smoking zone.

Mavis crushes her cigarette and moves into the kitchen. Her phone is tight to her ear.

"Holy shit," Kelly says.

"Was that Stephie?" Chloe demands.

Kelly nods.

"Who is Stephie?" Brit asks, unable to catch up.

"She used to be you. I mean, she lived in your apartment," Chloe says, upset. "Fuck. Fuck. Fuck."

The news called her a missing teen. Brit's mind replays the bulletin.

"We need to call the police," Chloe says and withdraws her phone from her back pocket.

"Put it down." Mavis's voice rises above the din of the television.

"What?" Chloe asks, her finger still on the screen.

"You can't call the police. Who do you think they're going to look at if you call the police?" Mavis takes Chloe's phone from her hands. "She was living *here*. Do you want the police all over this place, looking at *us*?"

"We didn't kill her," Kelly said.

"Yeah, but we're fucking men for money. Do you want that splashed all over the news?" Mavis hissed.

Brit doesn't want that splashed all over the news. She is sure of that.

"So what? That's my choice," Chloe whispers but not with her characteristic confidence.

"Sure, you can fuck whoever you want, but taking money for it is still against the law. You didn't kill her. You don't know anything about what happened to her, so you don't have anything to tell the police. She was living here, and I, for one, do not want the police crawling over this place."

"But it's Stephie. She was our friend," Kelly whispers.

Mavis turns on her. "And now she's dead. There is nothing you can do for her." Mavis softens her tone. "Who do you think they're going to look at?" Mavis speaks slowly, enunciating.

"Grant."

"That's right. And if Grant goes away, then this goes away." She indicates the apartment as if it were a mansion. "And we all go back to where we started. That means you, Chloe, with your teeth rotting out of your head. And, Kelly, you want to go back to where you started?"

Kelly shakes her head.

"God knows I don't. So we are not calling the police to invite them like vampires into our home to stir up our shit. You understand me? Grant didn't do *anything to her*, and you know it."

Brit doesn't speak, but her throat constricts the way it did when Grant closed his hand around her neck. Stars blink in her vision, and the voices around her lower to a dull roar. She's no longer listening, instead remembering his face above her contorted in ecstasy or rage.

Her vision clears, and she swallows. "I should probably call my mother."

"What?" Mavis hisses.

"I haven't talked to her in a long time. She's probably worried. She probably thinks that was me." A tear rolls down Brit's face. "Can I use your phone?" she asks Chloe.

Mavis hands over Chloe's phone but grabs Brit's wrist. "Fine, but you stay here. I want to hear everything you say."

Brit locks eyes with Mavis and contemplates telling her to go fuck herself. Mavis's pupils are dilated until the irises are just thin strips around the edge. "Fine. I'll stay here."

Breathe.

Brit does a quick search on the browser and finds her mother's phone number with Mavis standing over her shoulder. She never learned the number. It was just speed dial number 2. The alcohol is what's making her call. If she weren't drinking, she would talk herself out of it.

She steps a few feet away from Mavis as she dials but not far enough to be out of earshot. The buzz from her cocktail makes her head feel light, but she places her back against the wall and slides down until she's small and folds on the floor.

The phone rings.

"Hello?" someone with a deep male voice answers.

"Is Charlotte there?"

"Who's calling?" His tone sounds protective, as if he might not let her speak to her.

"It's Brit." Her voice cracks, and she clears her throat and says it again.

"Brit?" he asks, still sounding skeptical.

"Yeah, Tom. Can I talk to my mom?"

Chapter 53

Mom is hysterical. Brit can't understand her.

Brit says, "I'm okay, Mom," over and over, but it seems to have no effect. Finally, she sits silently, waiting for the hysteria to pass. With time, it does.

"Where have you been?" Mom sounds relieved but frustrated.

"I've been between places," Brit whispers, not wanting to tell her the truth of it.

"Why didn't you call me?" She sobs.

"I just... I couldn't. I needed to work some things out."

"I would have helped you!"

Brit breathes slowly. "You were out of town."

"Not since August. I've been looking for you. I thought you were dead. They found a body, Brit! I thought that was you."

Hysteria wells again, and Brit's stomach plummets. She feels guilty for making her mother sick with worry about the girl they found.

"It wasn't me, Mom. They just identified her."

"I thought you were dead. I thought Zack killed you."

"I'm not dead."

It has no effect. Her mother is beyond consolation.

Brit lets her work through her emotions, pressing the phone to her ear.

"It's been months. Why haven't you called me? Why did you let me think something bad happened to you?"

"I don't know. I'm sorry. It was really selfish of me. I'm sorry. I just screwed up, Mom. I'm sorry I made you worry." Tears erupt over her lashes. "I just made a mess of everything." Then she's sobbing and revealing what she never thought she would tell her mother. She admits she's a cheater, that she killed a girl in an accident because she was distracted. She stops short of telling her she's prostituting to pay rent. Her mother listens, supportive and not judging. Brit isn't sure she could have understood half of what she said.

"Oh, baby. It's going to be okay. We all make mistakes."

A weight lifts from Brit's chest, and the sobs ease. "I didn't want to bother you." She was too ashamed to tell anybody about the accident that killed Dee Martin.

"Bother me? Brit, I'm your mother. I'm supposed to be bothered by you."

Except when you weren't. The words are on her tongue, but she doesn't dare to say them. They aren't even fair. She's not a child anymore and understands better now what her parents were going through with their divorce. Mom invested years, and she managed to keep functioning. Brit wasn't even married to Zack, and she went completely off the rails. Not that it was all about Zack.

"I'm sorry. I didn't mean to worry you. I just felt like I had to get back on my feet on my own."

"Where have you been?" Charlotte asks, sounding bewildered.

"I'm still here. I'm in Newnan. I never left. I have an apartment. I'm looking for a job."

"Are you on drugs? Is that what's going on? You know your father had trouble with drugs. There's no shame in going through something hard."

"No, I am not on drugs. I don't have money for drugs." It feels like a slap in the face. Her father didn't have problems with drugs. He had problems with alcohol and younger women. Brit's eyes land on the glass she emptied, which is sitting on the coffee table. Drinking was a mistake.

"I've been worried sick."

"I should have called. I'm so sorry. I was just so ashamed of my-self." All these months, she's played through some version of this con-versation, but here when she's finally having it, she feels no shame in admitting how badly she messed up. Her mother isn't pointing fin-gers the way she expected.

"I just don't understand why you didn't call me," Charlotte says.

Brit can't understand it either. She didn't call because she didn't have a phone, because she was embarrassed and ashamed, and be-cause she didn't want to tell her mother about Dee Martin and what she did. Brit didn't want to hear her mother tell her that she was just like her dad. She didn't call because she didn't want to be forced to move to Florida and live in a house with a man she doesn't know be-cause she can't take care of her own shit. It's all true, but something else rises in Brit's awareness. She didn't call because she was punish-ing her mother, making her suffer for Brit not getting to go to college because she had to get a divorce. Though she wants to deny it, look-ing at it from this angle, she sees the truth of it. It was a shitty thing to do.

"I'm sorry. I should have called."

"We need to tell the police you're alive. They think Zack killed you."

An echo of a memory whispers in her ear. "If I ever see you again, I'll kill you."

"They know that wasn't me, Mom. They just announced it. It wasn't me."

"I'm telling you they think Zack killed you. Jason Jenkins, that little shit, told the police you said he threatened you. Oh my god, Brit. It's ruined that man's life. Do you know what it must be like for him to think he's going to be arrested every time he sees a police-man?"

She does, actually. Mavis begins making the wrap-it-up motion, and Brit nods. "I'll call the police. I'll let them know I'm here."

"I am so glad you called."

"Me, too, Mom. I'm sorry. I didn't know you were looking for me."

"Oh for god's sake, Brit. I'm you mother. You can't stop calling for four months and think I'm not looking for you."

The disappointment in her mother's voice takes her back to high school. The divorce wasn't good for anybody, and when Brit learned there was no money for college, she was a brat—looking back, she can see that. Brit took it for granted that her parents would pay for her college. She stormed out of the kitchen and went to her room. Her mother followed and stood in the doorway. Brit had looked up, expecting sympathy, but found cold eyes and folded arms.

"My marriage is ending, and you're acting like an entitled little bitch."

Brit was stunned. Her mother never cursed and certainly never at her. To be fair, she didn't call her a bitch, Brit thinks.

"I worked my way through college. If you want it, you will too," Mom said before she turned and walked away.

Brit figured out pretty quickly that she didn't really want college. She didn't want it badly enough to spend her money on it. She just wanted to go where Jason was so that she wouldn't lose him.

"Well, you need to go to the police and let them know you're alive," Mom says, the disappointment in her voice evaporating.

"I will."

"Good. That poor boy doesn't need to be arrested for killing you when you've just been hiding."

Brit wants to protest, but it doesn't matter. She *has* been hiding, and Zack didn't do anything to her that she didn't start. Her mother's right. She's just been hiding from her problems, and Zack didn't try to kill her. He just threatened her to make her leave. But Stephie—somebody did kill her. "Look, you're right. I should have called. I didn't do anything right, but I'm going to fix it. I have to go. Okay? I'll call you tomorrow."

Mom releases a heavy sigh into the phone. Brit can almost see her closing her eyes and forcing the air out, the way she always does. "I'm glad you're alive. I just wish you had called me."

"I know." Tears spring to her eyes. Brit has to do something with her life. She doesn't want to have sex with strangers so that she can avoid having sex with her landlord. Her mother is right. "I love you. I promise I'll let the police know."

A knock lands on the front door.

Chapter 54

Brit disconnects as Mavis turns to her.

"You are not fucking going to the police." Mavis glares at her.

"Not about Stephie. My mom says they've been looking for me," Brit explains and turns to look at Chloe with raised eyebrows.

She's not the boss. She can't tell Brit what she can and cannot do. Chloe meets her eyes but quickly looks away.

"I don't give a holy fuck. You are not going to the police so you can say you saw Stephie on TV and felt like you needed to make a statement. You live in her apartment. Are you fucking stupid?"

Brit looks around the room, bewildered.

The door opens. Mavis turns and faces Grant, unfazed. She walks the few steps to meet him at the door and leans in to speak so that Brit and the others can't hear. Brit suddenly realizes that Mavis called him when she walked into the kitchen with the phone at her ear. Mavis was protecting Grant, and there is no way any of them are getting out of here to go to the police. Brit doesn't really think Grant could have killed Stephie, but then she sees the wild look in his eyes when he enters the apartment.

A tense conversation transpires by the door. Grant is a wreck. Brit can't take her eyes off him. She has never seen him in disarray. He paces from the door to the window and back again.

"Did you kill her?" Chloe asks, and her hysteria tamps Brit's down. Chloe crosses the room until she intersects Grant's trajectory. "She was just a kid."

Brit still has the phone. The keypad glows.

Grant takes a step back, reaches into his waistband, and pulls out a gun. He aims it at Chloe's forehead. "Sit the fuck down."

Chloe retreats. As if directed to do so, Kelly and Brit sit on the sofa. Chloe sits between them, and they clasp hands. Brit places the phone on the coffee table, face down and in plain sight.

Grant paces. Mavis stands in front of the door, her arms crossed, as if she thinks one of them might make a break for it.

"Okay. Listen." Grant stops in front of them, pushing the coffee table back to give him room. The gun is still in his hand. He squats and crosses his arms so that the gun points toward the window.

Chloe cowers. Kelly and Brit keep their eyes averted.

"This is what we're gonna do. Okay?" He sniffs and shifts his hand until the gun rests alongside his cheek. "We're gonna just pretend she was never here. Okay? You never met her. She never lived here. Got it? She was just a runaway. She doesn't matter. Her life was all fucked up. She could have just died." He is trembling, his head vibrating. "Okay?"

They all nod.

"We'll go on like none of this ever happened. Got it?"

Again, they nod.

Grant rises and walks toward Mavis. They stand by the door, talking in quiet tones. He's still agitated but no longer vibrating. He replaces the gun back in his waistband and runs his fingers through his hair, taming it.

He turns back to the girls, saunters over, and lounges across a chair. "Who are we watching?"

"Cowboys," Kelly whispers.

"And Denver," Grant says, sounding more like the man Brit knows from the Dollar Store. He catches her eye and smiles. "Mavis. I need a drink. Anybody else need a drink?"

The three shake their heads, and Mavis disappears into the kitchen. She returns with a heavy-poured rum and coke, the cocktail of the night.

"Thanks, doll." Grant accepts the glass and slams the liquid in two gulps. "Damn."

He thumps the glass down on the side table and flexes every muscle in his arms and chest. Brit has to look away from him, feeling the constriction of his hand on her throat again.

"Come on, Dallas," he calls to the television.

A light flashes beyond the window, and Brit's attention shifts from the TV to the trees. They're on the second floor and can't see the ground, but the branches light then fade on a loop. She glances at Kelly. Chloe is unreachable, hunched into herself and weeping. Kelly catches Brit's eye and makes a small, nearly imperceptible nod before calling, "Touchdown," in unison with Grant as the Cowboys take the lead. He reaches a hand up, and she high-fives him.

Brit tears her eyes from the looping lights, and Kelly reaches forward to turn up the volume on the remote. Brit has also heard the sound of boots coming up the stairs. Grant glares at the three of them as Mavis goes to the window.

"Fuck!" Mavis shouts.

Grant leaps to his feet and joins her, looking down at the street. The gun is in his hand again. Brit screams as the officers rush in with shouts and demands. Kelly, Chloe, and Brit huddle together. Mavis stays apart and puts her hands up, and one of the officers tells her to get on the ground. Grant waves the gun past the girls and puts it under his chin.

The sound of gunfire causes a violent concussion in Brit's chest that feels like her heart has stopped. The top of Grant's head flies away from his body. Blood arcs in slow motion onto the perplexed Marilyn Monroe. He stands for a split second with his eyes open before he slumps to the floor.

Brit reaches for Chloe's phone and flips it over, displaying that it has an open line.

Chapter 55

"Ms. Addams?"

Brit recognizes him from his voice even before she looks up. He's the one who told her the DA wasn't going to press charges. This man is the one who said, "Somebody died. That doesn't mean you killed her."

"Officer Rathborn." Brit almost smiles. A warm sensation fills her stomach, as if they're friends, as if he isn't tied to the worst moment in her life—or at least one of them.

"Ms. Addams." The words flow from his lips in a slow sigh. "I'm very glad to see you."

He wasn't one of the officers who came to the apartment and escorted the four of them to the police station, where they were separated and asked for their statements.

"I didn't know anybody was looking for me," Brit tells him when he asks why she didn't contact the police after the press conference.

"You didn't think your mother would be looking for you?"

"I should have." Brit runs a finger over a scratch in the table. "I'm sorry I worried everybody."

"We should let your mother know you're alive."

"I already did. She knows." Brit holds his eyes for a second.

"Did you know Stephanie Colliers?"

"No. They said she lived in my apartment before me." Brit reaches for the bottled water and opens it with trembling fingers.

"What do you know about Grant Norton?" he asks.

"Nothing, really. He's a manager over at the Dollar Store. He let me and Am work nights stocking shelves sometimes."

"Who is Am?"

"My friend." She doesn't even hesitate to claim Am as a friend, but not so long ago, she would have, not wanting to be perceived as homeless. She has done worse than be homeless. "The old lady who walks with a wheelchair."

He nods as if he knows of Am. "She's your friend? So you were living on the streets?"

"Yeah."

"You didn't have a friend back in August, did you?"

"What do you mean? Back in August?" Brit just said Am was her friend.

"Would you like to tell me what happened after I last saw you?" Cliff leans back. "You told me you were going to the Leaf and Bean to wait for a friend, and you were going to spend the night with them."

Brit laughs. "Oh. No, I didn't have any friends."

"Where did you go?"

Her mind rolls back toward the summer. It's all a blur. Brit walked and slept at the edge of parking lots and under the bushes behind a house down by the square. She was peed on by a dog. She washed her hair in the Walmart bathroom and was kicked out of the store. One time, she saw Jason along with his wife and kid, but they didn't see her.

"I just walked. I got into the shelter for a week, but you know, they're always full."

"Where were you the rest of the time?"

Brit blows out a long breath. She doesn't want to talk about it. "I stayed with Am for a while." She says it as if Am has an apartment.

"Where was that?"

"Where'd we stay?" she asks.

He nods.

Brit hesitates. She doesn't know if it will cause problems for Am, Pudge, and Jed when they come back if the police know where they stay. "Around. Different places. Back in the trees beside the road. Out of sight." Brit protects the sheltered spot by the school. Her face flushes.

"I've not seen her around town in a while. Is she okay?" Cliff asks, leaning forward and folding his hands on the table.

"She went down to Florida."

"How does she get there?"

"They walk, I think." Brit shrugs, not comfortable telling the police about Am.

"I think I saw her about a month ago, down in Carrollton. Was she traveling with a man and another woman?"

Brit nods and smiles. "I guess they made it at least that far."

"I guess they did," Cliff agrees. "So you met Grant Norton because he let you stock shelves?"

"Yeah." Brit nods.

"How did you come to live at the apartment?"

"After Am left, he told me he had an apartment that was empty and that I could live there for a while," Brit explains, remembering how nice he was then, how generous. A flash of memory from the day he took her to the storage unit blooms in her mind. Then she sees the top of his head spreading across Marilyn Monroe and shudders.

"When was that?"

Brit shrugged. "Three weeks ago. A month ago, he told me, and three weeks since I moved in. I got a job at the gas station across the street."

"So you're working at the gas station?"

"I was, but they fired me because Grant said he'd give me a reference, but when they called, he must not have been there. They thought I lied. I didn't have any other references."

"You didn't feel like you could use your old law firm for a reference?"

She laughs. "They fired me too. I don't think they would have given me a good reference. They accused me of stealing money from them, but I didn't."

"I know." He looks down at his hands. "They figured out you didn't steal the money."

"Great," Brit says, but it doesn't make any difference. They shoved her out the door, and there's no going back.

"And all this time, you didn't know we were looking for you?"

"No."

"Ben Walton put up five thousand dollars as a reward for information leading to your whereabouts," Cliff says.

"Do I get that, since I told you where I am?" Brit says, trying for a joke.

"Possibly." Cliff smiles.

"I don't want Ben Walton's money."

Cliff releases a long breath. "So what are you going to do now?"

"I don't know. I gotta get a job and figure out how to do something with my life." Brit is back where she started, but she doesn't think she's the same girl she was in July.

"You could go down to Florida and stay with your mom for a while. She's been very worried about you."

"Maybe."

"There's no shame in accepting help."

Brit leans back and looks at him for several moments. "You think I didn't ask for help? Maybe I didn't say those words, because yeah, that's hard. But I asked for help. I asked everybody who saw me for help. But nobody fucking saw me. You think when I was walking down 34, carrying everything I owned, that I wasn't asking for help? When I was sleeping under the desk, you think that wasn't me asking Ben Walton for help? I asked Zack for help. And Jason." She remembers the day she stood in the entryway to Walmart and Jason and Mary Beth walked right past without even seeing her. "I asked everybody for help, and nobody even *saw* me. The only person who saw me was Grant."

Her voice drops as she remembers Grant, who was kind and gave her a pair of shoes when she needed them and a place where she began to feel like she could put her life together. Then she sees him as he was making up her rent, when his face was that strange mix of rage and ecstasy. She remembers him in those last moments, waving the gun and standing with his eyes staring for several seconds after the top of his head splattered across Marilyn's face.

"But I get it. I don't know how many times I drove past Am before because I didn't want to see. I wanted her to be invisible. *I* was invisible. Do you know what that's like? People look right past you because they don't want to see."

"What about your mom? You didn't ask your mom. She would have helped you. She wanted to help you."

All the heat and anger ebbs and washes away. "I know. I guess I was too ashamed to ask *her* for help. That's fucked up, isn't it?"

"So you could go live with your mom for a while. Figure some things out," he says.

"No. I love my mom, but she has her own life. She doesn't need me showing up and being the third wheel," she explains, but she is not the person she was before. She had to make this journey because she learned everything. Her mom would have wired money, but Brit suddenly understands that she would still be expecting everybody else to fix what was wrong with her. She didn't have to live any of this. But she *did*. It changed something in her that needed to be changed.

"So you want to find a job and get on your feet," Cliff says, pulling Brit out of her thoughts.

"Yes."

"Okay. Well, listen. I hear you. I don't have a job for you, but I'll tell you what." He slides a card across the table to her. "You put me down as a reference for anything. I'll vouch for you. Okay?"

"Why would you do that?" She lifts the card.

"Because I see you, Britany. I should have seen you before."

Chapter 56

Brit returns to the fourplex with Chloe and Kelly. Mavis is detained. Kelly splits off, and Chloe and Brit walk up the stairs toward the upper apartments. Chloe's apartment is sealed with police tape, and they stand outside Brit's for several minutes.

"I don't think I want to go in there," Chloe says.

Brit shakes her head. She doesn't either. "Do you think she died there?"

Chloe takes a deep breath. "Probably."

They go back down the stairs and knock on Kelly's door.

"Come in," she says as if she expected them.

They shower, taking turns washing away the day. It feels strange to do the mundane task of washing her body on a night when she saw a man die. The image of his skull departing his body replays as she washes suds out of her hair.

Brit dresses in Kelly's clothes, a T-shirt and shorts. Chloe does the same, and when they are all dressed like children for a sleepover, they slide into Kelly's queen bed with Chloe in the middle. They are different women tonight than they were this morning, and all the walls between them have been taken down. They hold hands and whisper the truth of their lives to each other until they finally sleep.

March 28

Chapter 57

Cliff always thinks of Britany Addams and Dee Martin when he drives past the intersection at 54 and Fischer Road. He pulls to a stop at the sign, and far down the road is a small group of people walking along the edge of 54. He squints. *Are they pushing a wheelchair?* He edges his car to the side of the road and parks well onto the shoulder then walks down the road toward the group.

As they come closer, the woman pushing the wheelchair stops walking. The others take a step but then return to her side.

"It's good to see you back in town," he calls, trying to sound friendly and nonthreatening. "We were afraid something happened to you."

When he reaches them, the old woman doesn't make eye contact.

"How was Florida?" he asks, trying to be conversational.

"Lots of waves. Waves," the chubby one says, rocking forward.

Cliff smiles. "Spent some time at the beach?"

"Uh-huh." She nods with a small sideways glance.

"What can we do for you, Officer?" the old woman asks, finally making eye contact.

Cliff squares himself to face her. "Do you know me? Because I feel like I know you."

Her lips compress into a line. She shakes her head slowly but doesn't take her eyes from his.

"You came to my wedding."

"She's a pretty girl." Her voice comes out in a whisper. "Is she good to you?"

"She is," he says, and his face breaks into a wide smile. They begin to move again with him joining their group and replacing the old woman as the one farthest into the street.

"Good."

They walk.

"How is Ant?"

His mother called Tony *Ant*. Cliff's stomach bottoms out.

"He's good. Thinking about getting married," Cliff says, smiling.

She nods, as if it's what she expects. "How's your dad?"

Are we really having this conversation? "He's okay."

"How about Carla?" The tenderness in her voice surprises him.

"She passed in November," Cliff says, and his heart pulls the way it always does when he thinks about Carla being gone.

"I'm sorry." She draws a long breath, and they reach his patrol car. They step around it and continue down Fischer Road. "She's a good person."

"Why did you leave?" Cliff asks and stops walking.

She walks another pace before turning to face him, and her face crumples. She puts her index finger to the side of her head and taps her temple. Then she shakes her head and closes her eyes, as if somehow, he should understand what she was saying.

"Are you okay? I mean, living like this. Do you need anything?"

It takes several seconds for her to bring her face under control. "I'm good."

"If you ever need anything, I'm here." He longs to touch her, but it seems there is a force field around her that keeps him at bay.

"I'm good." She turns to look at her two traveling companions.

"We found Brit. She doesn't think she would have survived without your help," he tells her, wanting her to understand that she did a good thing in helping her.

"Bee," she says with a smile. "Did she want to be found?"

Cliff shrugs. "I think she *needed* to be found. She's studying to be a cop. Says she wants to make a difference in the world."

"That's good." She glances at him then backs away. "We should probably go. It's been a long day. We gotta get to where we're going before Pudge wears out."

"I can give you a ride."

She crinkles her nose and shakes her head. "We're good."

"All right."

With a wave, she turns and rejoins her party. Cliff starts toward his car then pauses. "Miriam?" It doesn't feel right to call her Mom after all this time.

"Am. Call me Am."

"Yeah. Well, um, Maggie's pregnant, due in in July. Thought you might like to know."

She smiles, exposing missing molars. "Congratulations."

"Thanks. We're excited." He waves. "I guess I'll see you around."

Am nods and turns away. Cliff watches until they make the corner at Highway 34.

Chapter 58

Brit runs over a hard-packed path. Without missing a stride, she skips over exposed roots. The dog alongside her keeps pace and leaps into the scrub then back onto the path. Her hair is gold again, pulled up into a high ponytail. She checks her watch as it pings the three-mile mark and turns to make her way back to the other end of the trail. As she reaches the trailhead, she slows to a walk, checking her time and feeling her blood surging through her veins. The dog trots a few paces ahead.

"Come on, Cooper." As they reach the parking lot, she links his leash to his harness. It's a beautiful day, early spring hinting at summer.

Several cars are parked in the lot, and Brit passes a small family—a young boy, a mother strapping a baby to her body in a baby carrier, and a father. Brit is parked past them and tugs Cooper to keep him close. She doesn't really look at the family. Her mind is moving ahead toward the rest of the day. She has a test in her legal studies class, and she's ready but still feels nervous. After classes, she will go to her job at the Taco Mac. When she resurfaced, Ben Walton offered her old job back, but she declined. She isn't mad at him. It wasn't his fault that she fell off the rails. But she doesn't want to go back and work with Kay and Elise, who talked about her when she needed a friend. Anyway, she can't work during the day and take classes too. When she finally knew what she wanted to do with her life, she was eager to get started. In the blink of an eye, she decided to become a cop. When Cliff slid his card across the table and told her he *saw* her, she knew she wanted to be like him—but better.

"Brit?"

The voice breaks through her thoughts as she reaches for her car door. She turns to face the small family.

"Jason." Her eyes rest on him for a beat, and she's surprised that there is no flutter in her stomach, no emotional pull.

"Wow. How are you?"

"I'm great." She turns from him to face his wife. "Hi, Mary Beth. I don't think we've officially met."

Mary Beth makes a sour face. "I know who you are."

"You know who I *was*." Brit smiles, leaning down to pet her dog. "I'm glad I ran into you," she says, looking at Mary Beth instead of Jason. "I'm really sorry for whatever damage I did in your life. I hope you can forgive me."

Mary Beth's mouth opens, and she looks away.

"It was terrible for me to do that to you, and you didn't deserve it. I was wrong. I'm sorry."

Mary Beth nods and tilts her face until her lips touch the baby's head.

"You have a beautiful family." Brit smiles. She's talking to Mary Beth, not Jason. "I have to go."

Brit turns on a heel and opens the back door for Cooper, who leaps inside. Without looking at Jason again, she climbs into the driver's seat. As she turns the key, she makes eye contact with Mary Beth and nods, then she backs out of her spot. She drives past the family and out toward the road. At the exit from Line Creek, she comes to a complete stop and looks both ways, waiting until the traffic is clear before pulling onto the street.

About the Author

Angie Gallion has been a stage actor, an anti-money-laundering investigator, a photographer, and a paralegal. She has lived in Illinois, California, Missouri, and Georgia and has traveled to Greece, the Dominican Republic, Scotland, and Ireland. Angie dreams of traveling the country on wheels with her husband once her children are grown. She is currently rooted outside of Atlanta, Georgia, with her husband, their children, and their two French bulldogs.

Angie's writings usually deal with personal growth through tragedy or trauma. She explores complex relationships, often set against the backdrop of addiction or mental illness. Her first novel, *Intoxic*, was the 2016 bronze medalist in the Readers Favorite for General Fiction. That book was a twenty-five-year adventure in self-doubt and hesitation.

Read more at www.angiegallion.com.

About the Publisher

Dear Reader,

We hope you enjoyed this book. Please consider leaving a review on your favorite book site.

Visit https://RedAdeptPublishing.com to see our entire catalogue.

Check out our app for short stories, articles, and interviews. You'll also be notified of future releases and special sales.